# Keeping Up With the Joneses

ALSO BY P. R. HAWKINS

AIN'T NOTHIN' DOWN ABOUT IT

# Keeping Up With the Joneses

## P. R. Hawkins

www.urbanbooks.net

Urban Books
10 Brennan Place
Deer Park, NY 11729

ISBN-13: 978-1-60162-004-0
ISBN-10: 1-60162-004-7

First Printing June 2007
Printed in the United States of America

10 9 8 7 6 5 4 3 2 1

Submit Wholesale Orders to:
Kensington Publishing Corp.
C/O Penguin Group (USA) Inc.
Attention: Order Processing
405 Murray Hill Parkway
East Rutherford, NJ 07073-2316
Phone: 1-800-526-0275
Fax: 1-800-227-9604

To my mother, Helen Jean, and my Nanna Banana, Dimple, miss you much. To Carl and Martha Weber who took a chance on an unknown author, thank you. To Joylynn Jossel, girl, we are going to ride the bus until the wheels fall off! To all the people who have my back and help me hold my head up when things get just too damn hard: Sherri, Arthel, Sandra Lord, Lynn Freeman, Anita, Triana, Marcy Goodman, Vanessa Paul, and Sharon, thank you. To the people who do things and just don't know how much it helps me: Ann Young, Lynn Sogi, Marcy Mack, Lisa Bradley, and Charles, thank you. To all the people who get your props in the next book, thank you.

P

# *Acknowledgements*

Sisters, sistas, girlfriends, and divas! Sorors, confidants, and sounding boards! Thank you, thank you, thank you! And thank you! And to the special people in my life who provide support, support, support: Angelicque for inspiration, Becca for unwavering confidence, Carol and Georgia Mae for being my other mothers, Chevelle for being real, Linda who always supported me, Stephanie for being Stephanie, Roz for being so very supportive and listening to my crap, Andre for being his multitalented self and telling me I could do anything, Dion, who I love like family, Joann who has once again become my friend, Lisa Jason, who always makes time for me, Lisa Holly or Lisa Smith, whichever one you are, for just being there, Charla for having boundless energy, Tammy Anderson for being cheerful and Cydney for always telling the truth. You guys were right. I can be a writer and a comic. To all of you, a big fat thanks. What a party we are going to have!! And yes, I will pay.

# More Than Passion

**The talent behind the camera . . .**
Risa James spent long hard years cementing herself as a talented professional behind the camera on her popular local television show, *City Scenes*. Her determination and grit proved that she didn't have to rely on her model-perfect good looks to land major market interviews and stellar stories. She had everything a busy young professional could have, except a love life.

**The man behind the myth . . .**
JD Jones was a local boy done good. He was Dallas's own living legend, living a charmed life. An ex-professional football player, and successful businessman, he had the world by the tail. He had everything a man could want except a family to call his own. Who would be the woman to share his dreams and walk beside him as he built his empire?

**They meet . . .**
As soon as Risa and JD meet there is fire and passion so intense it is like a tangible thing. The question they must ask themselves is, "Is this more than passion?" Would what they share burn itself out, leaving the two of them spent and speechless wanting more? Or could Risa rise to the challenge and charm the six women in his life as surely as she had charmed him and become the next Mrs. Jones?

**Keeping Up With the Joneses** asks and answers the question: *If you have passion, do you need anything else?*

# Prologue

Risa James chuckled to herself as she listened to the words that rang in her ears through the mini-headset she wore while she engaged in her daily workout routine. Strenuous exercise wasn't necessary to maintain her naturally slim figure. She did it out of habit. She had been a star athlete as a teenager and maintained the active lifestyle as she grew older. Lucky for her, she still had an active metabolism. So, it didn't take much to get her heart rate up. She exercised to remain toned and keep her head clear. Exercise wasn't one of her passions, but it was a necessity. She indulged the bug by running several miles a week, swimming and working out on her StairMaster in her home gym. It had always been her motto to "Take care of your body and it will take care of you."

As she continued with her regime, the popular Dallas radio disc jockey she always listened to made a few more observations that Risa found incredibly funny. According to the local celebrity, who had the highest rated nighttime talk show in the tri-state area, a few things had changed. One, brown was the new black, and two, forty was the new thirty. It was the last observation that had Risa on the verge of outright laughter. He was right. She had made the same observation herself and had been pooh-poohed by her mother. She couldn't wait to call her and tell her she had heard it on the radio. It seemed only then would it validate that particular statement in her mother's opinion.

Risa's mother, Shelia Marcia Hooker James, was one of those people who believed a statement more if it was heard on the radio, seen on television or read in the newspaper. Having the media report on it made it true. Now that she had a computer, courtesy of Risa, she had fallen victim to believing more than one Internet urban myth. Risa was constantly monitoring her transmissions and trying to tell her that not all things in black and white were black and white. Sometimes there was a little gray. It was up to the informed listener to gather the facts and make their own opinions.

As a television talk show host who had started her career early as a reporter, she knew the importance of fact-finding. So anything she read on the net was subject to her normal scrutiny, just like the things she heard on the radio or saw on television. But since she was of the same opinion as the DJ, she decided to take his words at face value. The DJ was right. Forty was the new thirty. Today's forty-year-old was dynamic, sexy, and assertive. Today's forty-year-old was a new breed of woman. Today's forty-year-old was kicking butt and taking names! So the opinion that forty was the new thirty was not foreign to her and had some validity, especially since she was approaching forty herself and didn't feel a day over thirty. Today's forty-year-old was living longer. Now they were doing things at forty that people had never considered before. They were embarking on new careers, getting married for the first time and even having children. As a matter of fact, Risa's boss, station manager and mentor, forty-six-year-old Helen Jeffries, was about to have her first baby with her thirty-six-year-old husband, Isaiah. Their ten-year age difference meant nothing to Helen. Helen didn't feel forty-six. Helen didn't act forty-six. Helen didn't look forty-six. Helen and Risa had even joked that Helen would be sixty-two at her child's high school graduation. She would be a cool sixty-two just like she was a cool forty-six. Helen was vibrant, alive, and a grand diva. She would most definitely be the hippest mom of the Geritol set.

Risa wanted to be just like Helen when she grew up. Laughing at that, she thought that it was a good thing she had enough time. It would be a long time before she was forty-six. Funny, as of late she had wondered how she would react if Mr. Perfect showed up on her doorstep right after she turned forty-six. The thought of being in her sixties at her child's high school graduation was a challenge she didn't want to face. She didn't embrace the thought like her friend, Helen. Thank God she was a long way from forty-six and that decision wouldn't be one she would have to make any time soon.

Something was nagging at her and for the life of her she couldn't figure out what it was. Just as soon as she had the thought, she stopped in the middle of her workout. A thin trail of sweat rolled down her pretty face. She hated those commercials when they showed all those beautiful people at the gym. They were so unrealistic. Nobody sweated in those commercials. They glistened, courtesy of the water bottle used to add additional spritz to their hard, toned bodies. Realistically, if they worked that hard, they would be sweating like racehorses, not glistening and shining and preening for the cameras. Realistically they would be dressed as she was in faded sweats and mismatched socks. Realistically, those weren't even real people. Nobody looked like that! The thought of how she was dressed was fleeting as she dabbed at her brow with the towel that she kept handy.

It concerned her that she was forgetting something important. It was a gnawing notion that made her pause. Wait a minute, she pondered. What day was it? She glanced at the wall clock, then her sporty wristwatch, and then the calendar on the wall to verify the date. Her consternation with the unrealistic television commercials was quickly forgotten as she realized the importance of the date. It was exactly one month before her birthday. And this birthday was the special one. She was about to be one of the women she was so surrounded by. On her next birthday, Risa James would be forty! She knew it was coming. She just hadn't expected it to arrive so soon. Where had the time gone? She stood dumfounded, staring at the calendar then back at her watch. She had no idea how she had gotten thrown off track. She was a very determined lady who adhered to a rigorous schedule. Only by keeping it was she able to balance a very fulfilling personal life and demanding, high-profile job. So anything that threw her off track had to be corrected quick, fast and in a hurry or the entire ball of wax started to melt.

According to her inner biological clock, she was on schedule with everything in her life except for what she had once considered the most important thing, having her own family. According to her personal goals she should have a ten-year-old and a seven-year-old by now. If she didn't right this wrong immediately her entire life plan would be thrown out of whack. But how could she possibly do that? She didn't have a husband. She didn't even have a steady boyfriend. She couldn't even remember when she had been on her last date. She quickly reviewed her life milestones.

At twenty-one she had been a young fresh-faced reporter just starting out. Having graduated from Southern

Methodist University in the top 10 percent in her class, she had landed a dream job. She was the weekend reporter on the NBC affiliate in Waco, Texas. Waco was a small market, but it was television exposure and a decent salary. Her enthusiasm, skill, and competence had quickly caught the eye of the network brass. She had moved up the ladder of television journalism quickly and had found herself at thirty-one, a news anchor in the Los Angeles dog-eat-dog market by way of Waco, upstate New York, and Chicago. Once she had left Waco she had been on her way. Waco was the first and last market she worked in that wasn't in the top five.

She was a good journalist, but because of her picture-perfect highly photogenic face and supermodel-like figure, she had become more of a celebrity than a journalist. People were more concerned with who she dated, where she dined, and what she wore. The hard news she wanted went to the other, often male, reporters, and she was relegated to covering the celebrity beat. She was at all of the award shows sharing the red carpet with the likes of Denzel and Halle. Her picture was posted in *Vogue* and *Cosmopolitan*. She was a socialite and a jet-setter. Then at thirty-five, tired of all the paparazzi and fluff that was in LA, she went back home to Dallas, proud of her accomplishments but sick of the craziness of LA, LA land. She wanted to be around "real" people and do "real" things. It was her intention to rest, take a break, and find herself. But after one lunch with her old friend, Helen, Risa found herself accepting a position as executive producer and host of *City Scenes*, a new television show that in the past four years had become very popular in her hometown.

Exposing all the idiosyncrasies of Dallas life, it was Dallas's version of *Regis and Kelly*, *20/20*, and *The View* without Rosie, Elizabeth, and Joy. *City Scenes* starred its own chocolate Barbara Walters who sported a little humor, a great deal of talent, and a hometown freshness that the locals loved. Even in rest, Risa was an overachiever at the top of her game. Her little show had caught the eyes of network brass via satellite and they had come calling once again. Happy and content with her life, she turned them away. She had walked away from all the glitz and wasn't too thrilled about going back to it. Risa was happy in Dallas. She didn't need LA, New York or Chicago. Been there. Done that. Had the T-shirt in three colors. So she was content in her little job and with her new quiet life until just this moment when it had dawned on her that she had overlooked something. Without knowing it, she had once again found herself on the fast track and hadn't stopped to smell the roses.

"Oh, my," she said to herself as the realization hit her. She was thirty-nine. Thirty-nine! Thirty-nine! When had she turned thirty-nine? Sure she was successful. Sure she was single. Sure she was thirty-nine! Thirty-nine was almost forty! She was behind schedule! According to the life she had planned for herself, she was supposed to be having her ten-year wedding anniversary in three weeks. Wondering how on earth she had lost track of time and gotten off schedule, Risa walked through her spacious house located on historic Swiss Avenue and set her clocks to adhere to daylight savings time.

Risa's home was a nice house. It was filled with all the trappings of success: good furniture, expensive pieces of art, and an elaborate entertainment system. It was all anyone needed, except a family to fill it. There were three bedrooms and Risa lived in it alone.

Sighing with consternation, she decided to deal with it tomorrow. In one month Risa James turned forty. The big four-oh. It was one thing thinking about the milestone in theory, but it was another thing to live it. Realizing she had some choices to make, she fell into the large four-poster bed and eased under the covers. "Tomorrow," she told herself. "This could be handled tomorrow."

She knew what she had to do and tomorrow was as good a day as any to start. If she were going to get back on track, it was time for her to settle down, get a husband, raise a family, and move on with life. Tomorrow she was going to be very busy getting her life back on schedule. She had to make up for lost time. Tomorrow would be a new day and she would have to contemplate working on a husband then. She couldn't concentrate on that right now. She was tired. Sighing with the utter exhaustion of someone who had just spent forty-five minutes on the StairMaster, Risa fell into sleep determined to tackle her oversight after a full night's rest.

# Chapter 1

"Daddy! Daddy!" baby Eden called with glee as she waddled on short, stumpy legs that were a little bit bowed and surprisingly strong enough to hold up a body that supported what seemed to be a head too big for her body. Eventually she would grow into her body parts. But right now she was a fumbling, stumbling, comical eighteen-month-old that delighted her uncle, JD, James Derrick Jones, who watched from his comfortable seat on his sister's overstuffed sectional. Taking in the purely domestic scene, one of many he had been invited to as of late because his oldest sister, Angela, loved to entertain, he was still surprised when he saw his best friend, and longtime cohort from his football days, Larry Wheaton, on the floor playing horsey with the newest additions to their brood of four.

All in all, there was seventeen-year-old Hailey, fifteen-year-old Jacob, and eighteen-month-old twins Eden and Edison. Larry Wheaton was his real name, but everyone called him Big L. He was from Sulfur Springs, Texas and stood six feet, eight inches tall. This half-Mexican, half-

Samoan, who weighed almost four hundred pounds, had retired from the game of professional football ten years ago, but he was still solid as a rock. There was not an ounce of fat on him, which was hard to believe considering how much he liked to eat. And boy could he eat! Six feet and eight inches was a lot to fill up. He consumed a lot of calories and burned almost twice as many. His exercise regime was awesome, five miles a day, ten laps in the Olympic-sized pool, crunches, sit-ups, and jumping jacks. He wasn't a man obsessed, but he came from a long line of people who could either be big, fat or big and fat! Big L opted for big. Thus his name.

JD could only admire his friend. Larry Wheaton was a happily married man who had fathered four children with JD's oldest sister. He did his part in helping her with the brood. That said, he wouldn't turn to fat. Keeping in shape was the least he could do. He had explained this to JD on many occasions. Angela wanted them both to be around for a long time. So Big L did what made her happy. He exercised, ate right, and presented a pretty picture when she looked at him. His friend was in love. It showed. As JD watched them from behind half-closed lids, all he could think was what a woman his sister had to be to snag this notorious ex-womanizer and make him give up his philandering ways.

JD remembered the first time he brought Big L to his mother's house for Sunday dinner. It was then that his sister, Angela, set her sights on him. Back then he and Larry had been college roommates not sure of their futures. Although they both played on the college football team, the life of a professional football player was a dream they both aspired to. Angela, then a junior at local North Texas State University, had met her brother's college roommate and the rest was, as they say, history. All she had to do was bat those long eyelashes of hers and Larry Wheaton was a goner. JD watched as their love affair blossomed like a fertilized flower.

From college to the first-round draft to a career filled with sports highlights and good fortune, Larry and Angela had gone from college sweethearts to the old married couple that they had become. Now, so many years later, their little family had grown into the loud boisterous herd that it was. Watching them, JD wondered what kind of woman would he end up with? He hadn't really given it much thought until Angela had brought it to his attention that his birthday was fast approaching and in one month he, JD Jones, would be turning forty.

His best friend was the same age and had a wife and growing family. JD hadn't even started. He had no children. His sister had a head start on him. Just the other day she stunned him when she asked jokingly, "What kind of father are you gonna make if you're so old when you have children that you won't even be able to keep up with your kids?"

The older he got, the harder it would be. That's when it hit him. Time had snuck up on him. Although still in his prime, he was fast approaching forty. The big four-oh. By now most men his age were in the same boat with Larry, not him. How had he ended up in the boat alone? He had had relationship after relationship. Sometimes he had several relationships going on at once. None of them made him want to settle down and have what he was looking at as he sat there in his sister's living room. He had gotten close though. The relationship he was in now was by far the most serious and long lasting, but he suffered from no delusions. It was what it was.

"Want one?" Angela asked him as she passed a plate of homemade cookies beneath his nose.

"Of course I do," JD said, sticking his hand out.

He was a sucker for homemade tea cakes. He got one of

the warm cookies and a napkin from his sister as she went around the room with the cookies. It was such a domestic sight.

*Is this what I want?* he asked himself. "Yes," he said to himself softly.

"Huh?" Angela asked. "Did you say something?"

"Oh, uh, I said yes, these cookies are delicious." JD played it off then bit into his cookie, deciding this was an idea for future contemplation when alone. He reached for his wristwatch with the idea of setting it for daylight savings time. Suddenly, he had a lot on his mind and setting his watch was the least of his worries. He was running out of time.

# Chapter 2

Risa let out a sigh of agitation as she parked her late-model convertible BMW nearly a block from her assigned parking space. This was the third time this week someone had taken her spot and she wasn't going to take it any more. So with the same determination she used to tackle any project, she marched up to the security guard and had the offender towed.

*That will teach 'em*, she thought to herself. She was sure the gleaming black Jaguar that inhabited her parking space so comfortably belonged to none other than Richard Marconi, the 10:00 news anchor. Round, robust, and sporting a mane of orange-red hair, the Howdy Doody look-alike wasn't the lovable personality that everyone thought he was. Conspicuously closeted, he wasn't fooling anybody but the viewers; he was a virtual thorn in Risa's side. Resentful of the reputation she had from her journalism days and her meteoric rise to near cult status with the popularity of *City Scenes*, he was convinced her success was based on her ravishing good looks and not hard work, determination, and talent. He spent what she thought was way too much time and energy trying to undermine her at every turn. Risa was convinced if he would just come out of the closet, he would be happier. Surely hiding his "true self" was part of his problem and accounted for his nasty disposition. In all honesty she didn't care who he slept with, as long as he got out of her way and let her be.

On more than one occasion, she had asked him kindly to respect the decision of the parking committee and accept his assigned slot. In actuality, his slot was closer to the front entrance than hers. Risa had just had the good fortune to land a space beneath the parking structure. The covering provided protection from the occasional fickle weather conditions of Dallas. Sometimes the notorious Texas heat could set the car interior to boiling or a sudden unexpected downpour complete with golf ball-sized hail could wreak havoc on a well-maintained automobile or perfect coiffeur. The parking structure was a fantastic barrier to these unpredictable and unforeseen changes in the weather. Today it was raining and freezing cold. A thin mist of icy rain floated through the air. Without the protection of the parking structure, Risa had to lug a briefcase, purse, and portfolio through the icy downpour while wearing three-inch heels.

Frustrated, damp, and perturbed, she continued towards the office. Her teeth were chattering and she chastised herself for not grabbing a coat. She hadn't expected to have to make the walk to the front door unprotected against the weather. She was an easy target for the icy, cold rain droplets. The wet silk of her pale pink blouse clung to her skin beneath the wool of her dark-green pantsuit. The designer was Jones of New York and looked good on her lithe frame. It was a fully lined wool suit that she had been looking at for months before she had bought it. Even though she could afford it, she waited until the local Macy's had one of its notorious super Saturday sales. She had gotten the suit at a steal and hoped that she would be able to re-place it if the cleaners couldn't repair the damage that the drizzle mixed with sleet had caused. So concerned was she with her suit that she was almost thrown off guard when Cayce, her assistant, rushed up to her with a cup of steaming coffee and a worried look on her face.

"Risa, where have you been?" Cayce asked frantically.

Risa pulled off her jacket and reached for the coffee. The warm cup felt good against her cold hands. Gloves too had been left at home. In her mind's eye she could see them stuffed into the pocket of her calf-length double-breasted black Ralph Lauren coat that hung unused in her closet.

"What are you talking about?" she asked, sipping grate-fully from the coffee.

Cayce took Risa's jacket and hung it on the knob be-hind the door to the office.

"I called you. I texed you. I e-mailed you and I faxed you!"

Everyday Risa thanked her lucky stars for Cayce. Cayce, pronounced *Casey*, Lujan was more than an assistant. She was Risa's right hand. Standing five feet tall in her stock-ing feet, the ten-inch height difference between the two of them often provided comic relief when they had ani-mated, heated conversations as they walked side by side.

First-generation American, born of Haitian immigrant parents, Cayce was a hard worker who didn't complain about long hours and a sometimes hectic schedule. She graduated from nearby SMU with a degree in mixed media and typed one hundred words a minute. She was also a com-puter whiz, opinionated, and quick to assist. Unlike Risa, her hair was short and stylish, her makeup bold and her clothing led to the chic and trendy, displaying the eighteen-year age difference between the two. Today she was dressed all in black. Her short leather skirt, thick black sweater, and black tights were very fashionable. The ensemble was completed with a pair of three-inch stiletto ankle boots that were pointy toed and dangerous. She looked like a rocker chick, a biker babe, an ebony Carrie Bradshaw of the much-acclaimed *Sex and the City* reruns of which she was a big fan. Often time, she chose her wardrobe to be a reflection of the fictional petite beauty whose chutzpa she much admired. Mixed with her own personal style she had much panache and carried it off with much aplomb. Cayce was Risa's friend, as well as her subordinate. Risa couldn't live without her.

"Your interview is today!" Cayce reiterated. When she was excited, Cayce spoke in exclamation points.

"I know that," Risa said calmly.

Risa took another grateful sip of the steaming coffee. It was seasoned with a touch of cinnamon, a drop of honey, and a lot of cream. Who needed Starbucks when they had Cayce making the coffee?

"He's here!"

"What?"

Risa glanced at her watch. Even with her trek from the parking lot it was only 8:30 A.M. She had specifically told Mr. Jones's assistant to have him in the office at 9:00 A.M. JD Jones, ex-football player, restaurateur, business mogul, hometown boy, and entrepreneur extraordinaire was kicking off *City Scenes*'s new season with a special about hometown legends.

"He's been here for almost an hour and a half!" Cayce said as she paced with anxiety.

"It's only eight-thirty," Risa said calmly. Somebody had to remain calm.

"No, Risa, it's ten-thirty!" At Risa's blank look, Cayce continued. "It's daylight savings time! You were supposed to set your clock *up* one hour!"

Risa's first thought was that this couldn't be happening.

No wonder the usually levelheaded Cayce was agitated. *What to do?* Risa wondered briefly. She only had a few seconds to get this under control. She would handle this in a professional manner. One thing she prided herself on was being professional. Being prompt was part of that professional air she wanted to portray. Last night she had made it a point to set all the clocks in her house, including the ones on the VCR, DVD player, CD player, and microwave. She had set them all back one hour. But as Cayce shooed her out of the office and down the hall to the greenroom, where guests often waited, she realized her diligence should have been in setting the clocks up instead of back. So instead of it being 8:30, as she had thought, it was 10:30. No wonder she was so rested.

After her strenuous workout she had slept like a baby. She was an hour and a half late! She was also wet, wrinkled, hungry, and anxious about the confrontation she was sure was going to occur when she was confronted by Richard once he realized she had his car towed. So with all this going on, it was no wonder that she tripped just as she was walking into the greenroom. "Could it get any worse?" she asked herself as she fell. But, actually, as she felt strong arms grab her and steady her, it seemed to get better.

"Hey, hey, now. Are you all right?" the strong-armed gentleman said as he gripped her.

The first thing Risa saw was eyes. They were brown, luminous, sexy bedroom eyes.

"I-I-I'm fine," she stammered, at a loss for words as a jolt of electricity seemed to travel through her body from his touch as he steadied her easily.

This was no small task considering that he was holding a cell phone in one hand and had jumped over an ottoman in order to break her fall. The greenroom was very homey and decorated with furniture like that in someone's home. It was complete with couch, chair, ottoman, rug, and entertainment center. They maintained a family air at the television station and took every chance to make their surroundings reflect it. Walking in on her guest had been like walking into someone's house as they casually had a telephone conversation.

"Thank you," Risa said as she started to launch into an apology about keeping him waiting. "Mr. Jones, I'm sorry—" she began, but was immediately cut off.

"Here, have a seat," JD said. "I'll be with you in a minute." He immediately took control of the situation as he eased her into a chair. He was acting like this was his house and she was the guest. "I bet you set your clock back instead of up," he said with a smile and a wink, knowing he was right.

There was arrogance in his smile. He had perfect white teeth that gleamed from a flawlessly handsome male face. It was a perfect smile. His teeth were straight, even, and flawless. He could have been a model for a toothpaste ad. Risa had seen that smile before. She could not live in Dallas and attend social gatherings without occasionally running into JD. A party here, a fundraiser there, their paths had crossed before, however briefly. But never had they been so close to each other. Having never been in such close proximity, the power of his smile had been lost on her, until now. Now she could see it up close and personal. Now she could be mesmerized by it. He had the perfect mouth. Being the daughter of a dentist, she could appreciate a nice mouth. She knew that her father truly would. JD had the perfect smile wrapped around that mouth. She could feel herself being affected by it. It was as if she had been hit in her chest. For a moment she couldn't catch her breath. He had that kind of effect on her.

She took a deep breath as she sat in the chair gazing at JD as he continued on with his phone conversation. *What's happening to me?* she asked herself. She felt dizzy.

She put her head down and placed her hand on her forehead. *Am I getting the flu?*

Out of the corner of her eye she could see him watching her. Of course he knew he was right about the clock. She got the impression that he was used to being right. For some reason that rubbed her the wrong way. She righted herself and stood to address him. At six-feet-one inch in her three-inch pumps, she was sure they would see eye to eye. To her chagrin, the task could not be accomplished because he was still at least three inches taller than she. She liked her men tall. She had even dated a professional basketball player. It was such a pleasure to be able to wear heels and not have to slump to accommodate the height difference. With JD, she could stand tall.

"Yes, how did you know?" Risa finally answered his question.

"Pardon me?" he asked, placing his hand over the phone receiver.

"I did set the clock back instead of up."

"I just figured you did. Some people do. I had purposely cleared this morning allowing for some downtime. Your being late gave me some much needed personal time. I never get enough. Excuse me. I have to finish this call."

With that, he turned his back to her as he continued to coo into the phone. "I love you too, sweetie."

*How rude!* Risa thought, fuming that he had dismissed her with so little effort. She was forgotten as he continued with his phone conversation. The signals he was sending were mixed. First he kept her from taking a nasty spill against the floor, and then he turned his back on her and cooed to some bimbo on the phone. Risa could feel the hairs on the back of her neck rising with the slight he had just handed her. *How dare he.*

"Don't worry. I won't forget. I never forget," he said smugly.

Everything about him was smug. He had a confidence and style that bordered on arrogance. On a man with a less commanding presence, he could be perceived as belligerent. But on him, it was a cloak of confident arrogance that he wore with style and panache. He was so involved in his conversation that it seemed like Risa didn't even exist. She didn't like the slight. It wasn't the reaction she was accustomed to. Men found her attractive. It was in their nature to acknowledge her beauty. Oftentimes she had to ward off unwanted advances and put them in their place. But JD didn't even seem to notice her.

It had been a long time since she had deliberately sought out the attention of a man. She had been too busy building a career. It had taken all of her time and energy. That's how her deadline had slipped up on her unnoticed. She was too busy trying to be all the woman she could be. Oh, there had been a time when she tried the superwoman routine. She had tried to bring home the bacon and fry it up in the pan and love her man all night long, but had soon discovered it was harder than it looked. Painfully, she found out how having it all might be the one thing she would fail at. She didn't like to fail. She had just been too busy to tackle the new challenge. Balancing a demanding career and a man's fragile ego was time-consuming, emotionally draining, and painstakingly hard.

Risa knew that all men weren't emotionally immature babies who needed to be stroked, coaxed, and guided through a relationship while not stepping on their egos by being more successful than they were and giving them love and support as they struggled with the burden of living while Black and male in America. She knew that there was a man out there who could cherish and respect her as an equal. She knew there was a man who would be the Heathcliff to her Claire who would give her support and nurture her with long back rubs after she too had had a long day. She knew this. She could feel this. She had seen this with her friends and at one time with her parents.

As a news anchor, the chic and elite had courted her. From professional athletes, actors and moguls, she had had her share of admirers. But all she ever wanted was a man who rubbed her feet while they read the morning paper before she fixed him beignets and coffee. And she would make the New Orleans delicacy with love because she wanted to, not because she was *supposed to.* But as she continued dating, she became more and more jaded. Her "him" had made himself scarce. So after awhile she stopped looking. She made herself too busy to notice the men although they noticed her. So now, when she wanted a man's attention, she found herself rusty.

She didn't know the delicacies of flirtation that she should be using. Instead, she could only demonstrate the klutziness of a modern-day Lucille Ball. Sighing, she realized that she should have put more effort into her man search and not had given up just because she had kissed a few frogs. If she had done that, she would have been prepared for today.

Briefly she wondered if JD Jones was a frog or the elusive prince that all women were looking for. His physical appearance automatically put him in the prince category. He was, after all, tall, dark, and handsome. Quickly she forced herself to try to think of something other than his physical attributes. She knew it was because she was stressed-out that she was reacting so strongly to him. Otherwise he wouldn't look so handsome to her. The combination of the stress and anxiety that she experienced was most definitely because she was staring a deadline in the face. Were it not for those things, then surely JD Jones wouldn't be sending her into an emotional tailspin.

As JD talked on the phone, he had no idea Risa was waging a mental war with herself to stop being such a drama queen. Not being married at her age was no big deal. She didn't have to jump on the first man who came her way. She knew that. She had heard it on the radio! She was just thirty-nine! But as her birthday fast approached her mother's phone calls became more frequent and were littered with phrases like "old maid," "time is running out," and hints of finding "Mr. Right."

Forty would make it too hard to find a suitable mate and her chances were decreasing rapidly with every breath. She was starting to have second thoughts about her previous decision to hold off until Mr. Right found her. Suddenly Risa found herself second-guessing her actions and her motives. This wasn't like her. She usually made a decision and stuck to it. But as she sang the "Happy Birthday" song in her head, she was plagued with self-doubt. Could her well-intended, incredibly old-fashioned mother know something she didn't? After all, her parents had been married for forty years. Sure, they were divorced now, but forty years had to count for something.

As soon as these thoughts entered her mind, Risa shook them off. There were three things she had to do. The first thing was to talk to her mother and let her know that she wasn't going to live her life by her standards and rules. Who said a woman had to be married by a certain age? It wasn't written in stone tablets on the top of a mountain by a burning bush. It wasn't a law.

*No one considers me an old maid,* Risa reassured herself. *I'm not even forty yet. Forty is the new thirty. I have time.* The only deadline she was facing was a self-imposed one. Any other thinking had gone out with the introduction of Mary Richards and a whole slew of working women who blazed a trail in history. Women were living their lives fully and waiting before they got married.

The second thing she was going to do was talk to Richard Marconi. They needed to have it out once and for all. The parking situation was out of control. There was a reason for rules. He had to follow them or face the consequences, i.e., get his car towed.

The third thing she was going to do was reign in her feelings about JD. So he was attractive. And? She didn't have to have a man to make her whole. She didn't need a man. But she did want one. He was standing right in front of her. Suddenly it was as if she could hear her biological clock. It was ticking so loudly that she couldn't really focus on anything else.

*"Damn, he looks good while talking on that phone,"* Risa said, biting down softly on her bottom lip. She studied his attire. He was dressed in a pair of jeans that molded to his muscular frame like denim skin. His cotton shirt was starched but not stiff. His sports jacket fit over his wide shoulders so perfectly that it had to be hand tailored. His cowboy boots looked sexy and not hooky. If he wasn't Mr. Right, he was "Mr. look good enough to be right."

"No, I won't. I won't," JD insisted into the phone with a boyish grin.

Just listening to his voice, Risa could imagine the woman he was talking to on the other end of the line. She had done her research. JD was single, never married, never engaged, he played the field as effortlessly as he had ruled the football field. There was no doubt in Risa's mind that the recipient of his sexy bass voice was one of the beautiful women she had seen in the numerous photographs that filled her research folder on him. He was incredibly photogenic. Most of the photos had been taken at gatherings at which she had been in attendance. He always had a date. On more than one occasion, she had been alone.

"Love you too," he concluded.

His voice, deep and vibrating, took on a playful but soothing tone. Risa felt it like a caress against her skin and secretly continued to chide herself on being so affected. She had been around handsome men before. She had interviewed them. She had dated them. She knew how to behave like an adult and not like an adolescent around them.

As JD hung up his cell phone and turned to her she realized she would have blushed if he could have read her mind. But of course he couldn't. It was that realization that allowed her to gather her composure.

"Sorry. Sisters. Where were we?" he asked. Sister? That explained it. Risa watched as he placed the cell phone in his breast pocket. It was the smallest one she had ever seen. It was dwarfed by his large hand. The earpiece was also microscopic. Everything about him looked big. He was tall, at least six feet and four inches, dark and smooth with flawless skin and rugged features. His head was shaved and so was his face. He had eyes that were so brown that they were one shade away from being black. He was impressive. Oh, yeah, he was "Mr. look good enough to be right."

"I was apologizing for—" Risa started.

"Being late. I know. We covered that. Now, let's get down to business before another one of my sisters calls. I have five, you know."

Somewhere in the back of her mind she knew that. His sisters were integral parts of his business. She had read that somewhere.

"Mr. Jones, I copied those faxes that came in and sent them out FedEx next day as you instructed," Cayce chimed in from the doorway. Now she was her usual self as bubbly as she was efficient. She was no longer speaking in excited exclamations.

"Thank you, Cayce," JD replied. He said her name as if he were familiar with the taste of it. Risa bristled beneath the weight of his familiarity with her assistant.

"And I ordered a dozen roses for your sister."

"Very good. Make sure you order a dozen for yourself as well."

"Thank you." Cayce smiled but didn't break stride as she continued into the room. "You have a two P.M. lunch date with . . ." Cayce consulted her BlackBerry, "Elisha and dinner with Daphne."

"You're a busy man," Risa interrupted. She could barely keep the venom out of her voice. She knew she had been late but did this give him the right to commandeer her assistant and force her to juggle his schedule?

"Yes, I am," he said, glancing at his watch and then looking at Risa. "And I have spent more time here than expected. Had it not been for this remarkable young lady I might have been forced to reschedule."

"Now, we can't have that, can we?" Cayce chirped as she led the way down the hall with a follow-me gesture.

"Ready?" Risa asked. Of course she wasn't.

"Sure," JD answered.

"The studio is—"

"That way. I know."

JD started after Cayce. Risa had to race to keep up with his long-legged stride.

*When did I lose control of this day?* she asked herself as she struggled to keep pace with him. *And just what do I need to do to get it back?*

# Chapter 3

*D*amn, JD thought to himself as he followed Cayce down the hall.

He knew that he had met Risa a couple of years back, but he didn't seem to remember her being so attractive. Pretty, yes, but not drop-dead sexy-gorgeous like she was now. She was tall, dark, and sensual. There was something a little exotic about her. Maybe it was the slant and shape of her almond eyes. Or maybe it was the way her breast rose and fell beneath her jacket. He was intently aware that he was aware of her breast. Hmmm. He knew what that was about. He was a man after all.

There was no question about that but he didn't lust after every woman he saw. Even gorgeous, sexy ones like Risa James, who he suddenly found very appealing. Something hinted that she was growing into her beauty. Like a well-aged wine, she was getting better with age, ripening with a sensuality that he found slightly intoxicating. It was no wonder he had a purely physical reaction to her beauty. No one would ever question his masculinity. He just hadn't been prepared for his reaction to her.

Standing in her presence, JD suddenly found himself feeling like a teenage boy caught off guard. It would have been cliché to say that she had taken his breath away. But she had, so he made it a point to act as if she hadn't, hence, brushing her off. In all actuality, the closer she got to him the harder it was for him to breathe. He had to remind himself to takes short, controlled breaths. And also, like a teenage boy, he was suddenly experiencing a reaction he thought at his age he had mastered controlling.

*Strange,* he thought, careful not to let her see the confusion he was experiencing. He was a sophisticated thirty-nine-year-old man. He wasn't a teenager. He wasn't uncouth. He wasn't a teenager ruled by his libido. But he was a man. And she was a woman. Everything male in JD reacted to the subtle curves and graceful lines that were everything female in Risa. This surprised him. At first glance she didn't seem like his type. True she was a top shelf, dime piece, but she didn't seem to have that sister girl edge that he always found himself attracted to, that sense of self that was all lady wrapped in attitude.

Having grown up in the South, one of two men in a household full of true steel magnolias, JD knew the precarious line that women walked, especially Southern black women. Be strong. Be soft. Wear makeup. Wear pearls. Hold your household together. Let your man wear the pants. Stroke your man's ego. Support your man. So many women played the role of the Southern belle to the hilt that they lost themselves in the process. That wasn't the type of woman he wanted or needed. He needed a soul mate, a partner, an equal. He wanted a woman who didn't feel that she had to *let* him be a man. He didn't need any help in that regard. He was all man, secure in his masculinity and confident in his sensuality. He was proud of the fact that he could hem his own pants, not that that skill was ever needed because of his height, or he could prepare his own meals. He had been introduced to his feminine side, embraced it and continued to grow as a man. He wanted an uninhibited woman as confident and secure in her femininity as he was with his masculinity. He wanted a woman who fit into her role as easily as he fit into his. Actually, he wanted more than a woman. He wanted a partner. He wanted a wife.

When he made up his mind yesterday at his sister's house, he wasn't surprised at his resolve. He was a man who made decisions and lived by them, and his decision was that his bachelor days were numbered. It was time. So no more playing the field. It was time for him to settle down and tackle the role of husband, lover, and father. It was time for him to grow up. He had heard it before and chose to ignore it. Being a single man had nothing to do with his maturity level, but if he let his sisters tell it, his bachelorhood was an attempt to remain forever young, a playboy extraordinaire. But they didn't know everything.

For the past six months he'd been dating Lucy Belle exclusively. She was a youthful, widowed, Dallas socialite who was ten years his senior. She was a well-preserved, sinfully seductive chocolate treat, who easily moved her competition out of the race so that lately she had been the main thoroughbred chomping at the bit that was JD Jones. They looked good together. They had lively conversation. They enjoyed each other's company. She could have been his first wife, although he would have been her second husband. She was a complete woman, needing nothing from him but the companionship, good conversation, and great sex he provided. And oh, the sex was good. It was great. There were no games. There were no hesitations. She was a mature and skilled lover giving him what he needed and taking what she needed. They were good for each other and complimented each other. If only things were different they would be a perfect match, the age difference be damned. But things weren't different. Lucy was a widow and not a divorcée, therefore, no matter how good they were together, her and JD's union would never be as good as that of her and her first husband's, Marcus.

It was never voiced but her reverence for Marcus hung between them like an invisible cloud. She was a good woman. A fine woman. The ten years that separated them gave her the added confidence that he didn't often find in women his own age or younger. They had a lot in common. But she was not the woman he would take to be his wife. They both knew that. They were adults who played a very adult game that often ended beneath the sheets of his large special-order bed. He had seen it on a trip to Kenya and had it shipped back to the United States. It was made from mahogany and carved from one tree. It was a magnificent bed built to hold a magnificent couple. He and Lucy Belle spent a lot of time in that bed. They were good together in that bed. But they were not the magnificent couple it was meant to hold. They never tried to make their relationship more than what it was. It was good conversation and great sex. They had no intention of marrying each other. For that he was grateful. Nevertheless, he was gentleman enough to let her know when he was interested in someone else. It was only fair. And JD was always fair. It was what made him a good businessman and a fine human being.

"Excuse me, Ms. James. I have one more phone call I must make before we get started," JD said.

Before Risa could either consent or decline, JD flipped out his phone and began to speak in muffled tones. The cell phone was the constant companion of today's busy person. It was a convenience as well as a curse. Ringing at inopportune times, getting lost and being whipped out in the middle of conversations, they annoyed Risa to no end. She was the only person she knew who didn't answer her cell phone on the first ring. It wasn't too long ago when she finally gave in to peer pressure and purchased one. But she had only given her cell phone number to a select few and those select few knew that it was for emergencies only. If they wanted her, they had better e-mail her, leave her a message, or contact Cayce.

Watching with the ease in which JD used his cell phone, she knew he was one of those people who kept it with him at all times.

*Could he be that important?* Risa asked herself. Well, she didn't know if he was that important, but he was that arrogant. He carried on his second conversation as if two hours hadn't already been wasted. True, she wasted it. But still! She couldn't help but notice that his tone had changed as he whispered into the cellular phone. Although she couldn't make out what he was saying, there was no playfulness in his voice during this conversation. This wasn't a business call either. That was obvious from the sexy baritone and soothing tones he exuded. Everything about him was masculine and sexy. It was driving Risa crazy. It had been a while since a man's mere presence affected her this strongly. It had been a while since she'd even been with a man. She convinced herself that this was the reason JD was having this effect on her. It was the purely masculine lure of him that called to everything feminine in her. It was just physical. Nothing more. She didn't even know him.

As Risa strained to hear JD's side of the conversation, her curiosity was piqued as to whom he was speaking to. She could hear in his voice that he was deferring to this woman. *Hmm,* Risa thought. *Is the woman he's speaking with "the woman?" Is she "the one?"*

It always amazed Risa how men managed to justify and categorize their relationships. No matter how many others there were, there was always "the one." You know, "the one" who gets introduced to the parents and taken to family functions. "The one" gets taken out to dinner and presented to the friends. "The one" is special. The others are just that, others. Depending on the man, they could be treated with respect just at a certain level that never reaches that of "the one." Risa never wanted to be "the one" and she certainly never wanted to be "the other." She wanted to be "the only." Maybe that was why she turned and glared at JD with venom in her eyes.

In that brief walk to the studio she managed to classify him as one of the commitment-phobic playboys she had sworn off. It upset her because she found him appealing. Acting on her attraction to him would only give her stress. She didn't have time for additional stress in her life. She had a deadline to meet. She hadn't exactly mapped out her plan but in order to meet her future husband, she needed to be out and about. She couldn't be trapped in the studio on a cold, rainy Monday. Her man wasn't going to be delivered to her in the uncomfortable downpour. Risa's clothes were sticky and wet and she was starting to get a chill. All she wanted to do was get away from JD Jones so that she could break the attraction his proximity was having on her.

"If you can finish your phone call, Mr. Jones, we can start," Risa interrupted. She had to get him out of the studio so that she could clear a path for the man she was sure was going to find his way to her. Maybe he wouldn't appear in this downpour, but he would appear as soon as she made it clear that she was looking. She just had to open herself up to the possibilities and she couldn't do that with JD Jones filling the room with his scent.

"Shush," JD turned and said to Risa, placing his index finger over his lips.

"Shush?" Risa said under her breath. *Did he just "shush" me?* she thought.

Risa literally saw red. The only person to ever shush her

had been her granny and that was when Risa was a talkative five-year-old in church. *How dare he!* Risa's thoughts continued. *He is not my granny, and at thirty-nine I'm a long ways from a five-year-old that you could shush!*

She would not allow him to shush her. Risa had to restrain herself or she would have been all over him and not in a good way. She wanted to grab him and box his ears, but instead she spoke up and said, "Look, Mr. Jones, we have already gotten off to a slow start. . . ."

"Through no fault of my own," he replied.

"But—" she started to insist.

"Shush, woman. Don't you see I'm on the phone?"

And Risa did shush because with those few words, she had been put in her place. That was a first for her, but would it be the last?

# Chapter 4

JD could see the spark in Risa's eyes and the determination in the wrinkle in her forehead as she turned away from him to pretend to busy herself before he got off the phone, so that she could properly chastise him. He knew that much just as surely as he knew that he was going to ask her out.

She was all steel and lace, like his sisters and like his mother, women whom he admired. She would die before she was deliberately rude to him. That was the southerner in her. Southerners were bred to be polite. It was in the genes. Back in college it was a running joke among his Northern schoolmates that there was something in the water and mint-flavored iced tea that made southerners so gosh darn polite.

Risa was a Southern woman through and through. He could see that in her. It was the modern woman in her that forced her to try to get his attention because she obviously knew that he was speaking to a woman. It was the Southern belle in her that made her hold her tongue "in front of company." But when he got off the phone, watch out! He had shushed her like one would an annoying child or an inconvenient persistence. She was neither. She was an attractive, pretty wrapped package whose beauty wasn't daunted by her damp clothes. The perfect combination of Southern charm and modern woman was a combination worth exploring. He knew she was uncomfortable as the clothes dried against her body. Obviously she had walked in from the rain outside. If he had known he would have gratefully given her his parking space. He would have done anything to make her comfortable. He realized that from the start and wondered how she could possibly have such an effect on him in such a short time? If they'd been in New Orleans instead of Dallas, Texas, he would have thought that she practiced the art of witchcraft, for surely he was bedazzled.

The way Risa was making him feel confused him. He wanted nothing more than to remove the wet clothes from her body and warm her skin with his hands. He had seen beautiful women before. Beautiful women surrounded him. Even in his present relationship they pursued him relentlessly. As a gentleman he fended their assault with style, grace, and much aplomb. But this was one beauty he would not fend off. She could have her way with him. Knowing that, he had had to call Lucy Belle. He owed her that. Believe it or not, Lucy Belle took it like a trouper. No muss, no fuss, no d-r-a-m-a. She didn't even bitch or moan when he ended their long-term affair over the phone. And it was made so very clear to him what he already knew, Lucy Belle was more than his lover, she was his friend.

The phone call wasn't painful. The phone call wasn't sad. The phone call was inevitable the very moment Risa James had walked into the studio. JD didn't know off the bat what it was about her, but his heart pounded and his head told him that she was "the one." He didn't know how he knew. He just knew. He could feel it in his bones.

JD closed the cell phone and placed in into his breast pocket before he turned to the woman he planned on getting to know. Now she could chastise him for what he knew she thought of as poor treatment. He knew how to read women. Even though they were loquacious creatures, sometimes they said things with their body language that was so much louder than words. At the present, Risa's body language was screaming at him that she found his phone conversation inappropriate.

"You were saying?" he asked smugly. He knew she wanted him to ask her this or something like it. He could read it in her stance and the defiant way she held her head.

"You shushed me," Risa couldn't wait to say out loud.

*Oh, that was it.* Later he would get points for being a good listener.

"I was on the phone."

"You shushed me," she repeated as if that were enough.

"We already established that."

"Who do you think you are? You can't just walk in here, commandeer my assistant, take over my office, ignore my suggestions, and make personal calls. "

"Of course I can. I just did."

At his admission, Risa found herself speechless. What could she possibly say? He admitted to doing what she had accused him of. The wind had gotten knocked out of her sails when he just looked at her.

"But . . . but . . ." she sputtered, mad at herself for losing command of the English language.

"Okay, you have my full attention."

Again he had thrown her for a loop. Back and forth he took her, playing her like a fiddle. He was good at it and it annoyed her.

"I don't want your full attention!"

"Really? Well, what do you want then?"

He put it out there. He was instantly attracted to her

and he wanted to make sure she was attracted to him. Suddenly she had nothing to say. He knew what he was doing to her and he liked it. She felt as if she'd been hit with a big board and that the air was squeezed from her lungs.

They were standing too close to each other. She was too aware of him. He was too aware of her. She could smell the pure cleanliness of him, fresh linen and masculine cologne. If he took a breath, the scent of her Chanel Number 5, a classic, timeless scent, would fill his nostrils. She could feel the heat radiating from his body. Her clothes finally dried against her skin. The heat from her body dried them from the inside. She could feel herself being drawn into him as if her body was moving without her conscious thought. Before she knew it, she was in his arms. She didn't know if he pulled her to him. She didn't know if she pulled him into her. Maybe they just moved and were in each other's arms because there was nowhere else to go. This was the inevitable end result of their attraction. The kiss, when it came, was *the* kiss. It could be compared to no other. His lips. Her lips. His tongue. Her tongue. Their mouths fit together as if they were puzzle pieces fused from pliable flesh. She never felt like this before. She had never responded like this before. She had never been kissed like this.

Risa's hands moved like they weren't controlled by her brain. She found them around his neck. This was no small feat. He was a big man. She felt small, sexy, petite, and protected in his arms. No man had ever moved her in this way. No man had ever moved her this fast. No man had ever made her feel so alive and desired with just a kiss. But she discovered it was more than a kiss. It was *the* kiss. This kiss was better than any kiss she'd ever had and she fancied herself in love once. But with the touch of her lips to his, the interplay of their tongues, she knew that what she had before was a farce, a sham, a mere appetizer because this was the main course. With the touch of his lips to hers she was suddenly transported to bliss. It was as if she were no longer in the studio preparing for her weekly interview. With the taste of his tongue she was home.

Though they'd never kissed before, there was something so familiar about the touch and taste of him. Kissing him was something she felt like she had been doing all her life. She was meant to kiss this man. She was made for this man's touch. Her hands were on the buttons of his shirt. She wanted to feel his chest beneath her hands. She wanted to touch his skin as she tasted it. In turn, JD wanted her as close to him as physically possible. He wrapped his arms around her slender frame and crushed her to him careful not to expel the breath from her body by holding her as tightly as he dared.

She was so small in his arms that he wanted to protect her if even from himself. They were lost in the feel and taste of each other and threw caution to the wind as they danced the dance of lovers. And they didn't stop. It was as if the kiss set wheels into motion on a ride with no brakes. The kiss was the catalyst for the next thing. He took her hand and placed it on his belt buckle. He didn't say anything. He didn't have to.

"Well, well, well. Are all your guest treated this way?" Risa heard a gloating, mocking voice say.

Risa pulled away from JD so fast it was as if she had been scalded. If the earth opened up and swallowed her she would have been happy. The last thing she needed was for Richard Marconi to catch her in a compromising position. It would be so much better for her to be seen on television with spinach in her teeth or to walk out of the bathroom with toilet paper stuck to her shoe. Anything, anything, anything but this.

*My God!* she thought. *Here I am kissing a perfect stranger*

*and inches away from placing a well-manicured hand down his
pants. What's wrong with me?*

"I certainly hope not," JD said as he held his hand out
to Richard. "JD Jones."

And just as suddenly as what could be considered the
most embarrassing moment of Risa's professional career,
the awkwardness in the room dissipated. She watched as
JD flashed that 100-watt, Pepsodent smile and Richard
Marconi, her nemesis and pain in her posterior, turned
into a gushing, blushing, fumbling fan. He was starstruck.
He was awed. He was smitten.

"I know who you are," Richard said as he pumped JD's
hand with his big, soft, oversized mitts and grinned like a
fool.

Risa didn't know what to say. She had never seen Richard
like this. It made him look almost human. And for the first
time since she'd known him, he was a real person and not
some larger-than-life pain in her rump that took every opportunity to thwart her. Suddenly he was a person capable
of emotions and feelings. Suddenly he wasn't Richard
Marconi, problem too big to ignore. He was Richard Marconi, man. There were no tentacles or third eye or antenna.
She felt a great deal of gratitude towards JD. It washed
over her in a wave of relief. He made Richard Marconi
human by the power of his personage.

"I have been a fan of yours for years. I even remember
watching you play for Lincoln High School," Richard said.

Lincoln was one of the oldest traditionally African American high schools in the city. It, like JD, was an institution.

"Even back then, we knew you were destined for great-
ness," Richard continued as he pumped JD's hand vigor-
ously. JD accepted the compliment graciously. Although
he had retired from football almost five years ago, he still
got this type of reaction from fans.

"I was sure sad to see you quit," Richard said.

JD retired from football at the tender age of thirty-five.

"I got out while the getting was good. I might have been able to push it for two more years but my body had taken all it could."

"You're still in great shape!"

"Thanks, but man, every time it rains my right shoulder screams at me to give it a little TLC."

"And if you hadn't stopped playing you wouldn't have been able to devote all that time to JD Enterprises."

"True that. True that."

The two men were talking like old friends.

"Man, you have everything a man wants. How does that make you feel?"

Risa heard Richard slip into reporter mode and bristled. This wasn't his interview! JD heard him as well and had a moment of reverie. True, he had everything a man could want: good health, success, fame. It was everything except something he was sharing with a special someone. He was a king in need of a queen. Would Risa be that queen? If Richard Marconi hadn't of interrupted their kiss, he would have been able to explore the possibilities further.

"Well, Richard, you're just going to have to watch the young lady's interview to get my answer."

With that he took Risa by the hand and walked towards the studio, effortlessly getting her out of a sticky situation. All Richard could do was look at their retreating backs.

# Chapter 5

As Risa and JD took their seats in the large leather chairs from which they would conduct the interview, both of them were preoccupied with thinking of the events that had transpired. To keep him at arms length Risa donned her professional demeanor that she had somehow lost as soon as their lips had touched. JD could feel the subtle change in her body language. One minute she had been into him. He could feel her reaction as he had held her in his arms. The next minute she had turned away from him and masked her desire with a cloak of polite professionalism. He knew that everything had changed with the arrival of Richard Marconi.

He was astute enough to know that Richard, as her peer, could make her life uncomfortable. His sisters often talked about the double-edged sword of beauty and brains. Possessing the best characteristics of his mother, Lillian and father, Sam, he had five of the most stunning women in the city of Dallas as his siblings. All different, ranging in size and coloring from the extra-slim chocolate Elisha, to the model-tall Betsy to the statuesque honey-colored, redheaded Daphne who was the spitting image of his long departed great-grandmother, Pearl, to the bossy Angela and petite Carlie with the hazel eyes, brown hair, and coffee color soft as satin skin. They often discussed how men were ruled by their libidos and were condescending, lecherous, or just obnoxious beyond belief. As a man, JD never had to prove that he held his position because he was smart and qualified and hadn't slept his way to the top. But as a Black man, he was constantly proving he was where he was supposed to be, successful in his own right.

JD was constantly on display as an oddity because he didn't split verbs and drop nouns. So, he guessed he could understand Risa's discomfort. She got caught in a comprising position and he had put her there. Silently he cursed himself for being so ignorant of what his little slipup could cost her. With a kiss, witnessed by an adversary, her professionalism was undermined and a shadow of doubt was cast over her accomplishments. She was obviously worried. Since they had taken their seats, she hadn't so much as glanced at him or spoken to him. She was busy allowing the hair and makeup people to work their magic on her water-kissed hair and face. They didn't have much to do. As far as he was concerned she was already beautiful.

*This will be the mother of my children.* As soon as he said the words in his head, he knew that it could be a possibility. She could easily take her place at the table with his five sisters, mother, and grandmother and be the next Mrs. Jones.

As JD was adding Risa to his family tree, Risa's mind was racing. She was trying to figure out what it would take to keep Richard's mouth shut. She was convinced JD had no clue what that kiss could cost her. She knew Richard. JD did not. Richard was a pompous pissant who would feel important by having something to hold over her head. He would be like a little kid with a secret waiting for any provocation to spill the beans.

"Don't worry. I'll take care of it," JD assured Risa as the hair and makeup people left her side and they had a moment alone before the sound tech came over and wired them with tiny microphones.

"What are you talking about?"

"I'll autograph a couple of footballs for him. He can sell them on eBay."

"You have footballs with you?"

"I always keep two in the car."

She looked at him incredulously. Then he smiled, letting her in on the joke. And he had her. Just like that he had her. She felt herself falling for JD and tried to stop it, but couldn't. She was a rational woman who made rational decisions. If ever called to question she could say that she suffered from temporary insanity. Who would convict her if there were a jury of her peers—they would only agree with her. She was stressed-out because her birthday was fast approaching and she had gotten thrown off track. Therefore, her temporary insanity could be believed. Yes, that would be her answer. It had to be her answer. Otherwise she was as crazy as she was feeling. Only a crazy woman would risk her reputation and standing for a kiss. And, God, what a kiss! She forgot about Richard and the compromising position he had caught her in. She forgot about her ticking biological clock. All she remembered was the touch and taste of JD.

Maybe this was all a dream and she would wake up in her big mahogany four-poster bed, embarrassed at the raw reality of it. But as she caught JD's eye, she knew this wasn't a dream. And far from being a nightmare, it was her new reality. With the touch of their lips, Risa James had been knocked for a loop. JD wouldn't be so easy to remove from her list.

*Damn it,* Risa thought to herself. *There's no way I'm going to regain control of this day.*

# Chapter 6

Somehow Risa and JD managed to get through the interview without looking too awkward and without surrendering to the desire that they felt. They sat across from each other and pretended as if they were interviewer and interviewee with no history. The tension between the two of them was like a tangible thing when they acknowledged, if not to each other, at least secretly to themselves, it for what it was, sexual tension. It was a sexual tension so blatant that if it had a color, it would be red. It was that vibrant and floated in the air between them. Therefore, the air was crisp with static electricity.

Risa felt like she should get an Academy Award for treating him, in front of her studio crew, like he was just another ordinary guest on her weekly show instead of the man she just met who had shaken her to her very core with just one kiss. JD felt like he was in the middle of an endurance test to see just how much he could take and manage to restrain himself. With every breath she took, he could see the rise and fall of her chest and the outline of her breast. With every word she spoke, he could feel her words, soft as angel wings, brushing his skin. Everything about her was magnified. Everything about him was restrained.

As she had interviewed him and asked him the tough questions she prepared, she realized, as she had already known, that there was nothing ordinary about JD. He was an enigma. Successful in everything he had ever touched, from the pigskin to the construction company he ran, he was a desirable, eligible man with a Midas touch. He was everything her mother groomed her to look for in a mate. He was everything she and her Alpha Kappa Alpha sorority sisters discussed when they had talked about their soul mates. When she reviewed the list that she carried in her head concerning possible traits for her future mate, JD's name kept coming up. He was everything she had selected. From his demeanor to his knockout good looks, JD's face kept appearing over the image of the mystery man she had always carried in her head. It was like he was haunting her. That scared her. They just met.

The rush of feelings she was having about him couldn't be real. This couldn't be happening. All she could think about was the kiss. The memory of it enveloped her and invaded her mind so that it was all she saw. When his lips had touched hers her reality was altered. All she could think was, *What have I been missing?*

At thirty-nine, Risa was neither a virgin nor a wanton. She had had her share of relationships. Men had pursued her, wooed her, and chased her. Some even caught her. But none of her relationships, lasting in duration from four months to two years, had moved her the way JD did with just one kiss. She didn't know if she was heady with emotion because her deadline was staring her in the face or because he was so close to her. Until this day she never believed in love at first sight. Until this day she didn't believe in the saying, "when you meet Mr. Right, you'll know it." Until this day, those descriptions of emotions, desire, and feelings that made her light-headed and stirred her innermost romantic self were just a sinful indulgence she enjoyed when she had the time to read a romance novel. Until this day. Until this day, everything had happened to some make-believe creature who inspired thoughts of whimsy, fluttering hearts, and adventure. Until this day, that creature had never been her. This day changed her perspective. This day gave her new insight. This day introduced her to JD Jones, her hero. Yes, she had definitely lost control of this day. With a simple kiss she transported herself from reality into the pages of a romance novel.

"I want to see you again," Risa heard JD say, his words snapping her back to reality.

He was standing right in front of her. So very close. Too close. She took a step backwards. The heat between them was too intense.

They wrapped up the show nearly an hour ago. JD had spent the remaining time signing autographs and taking pictures with the crew. He did it with patience and a good deal of humor. Risa was pleased by how he handled her staff as if they were longtime family friends and acquaintances never getting tired of their adulation. Afterwards, now, when they stood awkwardly, looking at each other, all she could do was grin stupidly as he looked down at her. He noticed that she had taken a step backwards and wisely did not close the distance between the two of them.

She did want to see him again. All that smack she talked in her head suddenly dissipated as she thrilled at the thought of seeing him again. After all, she admitted to herself, *why not?* She wanted to see where this was going. Could it go anywhere? Could it go all the way? Could she be the woman to change him and make him see only her? Could she be the woman to wave a magic wand and convert the playboy into a prince?

Secretly women all dreamed of having the kind of power necessary to change a man. When she was a little girl she fantasized about having the magical powers of Samantha Stevens from the television show, *Bewitched*. Life would be so simple if she could just twitch her nose and make problems go away. If she had been born just twenty years later then Samantha Stevens would be replaced with Melissa Joan Hart. Sabrina the teenage witch solving problems in Technicolor was so much more interesting. But realizing that magical powers only occurred easily to TV characters, she would have to handle her problems with feminine wiles and get JD to bend to her bidding. She wanted JD to be desirous of only her.

"Tonight?" JD asked. He wanted to see her tonight.

"Tonight?" she croaked. *Be careful what you ask for,* she reminded herself. *You just might get it.*

Her mother had always said, "If you want a Cadillac, ask for it. If you don't, you might get a piece of junk." JD was the Cadillac she dreamed of driving. She had just envisioned herself behind the wheel. So when the opportunity arose why did she want to run from it? Was it too soon? Yes, it was! How could she see him tonight? She wasn't ready to be with him. She wasn't prepared. She had to plan and make sure that everything worked out just right. She couldn't afford to mess this up with her anxiety.

As JD stood there waiting for a response Risa didn't know what to say. She didn't know what would be expected of her. She didn't know what to wear! They had just met and yet they had kissed as longtime lovers. If they got together tonight when there was no crew, buzzing fans and groups of people, how would they act? What would stop them? What would they do? They had already breached the borders of decorum. With no one around to interrupt them, they would be out of control. Could they stop with just a kiss?

"Tonight?" she repeated. Did she want to stop with just a kiss?

"I want to see you tonight," was what he said, but what he meant was that he needed to see her tonight. He didn't have to say it again. They knew.

Again, he was standing too close. When had he moved? She could feel him through the layer of her clothes.

"I-I-I . . ." she started.

How far did she want to go with this man? How far was she willing to go? Her head was spinning. Her chest was heaving. She was confused. One minute she was telling herself that he was all wrong for her. The next minute she was telling herself he was all right for her. She was hot. She was cold. What did it mean when the object of a person's affection gave them flulike symptoms? This might not be a good sign. Then again, it might be a sign of love at first sight.

While she was having yet again another inner debate, JD made a decision for her. He reached out and circled the outline of her nipple with his thumb. The action brought Risa back into reality. She was shocked. He was shocked. She was aroused. She caught her breath. But she didn't stop him. She wanted him to touch her. She wanted to touch him. She placed her well-manicured hand against his hard chest. The nails were coated in a delicate French tip. She got her nails done every week. It was an indulgence she enjoyed. She couldn't concentrate on her fingers. She could feel his heart beating strong and steady beneath her hand. She had never moved so fast. She never kissed on the first date. The two of them were hurtling towards the sun. They couldn't stop. They were moving so fast and yet there was nowhere else for them to go. No, they would not stop with just a kiss.

Risa never had a one-night stand. Any man she had been with was a man she was in a relationship with. She didn't know the rules of the one-night stand. She didn't know how to behave or what to say. She could easily see herself going there with JD. The picture was so vivid in her head that she closed her eyes to block it. Even with her eyes closed it was as if the image of him was tattooed on her eyelids. All she could see was JD. She had to think. Prior to meting this man, the thought of a one-night stand had never even entered her psyche. It wasn't part of her frame of reference. She had never, ever. Ever. Ever. From her first lover to her last love, they had been involved. But this man, JD, was so different. It was too early for love. It wasn't too early for what lovers did in the dark when no one was around. He made her feel like bumping uglies. That's what her grandmother used to call having sex, "bumping uglies." Her grandmother had a lot of interesting sayings and funny thoughts. She wondered what her sweet Nanna would have called JD. Probably in her ever-funny way she would have called him a cool drink of water on a hot summer day. That's where her mother got all those sayings, from her nanna, she was sure.

Just thinking of her nanna made her smile. JD saw the smile and thought it was for him. In a way it was. Risa was thinking of things that made her happy, getting her nails done, talks with her grandmother, touching JD, JD touching her. All these things made her feel nice and smile as if her body was filled with sunshine. It was a good feeling to feel so full and so well loved. All this from a kiss and an indiscreet touch. What would happen when they completed the act? Someone loudly calling her name interrupted her thought pattern. She was so deep in thought it took her a moment to realize it was Cayce.

"Risa! Risa!" Cayce rushed in, tittering on her three-inch heels as she rounded the corner in a huff. She was frazzled. Her eyes were big and round and if possible, steam should have been coming from the top of her head. She was that agitated.

"What's wrong?" Risa asked not used to seeing the usually composed Cayce so out of character. Usually Cayce was a petite picture of perfect calm that only spoke in exclamation points. She never acted in them.

"They are towing JD's car! I tried to stop him but he said that it was parked illegally in your parking spot."

Silently Risa again thanked her lucky stars for Cayce. So many times, she had been there for her. This time, she saved her from taking a step forward that would not have allowed for a step backward. Cayce had stopped Risa from breaking a major workplace rule: Don't make whoopee in the workplace. For that Risa was grateful.

"No. Richard's car is in my spot," she mumbled, taking a much needed step back from JD. She still needed the distance. When she was close too him logic was thrown out the window and she behaved foolishly, throwing caution to the wind.

"Richard left over an hour ago!" Cayce said.

"What?" Risa asked.

What was wrong with her? She was acting like an accident victim with brain damage. She couldn't focus. She knew Cayce was saying something important but her mind was on JD. JD's lips. JD's mouth on hers. JD's hands on her body. JD. JD. JD. "Richard parked in his own spot today! It was raining when JD got here. I told him to park in your spot." Cayce looked up at both of them. Even though she was a munchkin in a land of giants, there was a presence about Cayce. She was a lot in a little package. She was pure dynamite. "Do you hear me?" She wasn't screaming. But she might as well have been. She was trying to get Risa's attention.

"Where is my car now?" JD asked. Unlike Risa, he seemed to be able to think straight.

"On its way to city impound," Cayce said, tapping her foot and fuming. "He told me to get my boss. He wouldn't listen to me."

Cayce wasn't used to not getting her way. She was furious. No wonder her eyes burned. When she was angry her accent was more pronounced. If she had had her way, the tow truck driver would have been burned at the stake. It didn't help matters that he had been so darned cute. She felt like he was being deliberately obtuse when she tried to explain the situation. He had even gone so far as to tell her to come down there herself and pick it up and he might not charge her the impound fee. Maybe she'd get her nana banana to put a spell on him. She didn't really believe in the old magic, voodoo hoodoo of her ancestors, but poking a voodoo doll in his image would make her feel better. He was trying to get her goat and he got it. She didn't like being manipulated no matter how attractive the puppet master.

"Come on," Risa said to JD as she grabbed her briefcase and purse.

He took her portfolio without her having to ask. He could see that she had a lot in her hands. It was like they were on the same page. She knew that once she left she wouldn't be coming back to the office. He was making it easy on her. "Let's go get your car." If it was one thing she could control, it was getting JD's car out of the impound.

"Will you be back today?" Cayce called after the tall couple as they strode from the building. She had no idea what was going on between them. She asked so that she could handle Risa's calls.

"No," JD called over his shoulder as he opened the door for Risa.

"Risa?" Cayce asked skeptically. She still reported to Risa although she had heard JD.

"I won't be back today, Cayce," Risa answered. "And you

can leave early if you want." Risa didn't even pause to see what effect her words had on her assistant. Cayce was hardworking, but Risa knew she wouldn't hang around if she was given permission to hit the road. On the way to her car she didn't even bother to correct JD in his assumption that she was going to spend the rest of the day with him. Whatever it was between them had to be addressed as soon as possible or they were both going to explode. It had to be now or never.

Watching Risa and JD walk out together, Cayce couldn't help but think what a striking couple they made. When she was a little girl her nanna banana had told her about having the second sight and clairvoyance. Cayce never put much stock in it. But as she watched the pair walk away with such haste and conspicuousness, all she could think of was that they should be together. Call it a hunch or a premonition or just a feeling. Whatever it was, her nanna would get a kick out of her feeling it.

The old Haitian woman would call it being blessed with having the second sight. She, younger and skeptical, would just call it having an insight into human nature. Laughing at the two different ways they—old-fashioned island wiles and newfangled technology—approached the same subject, she decided to go call her nanna. She knew how happy it would make her to think that Risa was well onto the road to finding a mate.

Her nanna, Consula, was fond of Risa. And in having her focus on Risa, who she considered another grand-child, she might, just for a moment, take her focus off of Cayce. For that reason, Cayce would gladly offer her boss, mentor, and friend up for sacrifice to her nanna's meddling ways. It would give Cayce a moment of peace. If Risa were in her shoes she would do the same thing. Laughing at her rationalization she started back to her office in order to have one of her many conversations with her beloved grandmother. For the first time in ages it would not be about her and her single-girl status. Then she would get her coat and head home. It had been a long time since she got out of the office before nightfall. She liked her job and thanked her lucky stars for the world's greatest boss, but she liked having a life too.

The walk from the front door of the television station to her car was one of the longest Risa had ever taken. They took it in silence and that made it seem twice as long. They huddled together beneath JD's small compact umbrella. JD didn't seem angry that his car had been towed; he was just deep in thought.

The car ride too was taken in silence. The two of them were so caught up in their own thoughts that they could not speak to each other. The oldies station was playing Diana Ross and the Supremes. The familiarity of it lulled them into a companionable silence, but the tension was so tight it was no wonder they were in each other's arms as soon as they found themselves parked outside the city impound.

Once their skin touched all the strain and tension they felt earlier eased and was replaced by something more insistent and more hungry. With ease JD pulled Risa over the stick shift so that she could straddle his lap. His desire was evident as he nibbled the corner of her mouth and traced her lips with his tongue. The strain was gone. This is what they needed to appease it. They didn't need words. The silence had prepared them for this moment. It was a prelude to this, yet another kiss.

As soon as the car had come to a stop, there was nothing else for them to do. They had to kiss. They had to touch. They had to try to crawl deep into each other's skin by going in through their mouths. Their lips were soft. Their tongues were wet. They tasted like each other. Although in good shape they were both tall people. In the front seat of the new BMW there was a tangle of arms, legs, elbows, and knees that was a hodgepodge of body parts that kept them from going any further. Yet if they could have, they would have.

"We have to get your car," Risa breathed against JD's lips as she adjusted her body so that she could be more comfortable and he less uncomfortable. Although dressed it was as if they were naked. Her center fit against his manhood as if they were two interlocking LEGO pieces.

"I can get it tomorrow," he growled, reaching again for her hips in order to reposition her against him. It didn't matter that they were clothed. Their two centers were doing a dance that worked with or without clothing. Unable to control the thrusting of his hips, his hands came up and tangled themselves in her mane of thick, dark hair. It was easier to maneuver her this way.

"No, we need to get it now," Risa said in an attempt to pull herself away.

She too was moving against him in the tight space. It was cold in the car, so she reached behind her and deftly turned on the heater. But it wouldn't work with the engine turned off. She didn't even have to voice the words. He reached around her and turned the key in the ignition. The motor roared to life then settled into a smooth hum. The windows fogged up quickly creating a camouflage of smoke so that they could continue with their love pay.

Risa ran her hands over JD's neatly shaved head. The skin felt smooth beneath her fingers. She had never dated a man with a clean-shaven head. She found the style very appealing on JD. Some men couldn't wear a shaven head and look sexy. He could. He could wear anything and look sexy. Just touching his scalp was agonizing because she wanted more. More. More of him.

"That's not what I need," JD said. His tongue was demanding as he continued to kiss her.

"We've got to stop," she panted against his lips.

She couldn't catch her breath. Being so close to him was literally taking her breath away. She needed to stop the madness but she couldn't because she was out of control. All of her upbringing was telling her to stop.

"I don't want to stop," JD panted right back.

*I do not make out on the first date!* Risa scolded herself. There were rules that she followed. She governed her life with them. If she ever sat down and put pen to paper she knew that one of them would have been "do not make out in the front seat of the car!"

"Me either," Risa gave in. Her mouth said the words that went against what her head was telling her. Her mouth agreed with her body and waged a war with her head. She didn't want to stop. So her mouth formed the words.

"That's right. Baby girl, don't stop," JD said, grinding against her.

Neither one of them wanted to stop. Deftly and skillfully, JD unsnapped one of the pearl buttons that held Risa's silk blouse together. He was very gentle with her. But she wouldn't have minded if he had broken the buttons in passion. The blouse was ruined anyway. It hadn't liked the icy rain.

He unbuttoned another button. She didn't try to stop him. He knew she didn't want him to stop. Looking into her eyes that were growing dark with desire, he slipped his large hand into the opening his hand created. She let out a sharp intake of breath as he traced her nipple with his thumb. He had done it before and she had responded as someone familiar with his touch. He weighed the heaviness of her breast with his hand, tested the feel of it against his skin before he bent his head and sampled from her. If it had been possible to lay back and open herself to him, she would have. But she couldn't. There was not enough room in the car.

Never before had Risa done anything so wanton and extreme and yet she did it easily as if it were second nature. She could feel how much JD was enjoying their union and conveyed it to her with his mouth and hands. She wanted to lie beneath him and feel his maleness inside of her. It didn't matter that they were outside in her car. It didn't matter that they were not afforded the luxury of privacy that came with making love behind closed doors in the comfort of a bed inside a house. She wanted him. She wanted him more than any man she had ever known. She wanted him now.

Through her clothes, in the cramped car, she felt the skill of his fingers and the deftness of his touch. There were no words as he slid his hand into the waistband of her well-tailored pants. His fingers grazed the delicate lace of her panties and eased past them into her woman's place. She parted her legs to allow him easier access to her. He knew what to do. As he kissed her, his fingers performed a complicated symphony against her most delicate nerve endings. She couldn't control the movement of her body or the sweet, delicate, womanly sounds that escaped from her lips. He didn't have to ask her if she liked it. He knew she did and her liking it made him like what he was doing to her even more.

"Tell me that you like it," JD said, deciding that he wanted to hear for himself what he already knew.

She had never spoken dirty words or whispered lover's talk in the quiet of her bedroom, yet here in her car as the cold rain fell against the window, she said the words easily.

"Umm, I like it," she moaned.

"I like you," she wanted to scream at the top of her lungs.

She could write a song about how he was making her

feel. She had never sung in her life, but right now, she could sing. She could scream. She could belt out a melody that would make Aretha Franklin give her props.

"I like you too," he said, placing her hand on him.

And just as soon as it started, it stopped. Faced with the reality of his maleness and the object of his desire, Risa was awash with a dose of harsh cold reality. She had just met this man. Was she crazy?

"Stop!" she shouted.

She had to put a stop to this madness. It had to be madness. Only madness would let her act like this. She was Risa James. She wasn't Carrie Bradshaw or Samantha Waters from *Sex and the City*. She didn't meet men and fall into a tryst with them because she found them incredibly irresistible and powerfully appealing. She wasn't a fictional character capable of bedding men without consequence. There was always a consequence. Didn't Richard Marconi just catch them in a compromising position?

Realizing that only strengthened her resolve to end this. She couldn't let a man she had known less than twenty-four hours drink from her like she was a piece of honey-drenched fruit. She just couldn't do it no matter what people said. And they always said it was a liberating and empowering thing to do, engage in casual sex. Risa James could not engage in casual sex. She could say that her mother had not raised her that way. Truth be told it had nothing to do with her mother. As a self-sufficient, educated, strong secure woman, she always felt that one-night stands were perceived as actions taken by desperate women with self-esteem issues. One thing Risa James had was a healthy dose of self-esteem. She didn't need to give herself to a man she had just met to feel empowered and whole. But even in saying that, she knew that wasn't the reason she would be giving herself to JD. She would be doing it because she wanted to. Were it not for the signal it would give and the message it would say, she would do it. But she didn't know how he would see it. She couldn't know. They had just met.

The litany kept repeating in Risa's head. *Would he think any less of me?* She didn't know and she didn't want to risk it. The uncertainty had her torn. *Do I give in to the desire that has me nearly blinded by the brightness of it? Or do I follow the rules of manners and good sense?* On one hand she was pleased that he found her so desirable that he couldn't keep his hands to himself. On the other hand, she was alarmed that he felt like he could treat her this way in such a short period of time. And if she had another hand, she would have been alarmed that she so easily let him.

"Stop," she said, and she almost meant it this time. If she let him go on, he might think of her as a loose woman. She wasn't a loose woman. Actually, she was sometimes embarrassed to admit how incredibly old-fashioned she was when it came to sex and relationships. She had never been casual with her affection and she wasn't about to start. Deadline be damned. "Stop."

JD placed her hand over his in a way that was intimate and familiar. "Do you really want me to stop?" he asked, looking into her eyes.

Faced with his passion, Risa found it hard to say her next words, because like him, she too was aroused. Her passion however wasn't as obvious.

"Really. Stop," she sighed.

Yes, she meant it this time. Someone had to be the voice of reason. JD stopped. He heard her. He looked deep into her eyes and knew that, again, something had changed. He didn't know what. But in the short time that he'd known her, he found it easy to read the subtle changes in her body language. She meant it. He stopped. He would not force himself on her. He had never had to do that before and he would not start now.

Tenderly, JD reconnected the buttons of Risa's blouse. If her delectable flesh were shielded from his eyes, it would be easier to control his passion. For a moment they sat quietly. The only sound in the small car was their heavy breathing and the pitter-patter of the raindrops that fell against the canvas of the BMW's rooftop. Until today she thought it was a good car for her. This was the first time that it seemed too small. She didn't make major purchases based on a whim. She researched everything there was to know before she traded in her practical five-year-old Saab for the new BMW. But now, as she found herself uncomfortably straddling JD's hips, she wondered if she had chosen correctly. Maybe a minivan would have been a wiser choice. She knew as soon as the thought entered her mind that it was simply to appease her desire to lay with him that she thought of cars more appropriate for that act. A minivan would have definitely been more comfortable than the BMW in that respect.

"I don't do things like this," she said.

She had to make sure that he knew that. She didn't want to lose his respect. It was important to her that he respected her. The thought of the minivan had her thinking of having children and a house with a white picket fence and soccer games and football games and Girl Scouts and PTA meetings. *We just met!* she repeated over and over in her head.

"Neither do I. But we're adults," JD reasoned. "We can do this if we want to."

"We just met and we're making out in the front seat of my car!" Risa exclaimed.

"We could have used my car, but it got towed." He made an attempt at levity.

"This is crazy." She wouldn't let him seduce her with humor. She was determined to approach this with a level head.

"I know."

Although they discussed the illogic of what they were doing neither one of them moved. There was a decadent innocence about their situation. Making out in the car was a fantasy of grand proportions in both the male and female mind. Being unable to not "actually do" anything only made the wanting of it more intense.

"We can't do this," Risa said with confirmation.

"Why not? Neither one of us is involved, or are you? Are you involved with anyone, Risa?" JD asked for the first time, suddenly realizing that she could have a commitment to another.

The thought both scared and angered him. He didn't want her touched by anyone other than him. Her delightful charms belonged to him. He suddenly felt possessive and jealous. He assumed he would not be her first. But if he had his way, he was going to be her last.

"Maybe I should be asking you that question?" There. She said it. She voiced one of the things that were nagging her. How many women were there? Neither one of them questioned the total inappropriateness of their questions. Neither one of them questioned why they suddenly felt so possessive towards each other. Neither one questioned it because it was just supposed to happen. Just like in sappy romantic comedies and dime-store romance novels they had found instant attraction and had gotten lost in the feel of each other.

"No. I don't have anyone special," JD answered.

Risa managed to ease her long-legged body from the straddle position it was in on JD's lap without further incident. "I don't want to play semantic games with you, JD. Does saying there isn't anyone special mean there isn't *anyone?* Is there a whole stable of women waiting in line for you to shower them with attention and affection?"

The mood in the car changed. Although she was in her

seat now and not touching him, she could still feel the heat radiating from his body. She was so aware of him. Ever since their meeting she'd been aware of him. She couldn't help it. It was like their auras were connected.

"Always the reporter, hmmm?" he asked, amused.

Finally, they were having the conversation they should have had before this whole thing started. It gave her a sense of comfort knowing he was willing to have this conversation with her. At least in this they would be conventional.

"I won't lie to you, Risa," he said. "We just met. Before you there were others. Sure enough. I am a single man. I have no attachments and women have found me appealing. There was one woman I was close to. But that ended, today."

"When did you have time—" she started before getting cut off.

"I made a phone call," he said simply.

Almond-shaped brown eyes stared into dark almost black ones as they contemplated the seriousness of what his confession meant.

"How could you do that? How could you know where this would go?"

"No matter where it went, if I felt the way about you that I did, I could not feel about her the way I thought I did."

They were simple words said with complete honesty and they said it all. There was a lot of feeling in those simple words.

"I don't know, JD," Risa said doubtfully. "I'm almost forty. I don't have the time or the inclination to play."

"Almost forty," he mused. "I didn't know you were that old. Maybe I should reconsider asking you out."

She knew that he was teasing with her but still she replied, "Old? Please. You're the one pushing forty."

"Forty? I'm thirty-nine. I won't be forty until November."

"I'll be forty next month."

"Oh, you're an older woman. I do like older women."

"Don't play with me."

He suddenly turned serious. "I am not playing with you, Risa. I knew it was time to stop playing as soon as I met you." He took her face between his hands and looked into her eyes as he got even more serious. "I am tired, Risa. I am tired of the chase. I am tired of the games. I want something meaningful."

She knew he was very serious. She could tell from the way his eyes beseeched hers. "I want that too . . . at least I think. JD, I didn't even think about marriage until last night."

As soon as she said the words she could have bitten her tongue. She only met the man this morning and already she was talking marriage. Did she want to send him running and screaming for the hills? Although there hadn't been that many men in her life, she knew that there were some things they didn't want to hear. "I'm late" and "marriage" were two of them. The men she knew were extremely commitment-phobic.

"I didn't ask you to marry me," he said the words as if he was tasting them for the first time.

"I know that," she began to clarify. He stopped her by placing his finger against her lips.

"Will you marry me?" he asked.

*Did he say what I think he just said?* she asked herself. *Was he serious? Did I hear him right? I've never had a hearing problem before. My hearing is very good. So is my eyesight. I've never worn glasses.* "What?" she asked.

She didn't know why she was thinking such inane things at this moment. Who cared about her twenty-twenty vision and good hearing although important senses that affected their time together . . . the better to see him with and the better to hear his moans of delight with, they had nothing to do with the issue at hand.

*Did he just ask me to marry him? No,* she thought. *That could not have possibly been it.* She knew she hadn't heard that. She could not have heard that.

"Risa James, will you marry me? I'd get down on my knees but I can't fit," he said.

*He's serious! He's crazy! Yes, that's it!* she thought. *I'm in my car with a crazy man. Only crazy men do things like this and only crazy women encourage them.*

"You're crazy," she said out loud. He had to acknowledge it. He was as crazy as a well-muscled Betsy bug.

"I'm thirty-nine years old, soon to be forty. Successful. Good to look at, or so I've been told. I'd marry me," he reasoned. His eyes held laughter and the corners of his mouth were set in a self-satisfied grin. He was having fun with her and she wasn't sure if she liked the joke. Yes, it was a joke. It had to be a joke.

"You don't even know me." She said it because she knew he wasn't serious. He couldn't possibly be serious even though as soon as he said it, she immediately flashbacked to the white picket fences and the soccer-mom minivan fantasy. She could live that life.

"I can get to know you. I can grow old with you."

She could detect the seriousness in him. The words were so right. It would be such a horrible joke if he weren't serious. If this was his idea of poking fun she didn't like his sense of humor.

"I can love you. You are perfect for me," he continued.

He wasn't trying to convince her. He was stating a fact.

"Let me think," she said nervously.

"Take all the time you want."

Every women who thinks of getting married dreams of hearing these words or some version of these words.

"I eat crackers in bed. I cry over old movies that I've seen over and over. I'm computer illiterate," she said, pointing out her flaws, rattling of her weak points to discourage him from making promises he wouldn't have to keep once he realized the error of his ways.

"So, so and so," he said, dismissing her excuses as if they were weak and insignificant. Even to her own ears they sounded like little bits of nothing.

"So?" she almost yelled at him. "Didn't you hear me? I eat in bed!" She said it as if it were the most heinous of crimes.

"I don't care." He punctuated each word with a close-mouthed kiss. Even without the tongue he still sent shivers up and down her spine.

"You're delirious because your car got towed. Let's go get it so you can get some air," she said as she reached for the door handle but he placed his hand over hers.

"I am neither crazy nor delirious. I am very good at what I do because I take chances. I want to take a chance with you."

If she ever thought that he wasn't serious, his tone and demeanor emphasized for her that he was, indeed, serious.

"I'm thirty-nine years old!" Her voice echoed in the confines of the car.

As the words reverberated in her ears she wondered if this was the powers that be trying to convince her that she needed to give pause to logic. This wasn't logical. This did not compute. Things like this just didn't happen to level-headed thirty-nine-year-old television executives. She was the demographic that read the romance novels of which she was fond of, not the demographic of the heroine. In her mind she wasn't glamorous enough or young enough or sexy enough for this to happen as it did.

"That's old enough to know what you want," he said, kissing her again. This time there was just the hint of tongue in the kiss.

"I know what I should want . . . but . . . it's too soon . . . too fast . . . too out of control." Her head was spinning.

"Okay. Let's approach this in a more conventional way. What are you looking for in a man?"

"What?" She still couldn't think straight.

"What are you looking for in a man?" He repeated the words, enunciating very clearly as if he were speaking to someone with a hearing problem who had to read lips.

"Ambition." She had always wanted a man with ambition. Her world was a very fast-paced, competitive field. Her mate would have to be able to stand on his own feet and exist in his own world. He would need ambition for that. Whatever his field, she wanted him good at it.

"Me."

"Drive." *Were ambition and drive the same thing?*

"Me."

"Sense of humor." She liked a man who made her laugh. Laughter was always the best medicine. When all else failed, laugh. Nine times out of ten you'd feel better.

"Me."

"Will you stop it? I'm trying to think." She began thinking to herself, *Just what else do I really want in a man? True, ambition, drive, and sense of humor would be nice to have. But if I gave it serious consideration, really serious consideration, what would I want?* "I want security and stability. I want someone who is nice to animals and old people. I want a man who keeps his word. I want a man who is faithful and listens to me when I talk."

Those weren't really outrageous things to ask for. She hadn't asked for a rich man or a handsome man. Riches could be earned and handsome meant nothing if he weren't kind and sincere. JD heard her and made a mental note of what she found important. To her credit, she didn't mention money.

He didn't know what type of salary she made in her present position or what she had managed to sock away during her career. He did have a good idea that her salary couldn't touch his. As CEO of JD Enterprises he was pulling in a six-figure income. It was very generous and came with perks like a company car and private jet. Before creating his own position he had a successful professional football career that had begun right after college. He was the number-one draft pick upon graduation, which led to a ten-year career with America's team. Any woman that married him would be afforded a very comfortable lifestyle. She had to be aware of it yet she didn't mention it. Good for her.

"I'm stable and secure. I'm nice to old people and animals. And I will always listen to you, " he assured her.

He smiled at her, white, even teeth gleaming against his ebony skin. He could win her over with a smile. She was mesmerized by his charisma.

"I want passion," she added. The man she married would be a man who always got her motor running. She deserved that.

"We have passion." He said it like it was a given because it was a given.

From the moment they met, there had been nothing but passion. They had passion when they didn't have words. Their bodies communicated better than their mouths ever could. He was handsome and he knew it. He was comfortable with his sexuality and confident in the reaction he got from her. She was a confident, accomplished woman, sexy, secure, and intriguing. She had to know that and what she was doing to him.

"I want more than that." She was running scared. Her

heart was beating very fast. For the first time, she didn't stutter. She knew what she wanted. If she was going to meet a man in one day, make out with him and accept a marriage proposal, she had better damn sure know what she wanted. "Can you give me that, JD? Can you give me more?"

"I can give you whatever you want or damn well die trying," JD replied.

Again, he kissed her. There was no hesitation in the kiss. The more they spent time together, the more confident and comfortable they became with each other. It was sweet and gentle and tasted like love or something very close to the beginning stages of it. Suddenly it didn't matter that things like this just weren't done. It didn't matter that at first she expected to wake up from a crazy nightmare. All that mattered was Risa and JD in the front seat of her car kissing like teenagers and touching like lovers.

Because she had to catch her breath she disengaged her lips from his and looked at him. She wanted to see him for the first time without being lulled into a sex-induced stupor. His eyes were so beautiful. She could drown in those eyes. She found herself actually contemplating his proposal. She couldn't find one reason not to accept. No one had ever made her feel like he had. No one had ever made her light-headed and aroused with a gentle kiss and a sexy sensual make-out session. She would be forty in a month. She didn't have any more time!

"I need to think about this." Yes, twenty-four hours would be what she would give herself. That was enough time to get him out of her system so that she could think like the rational woman that she was.

"The offer is on the table, Ms. James. I won't bring it up again. You have a few months to decide," he said without even blinking.

"Why a few months?" All she wanted was twenty-four hours and he was offering her a vague few months.

"Because I would rather be a thirty-nine-year-old groom instead of a forty-year-old one."

With that he opened the car door, got out and walked away without even closing the door behind him. Was she supposed to follow him? *I think not.* It was cold outside the car.

Risa watched with a combination of lust and wonder as he walked through the rain to the front door of the car impound in order to retrieve his car. She knew that even though things like this didn't happen to her it had just happened. She heard him with her own ears. She wasn't one for delusions and flights of fantasy. JD Jones just asked her to marry him.

She closed the car door. The insides were steamy. For a moment, she sat shivering from the sudden gust of wind that invaded the car when JD got out. With chattering teeth she turned on the car's heater again. The humming sound of the heat was comforting and in her confused state helped her think. *Maybe this really could work,* she thought as she put the car in gear and started for her house. She could take control of this day. It didn't have to spiral out of control.

# Chapter 7

"Lisa. Her name is Lisa or something," Angela whispered into the phone as she talked to her sister, Daphne.

JD and Big L were shooting pool in the family room. Angela was trying to hold her voice down so that they couldn't hear her. Originally, she had been working on her latest article for the PTA newsletter in her home office. Her job as vice president of finance for JD Enterprises afforded her the luxury of a flexible schedule. She managed a staff of three that were capable and independent. Therefore she had a lot of time to devote to her true passion, her family.

Angela was a busy, involved mother of four. She utilized all the flextime she acquired. While she worked on the newsletter she made a mental note of where her brood was dispersed. Hailey was at ballet class. Jacob was at karate and the twins, Edison and Eden, were spending quality time with her parents. She had snuck home with the intention of spending a little quality time with her husband, Big L, only to find him and JD shooting pool. They got suspiciously quiet when she breezed in with a platter of sand-wiches, chips, and beer and that had piqued her curiosity.

So when Daphne had called and interrupted her, she had been quick to pick up the phone so that she could gossip about her brother's crazy behavior.

*What could they be talking about that they don't want me to hear?* she thought as she sat the platter down. *Curiouser and curiouser,* she mused and made it a point to appear to be busy so that she could eavesdrop and report back to her sister. Their sistergirl network was strong. As the men continued their conversation in hushed tones she couldn't help but wonder why all the secrecy? No one had seen the girl and JD had stood Elisha up for lunch and Angela up for dinner. This wasn't like her brother at all. He never let a woman come between him and the close-knit relation-ships he had with his sisters. The only boy in a brood of girls, they'd always been somewhat possessive and protec-tive of him, Angela more than the others because she was the oldest and JD as the next Jones child in line was closer to her in age and temperament. All that said she knew her brother was a good man and would make some woman a good husband. But until that time she wanted to make sure that he wasn't caught by the wrong chicken trying to feather her nest with his money.

All the girls felt that their brother was a target for gold diggers, hoochies, and opportunists. Men just weren't al-ways smart where women were concerned. They didn't want him to make a costly and painful mistake. They were convinced that if they didn't help him along, he might not be able to decipher who was a legitimate candidate for his affection and who was just a candidate for good times and fun nights. He had no idea that they had influenced his choices. He thought he was in control. Men.

Of all the women who had paraded through JD's life and his bed, only one seemed even close to landing him.

That was Lucy Belle. She was the front-runner until this mystery lady came onto the scene. Suddenly the Jones girls had become very protective of their brother's current ladylove. No one, even Angela, who was of the unpopular opinion that Lucy wasn't "the one" for JD, wanted to see her mistreated. They wouldn't tolerate that from their brother. Sure he was a man, but he was a Southern man. Therefore, he must be an example of decorum and good manners. They wouldn't settle for anything else. So when JD announced to his third sister, Carlie, that he and Lucy had parted amicably, knowing that she would inform the rest, Angela suddenly realized she was fond of Lucy Belle. It was true that her stance had always been that Lucy Belle wasn't the wife that JD wanted or needed. Although Lucy Belle was a very beautiful, well-preserved woman who looked a lot like Angela Bassett, she was older than Angela's beloved brother.

At ten years his senior, with a child entering college and one in high school, Angela feared Lucy Belle would not be willing or able to give her brother the family he wanted. Every time Angela confided her misgivings, her sister, Daphne, the loudest and most headstrong, pooh-poohed her objectives. According to Daphne, if JD could love 'em, she could like 'em. Daphne admired Lucy Belle and wanted to be just like her when she turned forty-nine. But at twenty-six, forty-nine was a long way away for Ms. Daphne. Finally Angela had to hang up with Daphne because she couldn't manage to talk to her and listen unobtrusively to the men.

There was an old expression that said if you put two women in a room, eventually they'd start eating and talking about men. The same could be said about men. Angela knew this and wanted to stay and prove her theory, but she had to go get Hailey.

"I'm going to get Hailey," she called, hating to interrupt their conversation.

"Okay, hon. See you when you get back," Big L called after her.

She paused, waiting for her brother to see her off as well. There was silence. JD didn't even look up. She'd have a talk with JD when she got back. She was way too busy to give him and his new ladylove any more attention. With that, she gathered her things so that she could go and gather her child. The soccer moms they spoke about on television and in women's magazines had nothing on Angela. She was supermom personified and none of her children played soccer. As soon as Angela headed out in her Lincoln Navigator, Big L and JD broke out the pig-out food. There were leftovers from the night before, garlic potatoes, meat loaf, and green pea salad. There was half a chocolate cake on the counter, leftover Krispy Kreme doughnuts and lasagna from the freezer. The funny thing about it was that this was just a snack. As soon as Angela got in and prepared dinner they would eat again, not to mention they had already scarffed the sandwiches down.

"So, let me get this straight. You asked her to marry you?" Big L asked from between bites of the Krispy Kreme doughnuts he was so partial to. He had a notorious sweet tooth and kept his weight in check with daily exercise. His bites of the doughnuts were in between his turn at the pool table.

"Yeah," JD answered as he eyeballed the angle of the solid white ball and its position to the striped mustard-colored ball.

They had been playing pool for over an hour now and the score was Big L five, JD six. They were very competitive, but not as driven as they had been on the football field. Ten years ago and twenty pounds ago, they were lean, mean, fighting machines determined to demolish any and everyone on the football field. Now, more settled and not consumed with the football player killer lust, they could

play a game of pool and keep in mind that it was just a
game. There would be one winner and one loser. Careers
did not rest on how many touchdowns, passes and yards
were won.

"What did she say?" Big L asked. He was genuinely curious. Things like this didn't happen everyday.

"She has to think about it."

"Well, what do you expect? Nobody gets married after
one date, if you can even call that a date. It just doesn't
happen."

"I don't know," JD said as he finally took the shot.

Ever since he had asked Risa to marry him he'd been
thinking about his rash decision. But he didn't regret his
offer. The problem he had was convincing his new ladylove that the whirlwind pace they were traveling down the
road to romance was just fine. The more time they spent
together she was making every effort to find fault in JD
and their relationship, because no one could possibly click
as well as they did in such a short time. It just wasn't done!
He, on the other hand, was doing everything to prove that
he had made the right decision. He was right and he knew
it. To prove his point he had planned gifts and dinners
and outings so they could spend some quality time together. What he got in exchange for his well-thought-out
plans were evenings of sensations so delightful he was
about to lose his mind in his efforts to woo her. They had
gotten so very close to consummating their union that he
often had to leave her and take a cold shower. Each time
they fell short of the ultimate goal, consummation, he reminded himself that it would all be worth it in the end.

Risa was a prize well worth the effort. That said he
would take his time with her. So, each time they stopped,
he took his blows like the man he wanted her to know him
as. Sure, he was beside himself with desire, but he could
live with it, if she needed more time. When he analyzed

his feelings he realized he had never felt this way and found it hard to put it into words for his friend. As he attempted to explain just how smitten he was all the other men did was laugh at him.

"Looks like you've got it bad, bro," Big L said. JD had missed his last shot so Big L was now positioning himself to take his shot.

Big L took a great deal of delight in laughing at JD's dilemma. He had once been in the same situation and his friend hadn't been nearly as understanding. As a matter of fact, as he recalled, JD had teased him mercilessly.

"Looks like I do," JD consented. He was hooked and he knew it. He didn't need his friend to cosign for him. "Aren't you going to tell me I have lost my mind?"

"Who me?" Big L laughed. "Remember who you are talking to now."

He could easily remind his friend of the teasing he underwent when he first met Angela. They had gotten married without even dating. The difference between Angela and Big L and JD and Risa was that Angela and Big L had known each other for years and had been dancing around an attraction that was so obvious that it was comical. Around Angela, Big L was like a big, lumbering teddy bear that had knowingly walked into a trap laid by feminine wiles. Around Big L, Angela wasn't the bossy, loudmouthed know-it-all that she was with her sisters and brother. Around her husband she was a chocolate-covered Martha Stewart, a classy B. Smith, a domestic goddess capable of running a household and a business and doing it wearing pearls and high heels.

If JD needed a role model then his friend and his sister had laid the blueprint. Smiling, just thinking of Risa, he moved out of the way so that his friend could take his shot. *Let me see him make that,* was his thought as he contemplated his date with Risa scheduled for later that night. Would they be able to contain themselves this time like the times before? Would they? Should they? Would they?

JD and Risa didn't have the familiarity that Big L and Angela had that came from having known each other for a long time. But they did have chemistry. It was potent, viable, and blatant.

JD had always been a good judge of character. He was wrong rarely in his life. He wasn't wrong about Risa. He knew it. He knew her. He could touch her heart and feel her soul. She wasn't a woman of deceptive wiles, schemes, games, and tricks. With her, he got what he saw, and he liked what he saw. She was beauty personified. With those beautiful almond-shaped eyes, that creamy chocolaty skin, and that body that was anything but angelic, she was his siren and his kryptonite. She was a little skinnier than he preferred, but she wore it well, with full breast and sexy hips that swayed with a siren's come-hither song. That body was dynamite and he would risk the explosion. As they spent more time together, it was inevitable that they would get to know each other in the biblical sense. They were walking down a road that had only one of two destinations, her big four-poster bed or his. By mutual understanding they were holding off on the sex to prove that they had something else in common besides the obvious physical attraction. If they were to get married, they'd eventually have to talk to each other.

# Chapter 8

"Cards, roses, and a diamond tennis bracelet," Cayce chirped as happy as a lark, strolling around Risa's office with the flowers in her hand and the bracelet on her arm. Gifts from JD had been coming in a steady stream. As soon as they got over the thrill of one a new bobble took its place. It was like everyday was Christmas or Kwanzaa. The thrill of opening the presents was as exciting as getting them. "Me thinks he really likes you." She smiled, slipping into the singsong thick Haitian dialect that usually solicited a smile from Risa. Although she wasn't born on the island her heritage was thick and strong. Surrounded by her parents and a loving grandmother, who all spoke with the rich, thick, accents, she could slip into it as easily as she could slip into her clothes. She did it so well that it usually made Risa smile, but not today.

Risa was heavy in thought and could not be moved from her reverie with Haitian colloquialisms. JD was so relentless in his pursuit of her that she actually found herself giving serious thought to his offer. His attention was overwhelming and just a little frightening. She had never been paid this much attention and she found herself acceptable to it. It was fun and exciting and thrilling to be the object of someone's desire, especially someone as desirable as JD. She was flattered. But the pragmatist in her kept reminding her to think with her head and not her heart. Her main concern was that her fast approaching birthday not be the main factor in deciding to marry JD. She didn't want to make her decision out of desperation. She wasn't proud of the fact that she didn't want to enter her forties alone. Knowing this she had to take heed to the little voice. It was the voice of reason and she knew it. So when the practical side of her reared its ugly head and whispered in her ear, she listened, however reluctantly.

"And you look good together," Cayce added.

Cayce said it as if that was all it took to make a relationship work. Risa did smile at that. Although she wasn't totally involved in Cayce's monologue, she would occasionally allow herself to take a break from the battle in her head and check in and see what Cayce was talking about. The simple declaration that they looked good together was all Cayce needed to seal the deal. Risa, on the other hand, needed a little more than that.

"This might be love at first sight," Cayce persisted as Risa, once again, tuned to her inner voice.

If she followed her head, she could wind up forty, single, and alone. If she followed her heart she would be married to a beautiful man and could start on the family she always wanted. As she got closer to forty she could feel herself being swayed by him. She enjoyed his company. She liked the way he made her feel. Between the war between her heart and her head, her head was slowly losing.

"Doesn't he make you feel good?" Cayce asked, starry-eyed.

"Yes," Risa said. But *"Yes!!!!"* was what she screamed in her head. *"Yes, Yes, Yes !!!!"* She loved the way he made her

feel. So turning forty wasn't the only reason she was thinking about JD's offer to become his wife. The raw emotions
that ran through her body whenever they were together
were electrifying. At first she was ashamed of how she acted,
so wanton and uninhibited, bordering on desperate when
she saw him, giving in to a passion the likes of which she
had never known. But she slowly got used to it. After each
session, she was becoming more and more free. He was
bringing out a side of her she wasn't even aware she had.
Each and every time they came close to setting off water
sprinklers they were so hot. Once they had planned to
have dinner and talk, but didn't make it off her couch
where they made out like teenagers, stopping short of the
deed and spending the rest of the night overheated and
blissfully exhausted.

Never before had heavy petting been so painfully fulfilling. Risa had straddled JD in tight form-fitting 501 jeans
and pressed herself against him in ways that could make
her cheeks warm in the light of day. On another occasion
she agreed to meet him at his house for a Blockbuster
night and ended up topless in the Jacuzzi while he suckled
like a hungry child against her ample bosom.

He liked the taste of her and played with her with his
tongue and fingers until she squirmed. He teased and
suckled until she reached the climatic effect she so desired. And all this was just from playing above the waist.
Soon and very soon she would allow him to travel south
beyond her navel. Each time they were together they got
closer and closer to consummating their relationship.
They got so very close. They were stopped only by decorum.

She knew what made him moan with pleasure. He liked
to have his ears nibbled on and his skin tasted with small,
pleasure-filled, almost painful bites. She knew what made
him smile with delight. It was the sight of her nearly naked

and stretched beneath him hanging on by a delicate thread of endurance. She knew what made him look at her with a raw animal hunger and pursue her with passionate kisses. It was the sight of her in just her panties. He liked her in her panties. White cotton ones were his favorite so far. She knew all this and yet she didn't know his favorite color. She didn't know what kind of food he liked. She could not cook! Would he expect that of her? She would be forty on her next birthday. Did he expect her to have children? Would adoption be an option? Being an only child, Risa had always wanted a house full of laughing, smiling children.

As her birthday approached and she had not yet found Mr. Right, she had even contemplated adopting. She knew that she could love a child, any child, as if it were her own. Could JD? For that matter, how did he feel about children anyway? She didn't know anything about him. Shouldn't a couple have these conversations before they tie the knot? Just as soon as her mind said the word *couple,* Risa nearly fell from her chair. She considered herself and JD a couple. *When had that happened?*

For the past four days she'd been walking around as if in a drug-induced state. She was forgetful, preoccupied, and just dumbstruck. Things were happening around her that she was totally unaware of. In four days, Richard miraculously started parking in his own parking space and this was without her having his car towed. Whether it was because he witnessed just how far she would go when she was constantly pushed to her limit, or because he had gained a new respect for her after her show on JD aired, it didn't matter. Now, Risa could park in her assigned slot and walk into the building and benefit from the protection of the overhead covering.

Cayce started seeing the mysterious tow truck driver, Matthew Moab. He was a big man, tall, lean, ornery, and stoic. But Risa saw his rough exterior be wiped away with just one smile from Cayce. He and his four brothers ran a successful garage and tow truck business. He had only known the whirlwind that was Cayce for four days and they were already talking about expanding his business into car restoration, which was his true passion, together. Seemed like Cayce had found her Mr. Right by a stroke of luck. Unlike Risa, she wasn't questioning it. She accepted it for what it was. Neither she nor Matthew questioned the length of their relationship or the circumstances of their meeting. Risa wished she could follow their example. They made it look easy. Could it be that easy? Should she follow Cayce's lead? Were some people destined to meet and mate?

Risa's mother and father had been married for forty years until one day they just called it quits. At sixty-three and sixty-five, respectively, they seemed happier now that they weren't officially together. When they were together, Risa didn't even know that there were ever problems in their relationship. So did that make her a good judge of what works? Probably not. As she thought about this, she found herself coming up with an idea for a new segment for *City Scenes:* "Today's families, the many faces of Dallas's loving couples." She could show the diverse and new modern families, blended, step, traditional, surrogate, interracial, same sex, etc. She could ask the questions: "What was it that made some people mate for life, others over and over, others for short periods of time, and others after a chance meeting? What was it that made people go years without thinking about a husband or wife, and then be inundated with thoughts of matrimony and togetherness?"

Soon, Risa found herself directing the questions directly to herself. *What was it about JD that brought out everything sexy, wanton, maternal, and domestic with those two words, "Marry me"?* Just four days ago, before JD's proposal, she was anxious and concerned that she was so busy living her life as a "me" that she sidestepped, bypassed, and dodged the "we." Now, just four days later, she was thinking in terms of we and us and the two of them. In four short days she had readjusted her thinking so that JD's proposition didn't seem so far-fetched. He wanted to get married. She wanted to get married. Why not marry each other?

The practical businesswoman in her saw this as a win-win situation. Their combined assets alone made his offer very attractive. Each one came to the table with more than an appetite. That was one of Cayce's Haitian grandmother's sayings, "Never let a man come to your table with nothing but an appetite." Although her portfolio wasn't as diverse or as massive as his, it wasn't anything to sneeze at either.

Risa had never experienced unemployment or bad business decisions. She was a wise investor, so she would come to the marriage with something to offer besides the delights of her flesh. Any man would have to be a fool to not want to unite with her. She had to think in these terms. By marrying her he wasn't doing her a favor because she was just as good a catch as he. It was mutually beneficial. Win-win. Couldn't loose.

*You will be forty real soon!* was a constant litany playing in her head. She thought that she was putting up a good front by pretending to be listening to Cayce when she was really having such a busy conversation with herself.

"Earth to Risa. Earth to Risa," Cayce said. Risa finally looked up from her desk to Cayce who was still draped in the finery that JD had sent over. "Where are you?" Cayce asked curiously. "You are a million miles away."

Even though she said it she wasn't upset with her friend. She was having way too much fun parading around in Risa's presents. Although she never had a little sister, Risa would have been proud to have Cayce in that role.

"Just thinking," Risa said, unable to admit that she had missed more than half of Cayce's conversation.

"I bet I know about who," Cayce teased.

Cayce removed the tennis bracelet and placed it on Risa's slim wrist. Risa made a quick mental note to give Cayce the little tennis bracelet she had bought for herself last year. The bracelet that JD had delivered was at least three karats. The one-karet bracelet she had treated herself to on her last birthday would make Cayce smile. She liked it when Cayce smiled. Giving her the little trinket was the least she could do for her friend to make up for the crazy bipolar behavior she'd been exhibiting in the past four days. Had it only been four days? She felt as if she had known JD for a lifetime.

"Him be a fine man," Cayce said as she smiled at Risa with a knowing wink.

Why was she fighting this? There were just as many reasons for this to work as there were for it not to. How hard would it be to just go under the assumption that it could work? Fifty-fifty odds could be worked in her favor if she approached this with the right attitude. It could work. She wanted it to work.

"Yes," Risa conceded. "Him be a fine man." Risa mimicked Cayce and the two of them burst into giggles like teenagers comfortable in their friendship that allowed them to play and mock each other.

Cayce took a seat across from her boss and crossed her legs making herself comfortable.

"I'm glad you like him," she said, turning serious. "My mother always said a good man needs a good woman. Otherwise, he'll never know how good he is. I bet you can bring out the good in him."

"I don't know what I bring out in him, but it's so good it has got to be bad."

Cayce looked at her questioningly. "What do you mean by that?"

"My God, Cayce, he scares me." At her friend's look of alarm she quickly reassured her. "Not in a menacing, harmful way, but in a grab me by my heart, drop me on my head way."

"Honey child, it bees like that sometime," Cayce laughed, showing experience well beyond her years. "Sometimes, love scares you. But all the time love is good for you. This is love isn't it, Risa?"

"I don't know if it is love. But I do know that it is passion."

"Well, when you have passion what more do you need?" Cayce asked simply. What more did you need indeed?

Risa had never been one to gossip at work and she always kept her personal business just that, personal. But this thing with JD had her tied up in knots. Having talked with Cayce and gotten such a simplistic answer she could only turn to her friend and mentor, Helen, for what surely had to be another opinion and possibly the right answer. So after assigning Cayce the task of researching videotapes for footage on the faces of the new families, she scurried down to Helen's office for a little one-on-one woman talk with someone closer to her own age. She needed it. The more she stayed with Cayce the more she was seeing this thing with JD through the eyes of youth and optimism. She needed a cold dose of reality. Helen would give her just that.

"Risa, Risa, Risa," Helen chuckled. "There is no reason for you to say no." That wasn't what Risa had expected to hear. Her friend sat behind her big mahogany desk pregnant and as happy as a lark and looking like a sated cat. She was forty-six years old and had found love with a man ten years her junior who had been under her nose for years.

As a longtime cameraman for KKRL, Isaiah Hamilton had virtually gone unnoticed by Helen until one day he simply asked her out. At first she was taken aback. She had literally never paid him more attention than any of the cameramen. Sure, she spoke to them. She gave them all fruit baskets during the holiday season, birthday cards at the appropriate time and tried to keep up with work-related anniversaries. But to know personal details like he was infatuated with her skipped her altogether. She was just too busy.

When he asked her out, she had stopped to look at him, really look at him, and was shocked into speechlessness. He was a good-looking man, tall, but a little skinny. He was younger than she, obviously, but it didn't seem to matter. He had very kind eyes. She liked his eyes. He was dark like she liked them and very, very quiet. Otherwise she might have noticed him.

At the time she had been forty and he thirty. Although not his direct supervisor, as station manager, surely she was in charge of somebody who was in charge of somebody who was in charge of him. She could not date him. It would not be a good thing. So she poised her mouth to decline graciously but he had handed her a slip of paper. She opened it, not knowing what to expect. It read, *I Quit.* And he had. He was branching out on his own to start what was now a thriving photography studio.

Helen thought about the day Isaiah asked her out. She did end up accepting and they went out to dinner that very same night. Now, six years later, living together and expecting their first child, she was the domestic goddess she had often laughed at. Suddenly she was changing her tune. She was happy, in love and felt everybody else should be as well. So instead of pushing Risa away from JD, she pushed her friend closer to him.

"Why question it?"

"Are you crazy?" Risa asked, looking at Helen as if she had two heads.

"I'm not," Helen emphasized. "But what if you are?" she said between bites of a peach cobbler that she had delivered from her favorite restaurant, Cornbread and Brie.

"Come on, now, Helen. It's only been a few days."

"God created the world in seven."

"I need more than a few days."

"Why?"

"Why? Because it just isn't done."

"Well, Risa, maybe it's time to just do it. You're no spring chicken and time is just passing you by. Wouldn't it be nicer to spend that time with someone?"

Ever since she had found Isaiah, Helen had been spouting this kind of philosophy. Risa didn't know why she expected anything different when she sat down in her office. Despite what both Cayce and Helen seemed to feel, Risa felt herself still doubting that it could be this easy. No sane woman met a man and in days made a decision to alter her life. She couldn't do that. Or could she? If it were this easy, surely she would not have spent the past few years alone. But during this time she had never met JD. The more she thought about it she realized that she could, that he could, that they could. Things happen all the time. Decisions are made. People make choices. Life goes on. Everything doesn't have to stop just because she couldn't believe that fate delivered a man to her.

"So, what are you going to do, girl?" Helen asked. She finished the peach cobbler and started on the Caesar salad.

She had gained almost forty pounds during her pregnancy and just didn't care. Before her pregnancy she was what was considered waiflike thin. She was one of those women who didn't need a bra because she barely had a handful. Now, seven months pregnant she finally had the hips and breast she claimed she had always been denied. She was a tall woman, dark as mahogany with shoulder-length braids. Her eyes were wise, dark brown and brilliant behind horn-rimmed glasses that she was constantly losing. Every time she found them they were in some obvious place, on her head, in her pocket, on her desk. It was just one of the idiosyncrasies that made her Helen and so very adorable. She had the body of a ballerina and the bearing of a queen. Risa admired and respected her. If she said things like this happened then so be it.

"Okay, okay," Risa said in defeat.

"Okay, what?" Helen managed between mouthfuls.

"Me thinks I am going give this man a chance," Risa said in the singsong Haitian lilt.

"Cayce has had such an influence on you," Helen chuckled. This time she had a mouthful of salad.

"Bring me a doggy bag tomorrow when you come in. Being pregnant lets me be such a pig and I'm enjoying it." She rubbed her belly for emphasis.

Risa could hear Helen's delightful chuckle as she left her office. She'd bring her something good to eat from her date. That was the least she could do.

# Chapter 9

Risa had no idea what to wear. It wasn't like this was one of the many dates. This was the day she was going to give him his answer. Therefore everything had to be perfect. She had changed her clothes several times before settling on a black crepe wool dress that hung past her knees and flared into a ruffled fishtail at her calves. She paired it with a pair of black fishnet hose and three-inch black pumps. She put her mass of thick black hair up into a high ponytail and clipped it with pearls. Around her neck and in her ears were pearls as well. Her look was elegant and sexy.

She remembered asking Cayce what on earth was she going to do with a pair of fishnet panty hose? They were on sale at Neiman Marcus and Cayce insisted that she buy them. Now she was glad she had. They made her ensemble. A simple pair of hose turned the elegant winter cocktail dress into a delicately enticing affair.

JD sucked in his breath when he saw her. Although Risa and JD hadn't hit a home run, they had gone well past first base. They had done the things that couples do without being an official couple. It was important to her that he did things with her that weren't just shared in the dark of night and in the height of passion. Knowing this he ignored the heat in his loins and kissed her chastely on the cheek before he led her to his car.

He never wanted anyone as much as he wanted her. He never wanted to please anyone as much as he wanted to please her. So he reined in his hormones. For the first time since they started this, they were going to make it out of the house. He had asked his ladylove out for a night on the town and a night out was what she was going to get. Since his approach had been backwards he would reverse it for her. He would give her the ritual of tradition and courtship as she required. First he would woo her then he would wed her. That said he would behave as a man would on his first date. He would keep his hands to himself. This was a first but not impossible.

When he walked her chastely to the car and kept a safe distance between the two of them, their awareness of each other heightened. The anticipation of touching him like a lover intensified. Risa nearly stumbled as he had helped her into the car. Once again, he caught her in his strong arms.

"Hey, hey, now," he said, smiling at her. "Watch your step. I might not always be here to catch you."

As he held her, she felt the attraction that was so strong it almost hurt. She couldn't take her eyes off of him. He looked good enough to eat. Dressed all in black, he was an imposing sexy figure of mystery and appeal. She didn't want to let him go. The night air was cold as it surrounded them in its embrace; nevertheless she felt a heat radiating from his body that signified his desire for her. This time, she kissed him. She could feel him holding himself in check and she didn't care. She wanted him just as much as he wanted her. No words were necessary. His lips were soft and supple against hers. They parted easily letting her insert her tongue in order to play a dangerous game of cat and mouse with his emotions. He was the first one to break it off.

"Let's get inside or we'll never make it," he said. His voice was gruff with desire although his actions were gentle as he opened the door and eased her inside.

This was the second time in their short meeting that he had kept her from falling on her face. She liked it when he rescued her. She felt so protected and safe in his arms. All she wanted to do was kiss him and say thank you with her body. He felt the same way. She knew it and reveled in the knowledge that she was the cause of his growing physical discomfort.

It would be interesting to see how they managed to keep themselves in check out in public. JD's Jaguar was a smooth ride. The handcrafted leather hugged Risa's posterior and cupped her in comfort. She found herself being lulled nearly to sleep by the comforting sounds of India Arie as he drove towards their destination.

"Where are we going?" she asked him.

"Wait and see," he said, smiling mischievously.

It was a big secret. She liked him being playful with her, so she waited. They were only in the car less than two minutes when his phone rang. She was happy to see that he used his headset in order to keep his hands free while he talked on the phone. It was a pet peeve of hers when people drove and talked on the phone at the same time. Driving was dangerous business. A driver needed all their wits about them. Hands should be on the steering wheel and not the cell phone. She had actually done a story entitled " Cell phones, convenience or health hazard?" early in her career. Back then, cell phones were nearly as big as toasters. Now they were the sleek little numbers that fit into a breast pocket or evening bag with ease.

The one she had was a high-class high-tech model. She wanted practical, but Cayce quickly upgraded her $49.95 cell phone to the pretty little piece she carried now. Each day she was shocked to learn of another one of its functions. She had no idea it had games on it until Cayce got frustrated with her and took fifteen minutes to give her a cell phone lesson. Now she could actually enter phone numbers into the memory and look them up. The voice activation function was too intimidating to tackle at this time. That would certainly have to wait for another day. JD didn't seem to have any phone qualms.

"JD," he answered the phone, confident and secure.

It was a woman on the other line. Risa could tell because his voice changed dramatically. She opened her eyes and listened even though she was mad at herself for doing so.

"Hi, Hailey," he said.

At first Risa felt like she had been slapped across the face. *How dare he?* she thought. Then she realized that if he were talking to one of his bimbos, then surely he wouldn't do it while she sat next to him. He didn't seem to mind that she heard his conversation and it was obvious that his conversation wasn't of a proprietary nature. He didn't care if she heard what he said. That meant he had no secrets. Risa relaxed.

"I'd love to get together with you for lunch. But right now, I'm out with a very special lady friend," JD said, looking over at Risa and winking, removing the insecurities that were starting to develop. "Can I call you back tomorrow? Sure, sweetie. I look forward to seeing you too."

That last line changed everything. JD cooed into the phone before he hung up and eased the car into the parking lot of the very popular Cornbread and Brie. Risa's head was swimming. She didn't know how to digest what she had just heard. Either he had just made a date with another woman or he had made a date with another woman! Whatever it was he was acting as if it were nothing. Maybe it was nothing. A long time ago her father told her that the best way to get away with something was to do it out in the open. He had also told her that as a man acts, he is. And although she and JD had spent the past four days doing things that did not require words, she realized that JD only acted as a man infatuated with her. He didn't say or do anything other than that. The man she had gotten to know was charming and irresistible. If there were nothing to hide then he would tell her who was on the phone. She wanted the man she was contemplating spending the rest of her life with to come to her with honesty and true words. She didn't want to play games and spend her free time imagining him surrounded in a cloud of suspicion.

"JD . . ." she began; somebody had to address what had just happened.

"We're here," he said before Risa could say another word.

He kissed her quickly and smiled at her before he jumped out of the car and rushed to the passenger side to open the door. It was the smile that did it. It was the smile that made her swallow her words of concern. No man who smiled at her like that could hurt her either intentionally or with callous disregard. His smile was genuine and encompassed his whole face including his eyes. Liars and charlatans don't smile with their eyes. He had wonderful, honest eyes. She got lost in his eyes. If the eyes were a mirror into the soul then his soul was filled with boundless caring for her.

She wondered briefly if it were possible to be bewitched. Surely she had to be bewitched or common sense would have her running for the hills. Common sense said they could not possibly feel this way about each other in such a short period of time. But who listened to common sense when they were looking into deep, chocolate, soulful eyes? Nobody, especially Risa James, who found herself swimming in those eyes.

JD helped her out of the car before the valet approached. He was totally unaware that she was waging a war in her head about her new relationship. He was too wrapped up in her to notice anything but her fantastic beauty and the pitter-patter of his heart. She had him feeling like a love-struck teen and he liked it.

"Hello, Mr. Jones," the valet attendant said. "Good to see you, sir."

No sooner were they out of the car than JD was getting the royal treatment. A small Latin man with gray hair and kind eyes approached them in order to take his car.

"Hello, Hector," JD replied and smiled, happy at seeing the man. "How is your wife, Hazel, and the girls?" He sounded as if he were genuinely found of the valet.

"Everyone is fine and my littlest one loves that puppy you gave her. Thank you."

"Not a problem. Lacy had a nice litter and I knew the puppy would find a good home with you." He handed over the keys. " And Hector, call me JD."

"Sure. Sure. Mr. Jones . . . JD." He corrected himself as if the big man's Christian name was unfamiliar coming from his mouth.

"Hector is one of my oldest employees. When he retired he got bored so we let him oversee the valets here. But it seems like he still works harder than the men half his age."

All Risa could think to say was, "You have a dog?"

She didn't see a dog when she was at his house. But then again she hadn't seen much. If pressed the only thing she would be able to describe was his hard body and his Jacuzzi. It was a little larger than most, surrounded by cedar, and deeper than average. That she remembered.

"Don't let Lacy hear you say that," he started in a conspirator's whisper. "She doesn't know she is a dog. Actually, she is my mother's dog. A little pug."

Risa liked pugs. They were so ugly they were cute. He kept up a commentary about the difference in little dogs and big dogs and dogs who thought they were humans as he led her past the line and through the front door. It was a Wednesday night and the line to get in was still outrageous. According to the society page of the Dallas newspaper, Cornbread and Brie was booked up for an entire year. It would have been booked further than that but the owner refused to book more than a year in advance. The crowd waited patiently for a chance to sample the legendary cuisine. The restaurant had been opened over a year and yet the ever-growing crowd could not get enough of the scrumptious delights. Reservations had to be made at least a year in advance and yet JD sauntered past the waiting group as if he owned the place.

Having been in the limelight for so long early in her career, Risa wasn't impressed with the star treatment. The circle she traveled in back in Los Angeles had perfected it. They knew how to work the art of getting to the front of the line and not having to wait. She always felt a little guilty over the privileges her quasi-celebrity status gave her. But here in Dallas, with JD, there didn't seem to be that LA pretentiousness she'd grown to dislike so adamantly. He spoke to people as they walked by and even smiled an apology when someone made a face because they walked past them.

"I know the owner," he smiled an apology.

The few sour faces were dropped as quickly as they were shown as soon as they saw that it was JD. Everybody loved JD. He was a hometown hero. Risa couldn't help but wonder how much he was involved with Dallas's newest and hottest eatery. There was other local celebrity folk in line and no one seemed to mind that JD sauntered past them. No sooner were they inside then everyone was talking to JD. All the waiters and bus staff seemed to know him. He smiled and greeted them as he ushered her towards the back to an obviously private dining room. It was a privilege of his celebrity she was sure.

"JD. JD. Boy, I know you hear me," a female's voice called.

JD turned just as a statuesque beauty seemed to come out of nowhere. On closer inspection she appeared from the kitchen. It was the closest door.

"How dare you stand me up," she scolded. "Who do you think you are?" she asked with such familiarity that Risa felt a momentary twinge of jealousy. Totally oblivious to this the woman stepped in front of Risa and continued to scold JD.

"I'm sorry, Daphne," JD said as he kissed her on the cheek. "It won't happen again."

For a minute Risa was at a loss for words. Who the hell was this woman and how could she take such liberties?

"It better not," Daphne said. "My time, like yours, is valuable."

"I know. I know," he apologized.

Risa watched in awe as the beauty fell beneath his spell. Risa would love to meet the woman who could resist his charm. Coupled with that smile, it was deadly. Any woman who wasn't affected would have to be dead or ninety. Actually, age might not even shield a woman from the wattage of his charisma. A ninety-year-old woman was still a woman. Even grandmothers weren't safe from the magnetism of JD Jones.

"Okay, okay," Daphne relented. "Get in the back. Everybody is waiting on you. I'll stick my head in, in a second."

"You aren't going to join us? I need you," JD pleaded.

"I'm afraid you're on your own, James."

The two of them obviously had a past that she could not be a part of. It provided them a comfort level that was easy and carefree. Risa realized that she had been nearly naked with this man and she had not called him by his Christian name. Like the valet, *James* was an unfamiliar word in her mouth. Maybe this woman was more than a past lover and their relationship was one in which he felt that he could bring Risa to the restaurant and not be afforded a scene. Risa never had that kind of relationship with any of her ex-lovers. When it was over, it was over. That's why they were exes. She wished them well but they certainly didn't hang out together. No way. No how. Un-uh.

"JD. JD. Don't call me James," he said, cringing.

Until she heard it, Risa had forgotten that his given name was James. That was part of the reason she didn't use it. Risa James and James Derrick Jones. Was that an omen?

Laughing, the stately women started off and bumped right into Risa.

"I am so sorry," Daphne said, seeming to notice Risa for the first time.

"I'm Daphne." She held out her hand.

"Where are my manners?" JD interrupted. "Daphne, this is Risa. Risa, this is my loudmouthed sister, Daphne."

*His sister?* Risa thought as she looked from one to the other. The only thing the two of them had in common was height. Daphne was a honey-colored strawberry-blond delight with strategically placed freckles and a knockout hourglass-shaped body that was ample of hip and breast without being fat. She was a male fantasy, a fifties calendar girl dipped in toffee. She was a configuration of light colors with tinges of reds, beiges, honeys, and almond. She was exotic and interesting looking like a Beyoncé Knowles from the popular singing group, Destiny's Child, but taller and older by a few years. But unlike Beyoncé, Daphne was an exotic mix, the kind that came from recessive genes that families long forgot they had until they appeared in a multicolored mix like Daphne. She was so odd she was pretty and so pretty she could be beautiful if she wore makeup and did something with that hair.

Unlike Risa's thick flat-ironed mane, Daphne possessed an uncontrollable natural mass of multicolored curls. Risa knew women who would pay money to get their hair to look like Daphne's either in color, texture, or haphazard array. If this was his sister, what did JD's parents look like? What would their child look like? Would two chocolate-skinned people find themselves with an auburn-headed munchkin? Chocolate skin, red hair and eyes that would probably be hazel, their child would be an interesting mutt. If the genes aligned correctly, it could be beautiful and exotic. But Risa wouldn't care as long as it was healthy. A healthy redhead baby from their union? Stranger things had been known to happen. There was a Web site that showed crazy pictures of what the offspring of celebrity couples would look like. Although she was sure she could find a picture of JD, she wasn't sure her cachet was enough to rate a picture on the Web site so that she could see what their child would look like.

*Their child?* She had to stop daydreaming or she was going to miss something. The statuesque creature that was Daphne was pumping her hand.

"Risa? So you're the one. I have heard so much about you," Daphne said.

"Don't start, Daphne," JD warned, suddenly trying to steer his sister away from Risa.

"Of course not from him," Daphne continued. "He has been absolutely tight-lipped about you. But my other sisters, honey, you have been the topic of conversation for at least a couple of days."

Risa didn't know what to say. Before she could respond,

JD took her by the arm and started towards the private room.

"Don't you have a restaurant to run?" he called over his shoulder to his sister.

"You might sidestep me. But just wait until the others get to you," Daphne said with a laugh and hurried back into the kitchen.

She had already spent way too much time gabbing with JD and she was a hands-on restaurant owner who was also chef/waitress/hostess. She'd have more than enough time to see how Risa fared with her clan. Right now she needed to get back to her soufflés. If she didn't time it just right, they'd fall flat. They'd still be good, but flat. Daphne didn't serve flat soufflés.

As JD walked Risa towards the private room that his family occupied once a week, he hoped he was making the right decision in choosing this as the perfect place to introduce them to Risa and vice versa. It was important to him that they all got along. He grew up with the Jones women and knew how ruthless they could be when interrogating a potential mate for him. He learned early that how his women friends fared with his sisters could be the barometer of the success of the relationship.

Luckily, Lucy Belle had been able to hold her own with them. But Risa wasn't Lucy Belle. Risa was Risa, plain and simple. Whenever he thought of her, and that was often, he caught himself smiling. He was so happy to have her he was almost walking on air. When he had picked her up at the beginning of the evening all he had wanted to do was lay her down and finally consummate their union. In the black dress that clung to her he heard her siren song as surely as if she were luring him to her bed. He would have gone willingly.

Fate must have made him accept the offer to do her show. Reporters had contacted him before but he had always managed to find something else to do. This time, it was to his benefit that he had not been busy. His sister, Betsy, vice president of his public relations department, insisted that the publicity couldn't hurt him. As far as Betsy was concerned, she wanted JD's name on everybody's tongue. No publicity was bad publicity and no public appearance could tarnish his hometown hero image. She wanted his name on everybody's lips. That way when he submitted a bid for a project, his public image, combined with the good work he did, would make him a shoo-in. So, despite his protest that his work should be able to stand on its own, he relented, so he had started making more public appearances.

Meeting Risa hadn't been chance. He had gone on *City Scenes* just to appease his sister. He and Risa were destined to meet and explore the attraction that was new, fresh, and exciting. Because she hadn't realized that yet and was still skittish around him, he didn't want to expose her to his sisters' scrutiny in an uncontrolled environment. So Cornbread and Brie it would be. In public they would have to be on their best behavior. He was counting on that because he couldn't risk Risa bolting from the room in tears. He didn't think she was a fragile waif unable to hold her own, but he knew that his sisters were formidable. He wanted this woman more than he had ever wanted another. It was important to him that all the women in his life got along, because anyone who was with him was with his family.

His family was composed of a mother, grandmother, five sisters, and a father who seemed to take it all in stride. He was a lucky man to be born into this family and he wanted his future bride to feel the same way. He had heard horror stories of men marrying women who didn't get along with their mothers or marrying into a family where their bride's mother was a dragon. His family was nothing like that. The Joneses worked together, partied together, vacationed together, and had dinner together at least once a week as a whole unit. Throughout the week, he often spent time with his father, had tea with his mother, lunch with one or two of his sisters, and a beer with Larry. There wasn't a dragon in the group. If there was, he didn't know it. Even Angela's bossy nosiness wasn't enough to make him avoid her and her ever growing brood.

It was important to JD that Risa fit in with this group. But right now he didn't know how to play it. There was no playbook or well-thought-out business plan. They were already moving too fast for her. He kept his promise not to bring up the marriage proposal again. But he didn't promise not to pursue her. He didn't promise not to woo her. He didn't promise not to call in reinforcements. So he was going to use everything at his disposal to get her. That meant that he needed the aid of his sisters. Those were the best people to have on his side when he was planning anything. JD was planning a seduction. Who better to consult than a roomfull of women?

# Chapter 10

"Here they come," Angela whispered as she peeked through the French doors that separated the private room from the rest of the restaurant.

The private dining room, usually reserved for corporate parties and private functions, was more than large enough to accommodate all of them. Also, by meeting at Cornbread and Brie, they were able to give their respective host a break from the large group. At the restaurant no one had to do the dishes or clean the house. Daphne had a staff for that. Originally they all met at the restaurant with the intention of supporting Daphne in her endeavor. But the restaurant was so popular there wasn't a moment of struggle that often accompanies a fledgling business until its clientele was established.

Daphne had hit the ground running. She started out in the black, so her family's well-intended intentions weren't necessary. Nevertheless, faced with the meeting room, they found it perfect for their new meeting spot. They continued with their tradition of meeting once a month and Daphne's restaurant became the unofficial meeting place. The monthly meetings always ensured that they got to see each other even though they were all busy. Here it was like the large Sunday dinners they had had as children. Here they got to catch up and make up for lost time. And like customers, they paid and even tipped.

"Honey, get away from the door," Big L said. "You'll scare her away."

It was possible that he alone knew how important this woman was to JD. He didn't want her to go running for the hills when faced with the Jones women. The thought of facing all of them at once was daunting even to him and he had been a surrogate member of the family well before he and Angela had gotten married. He could only imagine the girl on the other side of the door. He would bet money that her knees were actually shaking. He'd seen women crumble beneath their scrutiny. Only Lucy Belle had managed to keep her composure and he took an instant liking to her because of it.

"Telling Angela to get away from that door is like telling her to quit butting in," twenty-eight year old Betsy teased.

Her real name was Bethesda. Bethesda Mary Ann Jones. She had taken a lot of ridicule because of it. They had been calling her Betsy since she was a toddler. At five feet six inches, she was the most petite of the group. They were all tall. Both parents were six feet.

"I do not butt in," Angela said as she feigned a pout as she left the door and took a seat next to her husband of eighteen years. " I just give you my opinion."

"She can't help herself," Elisha quickly came to Angela's defense. At twenty, she was the baby of the bunch. "It's part of her genetic makeup. It has something to do with birth order. She feels she has to butt in." She said it matter-of-factly as if that explained everything.

"Okay, I am obviously out of the loop. What has Angela

done now?' Carlie asked as she nibbled on a cherry tomato.

Carlie was one of those women with a metabolism that allowed her to eat anything without gaining weight. She ate like a trucker and maintained the same weight as she had in high school. She ran five miles a day four days a week. She could ride a horse or eat it and still not gain a pound.

"Whose boyfriend isn't up to snuff? Or who did something not befitting a Jones?" Carlie teased, mimicking her eldest sister.

"Okay, everyone stop picking on your sister," Lillian called from the head of the table. Sitting next to her husband of forty-three years, she looked out on four of her five daughters. They were beautiful girls. They were smart girls. They were girls who spoke their minds and took a great deal of pleasure out of teasing each other. JD often endured his share of ribbing and teasing. But it was always in fun. Overall, the Jones siblings were a half dozen special people. Lillian was proud of them. Each and every one of them was unique and successful. She and Sam had raised them right.

Now Sam pretended not to have any idea of what was going on. He was very good at pretending to be oblivious to everything. His facade was that he was easygoing and laid-back, but in actuality, he ruled his house the best way he could. He let Lillian run things. She, on the other hand, pretended to let him let her run things. In all actuality, they ruled together, he giving when she took and she giving when he took. They had a relationship based on mutual respect and a lot of love. They had lasted forty-three years because of it.

"They're always picking on me, Mama," Angela pretended to whine as she snuggled into her very large husband's embrace. If there ever was a match made in heaven, she considered hers to be it. She was so happy she glowed.

"Whine, whine, whine. You are such a baby," Carlie said. "If I didn't know any better, I wouldn't believe that you were forty."

As soon as she said the words, Carlie was immediately contrite. A hush fell over the group. Everyone looked to Angela expectantly.

Angela turned forty on her last birthday. She did fine for the first few weeks until one day Elisha quipped that she looked good for someone middle-aged. What did she say that for? Angela burst into tears. Until that very moment she had not realized the truth in what her younger sister said. It was possible that she was middle-aged. But she would not claim it. She looked good. She felt good. She had a wonderful husband, four beautiful children, and a successful steady career. Her age meant nothing. She had it all, except her youth. At forty, if she were truly middle-aged, then it was only downhill from here on in. It took half the night and part of the next day for her husband, sisters, and mother to convince her that she wasn't old. So if life truly begins at forty, then her life was filled with a beautiful beginning.

"Ouch," Carlie grimaced when Betsy pinched her.

"Don't get her started," Betsy whispered. Betsy and Carlie always stuck together.

"I don't know why y'all bothering to whisper," Elisha said as she speared one of the tomatoes from Carlie. "She's sitting right there," she whispered, obviously making fun of her sisters.

And just as suddenly as the mood turned serious, there was a shift in the mood when Angela burst into laughter as if realizing for the first time just how ridiculous she had been about the whole age thing.

"I'm holding at thirty-nine. And I'll be thirty-nine until I'm ninety," Angela said.

"And when you live to be ninety you will have proved little Miss Elisha wrong," Big L said, kissing his wife's forehead and winking at Elisha to show her there was no hard feelings.

"I'm sorry, Angela. I know how sensitive you are about your age," Carlie managed while rubbing her arm where Betsy had pinched her.

"Drama. Drama. Drama. You should have been an actress instead of an accountant," Elisha said as she reached over her sisters and grabbed another tomato.

There were small bowls of cherry tomatoes that Daphne placed on the tables. They were sautéed in sugar, olive oil, and rosemary. They were sweet and tasty, a simple little appetizer to be eaten with glasses of merlot.

"We leave the acting up to you," Angela shot back.

Elisha, a theater major at local University of Texas at Arlington, had been in plays, musicals, and beauty pageants since she was a teenager. She was the only Jones child to go to the University of Texas at Arlington. The rest had gone to SMU. She chose another school because she wanted to make it clear that she was sick and tired of following in her siblings' footsteps. She wanted to make her own path in life. So her path was so different from the rest of theirs. She was currently the reigning Ms. Juneteenth and had once held the crowns of Miss Jr. Black Dallas, and Miss Teenage Fair Park simultaneously. She was a coffee-colored elfish beauty who was confident and secure well beyond her meager twenty years. She was a pretty girl and parlayed her beauty into a lucrative side gig.

"Okay, already. I've had enough attention. Can we focus on JD for a minute?" Angela said the words just as JD entered with Risa.

"Did I hear my name?" JD asked, leading Risa by the hand into the room.

"Of course you did," Angela said.

Risa finally figured out that JD was taking her to meet someone. She wasn't prepared for so many someones. The room was filled with five of the most striking women she had ever seen in one place. From pretty to prettier, they sat around the table headed by a couple that had to be JD's parents. Instantly she knew where Daphne got her unique blend of reds.

JD's father had a neat skullcap of russet with tinges of gray mixed in. Like his daughter, there was a freckle or two that graced his face. His beard was a mix of red, blond, and gray. It suited him. But only Daphne seemed to inherit his red hue. He was the man that JD could easily grow to resemble in his later years. Tall, he had kind brown eyes and a body that hinted at earlier years spent at hard labor. In his sixties he was a good-looking man made even more interesting by the unexpected red hair. He wore a pair of very modern glasses, a pair of black pants, and a sweater that made him appear youthful and vibrant although he sat quietly next to a woman whose genes were obviously the most dominant, because next to Daphne and JD's father, no one had freckles or reddish-blond hair or skin that wasn't a coffee blend.

She was a woman who had been used to turning heads in her day. Tall, like Risa, she was a mahogany-colored goddess with a head of hair so white that there was no hint at its original color. Were it not for the roomful of heads that were brown, sable, chestnut, and black, Risa would never have guessed that the snow-haired diva once had hair that was a thick and luxurious sable. Now, in her sixties, she wore it well, short, white, and natural. It was a good contrast against her dark unlined face. Her mouth was wide and filled with straight white teeth that she showed to Risa in a genuine smile. This was the only reason Risa could bear it when JD left her alone to go to his mother's side and kiss her cheek. She was forgotten in an instant as soon as he took on his role as dutiful son. A long time ago, her mother said to her, watch how a man treats his mother. It will have a reflection on how he treats you. JD revered his mother. It was obvious in how he rushed to her to bestow her cheek with a kiss.

"JD," his mother scolded, gently, "don't forget your guest."

All eyes turned towards Risa. For a moment she felt like she was on display. Were it not for the smiles and signs of welcome she might have bolted. Women could be a catty lot, making judgments and choosing to accept you based on shoe brand or clothing choice. She wasn't getting that feeling from the women in the room. They weren't judging her or criticizing. They looked at her with interest and nothing more.

Although Risa was happy with her choice of attire, had she known that she were to meet his parents she would have selected something more demure and less formfitting. The dress she was wearing had been chosen for seduction, not to impress his parents. For her first impression she would have chosen something that showed less cleavage and didn't cling to her slender curves so enticingly. First impressions were sometimes all you got and she didn't want JD's mother thinking that she was a trollop bent on seducing her son. And yet that was exactly what Risa had in mind.

From the moment she kissed him outside her house, she knew that tonight would be the night. Until the phone call came she even contemplated beginning her se- duction in the car. They had danced this dance long enough. It was time to come to the final waltz and per- form the finale. But all that had changed with first the phone call, and second the introduction of his family; Risa felt like she had been blindsided. She wasn't prepared for this meeting. All thoughts of seducing him were erased as she instead concentrated on making a good impression.

"Risa," JD said as he held out his hand to her. "I'd like you to met your future mother-in- law."

Although JD said the words playfully, there was a ring of truth to them. He wanted her to accept his proposition knowing what she was getting. He was a man with baggage. He had a ready-made family and the women who walked beside him needed to know that she would make that walk surrounded by these people. Once, Big L had even joked with JD saying that marrying Angela was like marrying her whole family. Just like coming into a relationship as the second husband there was all the stuff from the first marriage. But instead of an ex-wife and kids, JD had sisters.

Risa counted four plus the one outside running the restaurant. Five sisters and a mother was enough estrogen to make a strong woman faint if they weren't with her. Sisters could be more daunting than an ex-wife and children. Sisters were on another level. They could say and do whatever they wanted and not fear any consequences. Eight sets of eyes turned to her.

"What did he say?" a whisper went through the room.

Risa's mind was in a whirl. How dare JD make that kind of statement without consulting her? All night he had been taking her on a roller-coaster ride of emotion. The dynamics of their relationship was changing in front of her eyes. She hadn't said yes, yet. Actually, she hadn't said anything. She just made up her mind that she was going to sleep with him tonight, not meet the whole damn family.

He seemed to take it for granted that she was going to

say yes and marry him. Well, if he thought she was that easy, he had another thing coming. He put her on the spot and this was unacceptable. She wouldn't make a scene because that wasn't her style, but later he would get a tongue-lashing for springing this on her.

Smiling brightly, Risa made the walk to JD's side with trepidation because there were eight sets of eyes on her.

"JD is such a joker," Risa started, intent on taking the pressure off his words. "We just started seeing each other. It hasn't been time for us to make any decisions about our relationship yet." She held out her hand to the woman and noticed that her smile didn't waver as she absorbed Risa's words.

"It's just a matter of time, Mama. Just a matter of time," JD reassured his mother, dismissing Risa's attempt at dismissing their attraction.

"My son has always known what he wants," Lillian said with gentle authority as she pulled out the chair next to her. "And it seems like he wants you. Sit. Join us."

And Risa did sit because with those simple words, Lillian Jones made it clear that she had accepted Risa into her heart and into her family.

# Chapter 11

Nothing was as it seemed. The women were friendly. They weren't angry or manipulative or conniving or threatening. They were fun. The dinner was quite enjoyable. Risa found herself feeling as if she had always been part of this loud, rambunctious lot. Her earlier trepidation was replaced with a feeling of contentment and comfort. Having been the only child, born to two only children, she had only imagined what a large family gathering would be like. If they were anything like what she experienced with the Joneses, then she had truly been missing out on something.

In her mind she always wanted the TV family ideal that had been portrayed by the Cosbys. Faced with the reality of the Joneses, she realized just how easily it could be hers. In one night she discovered that they were a supportive, funny, diverse group of individuals that she found appealing. Throughout dinner she had looked up to catch JD's eye only to see him looking at her with an "I told you so" grin. She wanted to wipe that knowing smirk off his face. It galled her to know that he was always right. He knew how this was going to turn out. He knew she was going to fit right in. It would be so easy to give in and just let things take their natural course. But she couldn't do that. Not yet. She always wanted her marriage to last. Till death do us part was an edict she believed in. To find that kind of love there had to be some commitment and some kind of time spent. She couldn't have stumbled onto that kind of love in just a few short days. *Nobody does that!*

Risa had never been one to enter into things blind and uninformed. She was totally convinced that she was being led willy-nilly by her hormones down a path that was getting her closer and closer to consummating her relationship with JD. She felt powerless. She felt overwhelmed. She was in over her head. She needed reinforcements. The first thing she was going to do when she got home was call her mother. Somebody needed to be the voice of reason. For the first time, it wasn't Cayce or Helen or even Risa herself. Somebody had to give her a wake-up call or she was going to be the next Mrs. Jones. The only incident occurred when Angela asked her after a couple of glasses of merlot, "So, Risa, do you have any kids?"

Risa felt the room get suddenly silent.

"No, I don't," she answered.

"Do you want any?"

Risa's cheeks burned because she felt that Angela could read her mind. If she were going to have children, she had better get on the ball as soon as possible.

"I would love to have some children," Risa said with a soft smile.

"Women aren't like men," Angela said. "They can keep shooting them out like it's nothing. We, on the other hand, have to decide when we're going to start and when we're going to stop. I'd hate to be fifty with a ten-year-old."

Risa and Angela were about the same age and yet the difference was that Angela had four children. She was winding down where Risa would just be starting. It was something to consider. If she did decide to go ahead with this thing with JD, they would have to start a family immediately. That wouldn't give them time to get to know each other. This thing was getting more and more complicated.

"Babe. Babe. Come on, let's dance," Big L said, summoning Angela's attention.

"Sorry, girl. My husband's calling," Angela said, cutting the conversation short as she got up to dance with her husband.

They were playing the Dells. The music was soft and slow. The mood was somber. JD was playing checkers with his father. Risa was left alone with her thoughts. She didn't feel old. She wasn't old. But if she conceived tonight, this night, she would be fifty with a ten-year-old. Did she want that?

"Dance with me," Risa heard JD's call.

Angela had touched on a sore spot with her and she was mulling over that, so she hadn't really noticed him until he was actually standing in front of her with his hand out for her.

He eased her from the chair into his strong arms. His sisters, Carlie, Betsy, and Elisha, were acting like an old Motown singing group. They were snapping their fingers and dancing to the music complete with choreography. JD held Risa to his body and danced with her. Could she live her life with this man? Could she raise children with this man? Could she be a fifty-year-old woman with a ten-year-old with this man? As he danced with her and smiled down at her and she looked up into his eyes, she knew that she could. She could do anything with this man. He had the eyes of an angel. She would be the mother of his children. While his family looked on she kissed his lips.

"I can be fifty with a ten-year-old," she said.

"What?" JD questioned, not having the slightest idea where her statement was coming from.

"Nothing." She smiled. "Nothing." And they continued to dance.

Because his family was there, they behaved, but soon, and very soon, they would be alone in the dark of night and it was time to heat things up.

The ride back to Risa's house was spent in companionable silence as they were both deep in their own private thoughts. JD was thinking how lucky he was to find the woman sitting next to him. He wasn't a novice to dating. There were women in his life before. A very few had gotten the privilege of meeting his family. But none had ever been as easy a fit as Risa. She took to the Jones women like a fish to water. His mother had actually called her "dear," and his father, Samuel, the quiet and gentle giant who he would look more like if he didn't keep his rust-colored hair at bay by shaving his head, had told her to call him "Sam." And he had even shared his apple peach pecan pie with her. Lillian didn't even get to taste his dessert! Actually that wasn't fair. JD smiled. His mother was allergic to pecans. Daphne always let her father sample a new dessert before she added it to the menu. It was a long-standing joke that she was his favorite because of the fabulous desserts and not the red hair they shared. That said, she always made him something special and paraded it before the others as she sat it before him to taste. He would make a big show out of sampling it and teasing his children by not giving them any. Once he gave the okay, then everyone else got his or her fair share. Tonight he shocked them all when he offered Risa a taste—mind you a small taste—but a taste of the sugary treat. Unaware that she was being offered a remarkable first, Risa nibbled on the confection and rolled her eyes in the back of her head and declared that next to her dinner of crab cakes, pan-seared pork chops, garlic potatoes, and Caesar salad, it was the best thing she had ever put into her mouth.

She liked his sisters. His sisters liked her. She liked his sister's cooking (although that wasn't fair because everybody liked Daphne's cooking). She fit in with his family. There was no reason to weigh these things. JD had already made up his mind about Risa. But when she had danced with him, the deal had been cemented for good with JD. He was going to make her his wife. There were no ifs, ands or buts about it. His mother liked her. His father liked her. And his sisters, even Angela, liked her. It was meant to be.

He stopped the car outside Risa's house and got out to open her door. Before this night started Risa was hell-bent on inviting him in once they returned. Even though she had waffled during the night, she had finally decided to go back to her original thought. Tonight was going to be "the night" for them. The problem was that she wasn't sure how she was going to play it. He was too sure of how things were going to turn out, and for once, she wanted him a little unsure and unstable. She would like to see him in her shoes. She would like to see him completely naked and stripped of his confidence. Just once she wanted to see him vulnerable.

The walk to her front door was cold and she shivered in the chilly wind. Her expensive woolen stole seemed to be more for show than warmth. She bought it on sale and thought she had gotten a pretty good deal, a steal. As the wind penetrated the soft wool, she knew that her double-breasted lined coat would have been a better choice. But as she donned the beautiful evening dress she realized she would tolerate the cold so as not to mar its perfection. The woolen shawl was the perfect accessory to complement the sexy dress. It was worth being cold. Wordlessly, JD put his arm around her as she unlocked the front door.

She could feel the heat radiating from his body. He always seemed to be ten degrees hotter than she.

"Thank you, JD. I had a great night," she said, turning to him. Her back was against the front door.

"I'm glad," JD answered.

He stood in front of her blocking the wind from her. She was attracted to the heat his skin was generating. What was it about this man that made her mind go numb when he was close to her? Common sense told her to stand her ground and stick to her guns, but as always, where he was concerned she had no common sense. She was working on raw emotions. She was flying by the seat of her pants. Everything was happening on autopilot. She was moving without thinking. That was so dangerous. She needed her wits about her and needed to play this right. So no games. She had already made up her mind. Her daddy always said, "Go with your first mind."

Her first mind said she was his for the taking if he were interested. He was interested. She knew that. He knew she knew that.

*Damn it,* she said in her mind. She didn't even have to say anything. No words were needed. He was going to conquer her. She was going to let him conquer her. His lips were on hers in an all-consuming kiss. His tongue parted her lips and sought the warmth of her mouth. He reached out and cupped her breast ever so gently. The combination of the cold night air and his warm, leather-encased hand had her reacting with a moan as he brought her nipple to a tiny pinpoint of ecstasy. The cold aided in her excitement. It was like an aphrodisiac and spurred their lovemaking on. They were outside on her porch and she didn't care. The warm house and comfort of her bed were just a few feet behind her and she didn't care. It was late night. Her neighbors had long since retired and her house was placed far back on the lot and shielded from passersby on the street by well-placed shrubbery and trees that lined the walkway. The odds that anyone would see them were rare, but it still didn't matter.

As if on its own her long legs parted and her right one wrapped itself around his body, drawing him into her warmth. She could hear the sharp intake of breath he breathed against her throat as he nibbled on her neck. She could feel him growing strong and proud against the center of her thighs as he pressed her into the door for support. But this wasn't enough. In one quick, easy motion, he picked her up. His strong hands cupped her bottom easily. Her legs wrapped themselves around his waist. The only thing that separated their desire was the material of their clothing that suddenly seemed way too dense.

"I could take you right now," he growled against her throat.

She arched her neck. inviting him to lick, suck, and kiss her like she liked. "And I'd let you," she moaned back.

He paused for a moment to look into her eyes to see if what he just heard was the truth. It was. Her eyes were passion filled. No other words were necessary. With that, he took her into his arms again. His kiss was so intense it was like he was trying to brand her with his lips. Warm kisses that turned hot with their increasing passion seared her skin as he started to make her his.

"I want you," he breathed against her mouth.

It was obvious. Her body was weak against his onslaught. Her emotions fell victim to his desire. He opened the door and managed to carry her inside and shut the door with his foot. Before either one of them could go back to their conversation, his mouth was once again on hers. He carried her to her bedroom and deposited her in front of her large four-poster bed. Her room was decorated in lush earth tones supporting a California king-sized bed that she had shipped from Los Angeles and a huge antique armoire and couch that was her most favorite spot for reading. Lush pillows, candles, and baskets of potpourri filled the room. Her home was decorated with a combination of antiques and modern pieces that worked well together. It was an open, inviting home. He had commented on how comfortable he felt the first time he ever came to her house. The furniture was sturdy and well made, enough to support his large frame. He didn't feel as he often had when visiting a woman that he was sitting on doll furniture that was pretty, uncomfortable, and not made for his six-feet-four-inch muscular frame. And now, standing in front of her, as he undressed, he looked like he belonged in her bedroom. His large frame fit perfectly.

The first piece of clothing to go flying was JD's cashmere coat. He removed it and draped it over the chaise lounge at the foot of her bed. Next were his sweater, his belt, and his pants. He took his socks off one at a time and placed them inside of his shoes. In nothing but Calvin Klein white cotton boxer briefs, he was a magnificent creature sculptured and defined. There was an art to wearing boxer briefs. Not every man could do it. But JD could. He was a chocolate Apollo, smooth, chiseled, and anxious for her. His desire was evident and obvious despite it being shielded from her eyes by the thin gray material of his underwear. Deliberately he hooked his thumbs beneath the waistband of his boxer briefs and slid them down his toned body as he watched her watch him. His years as a professional football player had honed his body to perfection. And even though he hadn't played in a couple of years, he still had it. He knew it and she did too as her eyes took in all of him. And by saying all, she meant all of him. His manhood was perfection itself, proud, erect, and ready to join with her. It excited him to be watched by her. There was no shame in his bearing and he wanted her to feel none in making a frank assessment of him.

"Take off your clothes," he ordered her, his voice thick with desire. But he didn't have to tell her to get undressed. She felt out of place in her clothes.

Suddenly the material was oppressive and restrictive. He crossed the short distance that separated them and placed his hand over hers and guided it to the first button at her neck. As soon as she unsnapped it, he kissed the exposed flesh. She knew what to do. She undid the next button. Again, exposed flesh was met with lips that were succulent, gentle, full, and lush. Soon, in nothing but her white lace Victoria's Secret ensemble, she stood before him, shivering not with cold but desire. For so long the silky garments had lain untouched in her dresser drawer. When she had donned them, she was surprised at how sexy and alluring she appeared even to herself. Before she got dressed she took inventory of her body and was pleased. Judging from his reaction to her, JD was too. It made her feel good to know that her body pleased him. It had been a long time since she found herself in this place with a man so anxious for her. It was intoxicating to know that she could be an object of such desire. She felt sexy and empowered. Taking him by surprise, she led him to the bed and pushed him back onto it. He looked up at her with a combination of surprise, delight, and desire. She turned on the CD player. The room was filled with the sounds of vintage Prince. She could never call him, "the artist formally known as." He was Prince in the beginning and Prince he would always remain.

She had a friend named Michael who had changed his name to Malek. She could never remember to call him Malek. Therefore Prince would always be Prince to her. His music wasn't what she would have chosen for the seduction. She needed Roberta Flack, Teddy Pendagrass, or maybe even Barry White. Not Prince. The pulsating beats and sensual undertones were so very harsh. They were seductive sure enough, but not the soothing tones for love-making. When the dance was done to Prince there would be nothing gentle about it. It would be sexy and raw and passionate and fierce. She was about to change the selection but he held up his hand and stopped her.

"No. Leave it," he said.

She could feel the music pulsating through her body. Her blood seemed to flow to the beat. She felt herself growing excited with the undertones.

"I like that," he said.

He was enjoying listening to the music and watching her. He made himself comfortable by positioning himself upright against her headboard and by stacking her bed pillows behind his back.

"Dance for me, sexy," he commanded.

He had given her that nickname, sexy, and she liked it. The entire mood changed with the introduction of the Prince music into the boudoir. Risa began to move to the music. He watched her with eyes filled with desire. She was doing something she had never done before. She was dancing for this man, performing a seductive striptease made even more alluring by her inexperience. In college she took a belly dancing class and reverted to those moves, giving in to a moment of whimsy that was so unlike her. He watched unself-conscious in his nakedness as she danced for him, his desire evident. The music surrounded her and Risa felt herself giving in to its commanding sensual undertone. It was too much for him.

"Risa, enough. Join me," he said.

For the first time in her life, Risa discovered that she didn't mind being ordered around. He held out his hand. Abruptly, she stopped dancing and walked to the bed as if under the spell of his magnetism. He lifted her and placed her over his lap. The thin material of her panties was the only thing separating his manhood from the treasure it sought. He put his hand into her hair and released the pearl clip that held her hair away from her face. Thick black hair fell to her shoulders in long, thick strands. With her hair down, she felt liberated and uninhibited. He placed the intricately designed pearl clip gently onto the nightstand. He handled it with such delicacy she couldn't wait to feel his hands on her body, touching her in such a gentle manner. With expert hands, he unfastened her bra and placed it too onto the nightstand.

For a brief moment he looked at her getting his fill of the delightful sight of Risa straddling him. Gently, he reached up and cupped the fullness of her breast. They were so heavy with wanting him all she could do was moan as he traced her nipples with his thumbs. The kiss was inevitable. He sucked and kissed on her lips as he slipped his hand into the lacy silk that separated their mutual desire.

Risa arched her body with wanting as he slid one of his fingers into the juncture at her thighs. Mirroring the action of his tongue, he manipulated the finger until Risa could stand it no longer. Her body moved in a rhythm bent on fulfillment. She arched and moved until she reached the pentacle of ecstasy against his hand and collapsed against his chest. When she could raise her head to look at him he was smiling at her. That same knowing, galling smile that let her know he was pleased with his handiwork.

"You're such a know-it-all," she said.

"It's a character flaw," he replied.

He rolled her onto her back and lay on top of her. The playfulness was immediately replaced with passion and desire. It was time. Although Risa hadn't been in this position in a very long time, she remembered the dance. She reached out and captured him with her hand, getting the full measure of him.

"JD . . ." she began, hating this inevitable moment.

Things had changed so much. She could not continue
without asking for the required protection. His breath was
short and controlled.

"Wait," he said, cutting her off.

He got up and went to his pants pocket. He returned
quickly with a small package. It pleased her tremendously
not to be the one to have to broach this subject. No matter
how excited they were, they had to be responsible.

He tore the cellophane with his teeth and slipped the
required sheath on just before he removed the lacy strip
that kept her from him. He didn't have to ask if she was
ready. He knew. Her reaction to him was evident. His
hand was wet with her desire. He completed their union
with one quick thrust that made her let out a moan that
made him pause.

"Don't stop," she breathed, adjusting to the fit and
curve of him as they molded their bodies into a tight fit.
She soared to heights that she only dreamed about. This
was like no other dance. The rhythm and pace were so different she was surprised she didn't lose her step. But she
kept up. So did he. Afterwards, Risa realized that she was
in over her head. This was much more than she ever bar-
gained for. She was in love. It had to be love because nothing but love could make her body betray her so completely.
She lost control and had fallen under the spell that was
JD. He had won. She could only give in and marry him.

JD didn't know what to say. They lay entwined, naked
against each other. The pale, pink cotton eyelet sheets
with high thread count draped their bodies seductively. It
was chilly in the room. The heavier covering, a down comforter and a woolen blanket, had been kicked off in their
passion. Under normal circumstances JD would have
pulled up the covers and maybe even gotten up to light
the fire. There was a brick fireplace in the bedroom. He
liked that. It was the centerpiece of the room. The furni-

ture was placed decoratively around it. It was a good room, a comfortable room. He could be happy in this room. But these weren't normal circumstances. His concentration was split. JD found himself nearly dazed. He didn't expect it to be like this. He didn't expect her to be such an enchantress.

When Risa did that impromptu striptease, he was shocked, but aroused, by her boldness. He didn't expect that from Risa, who didn't appear all that experienced. He liked that about her. She was so perfect, as if she were untouched until he came around. Now, he wasn't naive enough to think that no other man had lain with her. But he couldn't imagine that the Risa he had gotten to know had done these things with another man. He couldn't imagine her sweet lips and greedy mouth delighting anyone like she had delighted him. He found himself jealous of the other man, or men, who had been privy to that delightful body and those delicious moves.

When JD and Risa finally got into the act, his little kitten turned into a wildcat that gave as good as she got. He found himself wanting to know who taught her that. She didn't get that good from reading books and talking with her girlfriends. How many men had there been? Was she not what she appeared?

A man in JD's position had to be careful. He didn't know his net worth. He could always ask Angela. She could rattle it off and not even blink. There were women out there who set traps for him with acts that weren't nearly as convincing as Risa's. He had always been lucky and sidestepped them before, but Risa had fooled him. He believed her naïveté and had almost fallen for her hook, line and sinker with that pretense that he was taking it too fast for her. He was delighted and honored that she let him into her woman's place with a response that looked so real that he had almost been fooled. But nobody moved like that without practice. Practice made perfect and she had obviously been practicing a lot. And to think, he had wanted to marry her. He had asked her on the first day that she had kissed him with that warm, fantastic mouth. A mouth he suddenly found a little too talented for his taste.

There was something to be said about a high thread count and scented sheets. They smelled like lavender and vanilla and could easily lull him into a contented state. Risa's soft, gentle lips were tattooing his body with gossamer-light butterfly kisses that was arousing him again. He was getting there even though he was torn. She was practicing her previously mastered tricks on him. They were working. *Who had scented sheets?* He closed his eyes and tried to think but it was hard with her playing with him. He wanted to be the one to teach her tricks and hear the moans for the first time and yet she had been the one to have him shaking with desire and quivering awaiting her touch. *What was she doing with her hand?* Suddenly the teacher was the student. The tide had been turned and JD didn't like it. He didn't like it one bit.

Risa felt good lying next to JD. No other man had shared her bed since she purchased it. His large body was a good fit for it. Together they fit perfectly. His chest felt good beneath her fingers. His skin tasted good on the tip of her tongue. He tasted like pomegranates and pumpkin seeds. He smelled like rain. Her head lay on his chest and she gloried in the feel of his naked body. She was cold and wondered if he was thinking, like she was, that a fire would be a good thing right about now. She wouldn't be surprised if they were on the same page. Everything about the two of them worked well together. She decided that he was right. If it was this good, they could make it work.

"Yes!" she said out of nowhere, elated, happy and excited.

"What?" JD asked. His energy was split. He was concentrating on something. She could tell.

"Yes, I'll marry you," she said, then thinking, *that should get his attention.* She moved closer to him so that she could see his eyes when she said it.

"So, you want to marry me now?"

Her words rang in his ears. Was this was a well-constructed ruse to get him? Had she been pretending to be overwhelmed by his attention? He felt betrayed and used. He wanted her more than he could remember wanting a woman. But the time they just spent together had him doubting his hasty decision. He didn't want to be controlled by his rampant desire and be a fool to his hormones because he found her appealing and enticing. He needed a moment to think and he could not do that if she were draped so precariously around his naked body. He was, after all, still a man. His body was betraying him as she traced his nipple with her well-manicured finger.

"I thought you wanted to wait," he said.

He could feel himself growing aroused again. The mere presence of her had him reeling. She was just touching his nipple and kissing his skin. There wasn't anything overtly sexual in what she was doing and yet he was becoming rampant with desire and raging with fire as she touched him.

"Well, you said yourself, I'm not getting any younger," she said, chuckling. The countdown to her birthday was fast approaching.

"Maybe we should take it a little slow," he said.

"What?" She wasn't sure she heard him correctly. Up until now he had pursued her with a single-minded determination that had her doubting her common sense and good judgment. "But we can't," she stammered. Hadn't she just lain with this man?

"Why? You can't be pregnant."

"What?" She sat up confused at his reaction.

Something was wrong and she didn't know what. As she faced him, the sheet fell from her body, exposing her radiant and magnificent nakedness to his scrutiny.

*She really is beautiful,* he told himself as he restrained from touching her flawless dark skin. His hands were straining with hunger to touch her. But whenever he did, he lost all control. She had him mesmerized by her body, lulled by her song. It was all such a deliberate trick. He felt fooled by her duplicity.

"Don't play innocent with me, Risa. I am a grown man. I've been around and obviously so have you."

His words were so filled with venom that Risa reacted as if he had physically struck her. She fell away from him and clutched the sheet to her body.

"Surely you didn't expect me to be a virgin, JD?" she said. "I have been in relationships before. Did you expect to be the first man to my bed?" *Why is he acting like this? He wanted to do it just as much as I did.*

"Obviously not. But I didn't expect to be one of many," he said as he threw the covers back and began to dress hastily.

She watched with a mixture of shock and desire as he pulled on his pants. He was in such a rush that he didn't bother with his formfitting boxer briefs. He stuffed them into the pocket of his dark trousers.

"One of many? JD, I've only slept with four men in my life. You were the fourth."

Why were they having this discussion now?

"Risa, Risa, Risa, such a beautiful mouth. What a shame it is filled with so many lies."

He didn't put on his socks, or his sweater. He just threw the cashmere coat on over his slacks.

"I do not lie. Especially about my sexual history," she said with as much dignity as she could muster in her nakedness as she followed him through the house. He hadn't given her time to dress so she just wrapped a sheet around her slender curves.

"What kind of game are you playing, Risa? We're adults. I know what I want. You know what you want too. You didn't have to trick me into proposing marriage just to get me in your bed," JD said accusingly.

"I don't do things like this!" Risa exclaimed.

"You could have fooled me."

He was so angry. Each word out of his mouth was aimed at hurting her. She felt like she was being punched and slapped by him. She had never been in an abusive relationship, but surely the physical punches could not have been worse than these innuendoes and cruel words.

"Did you expect a thirty-nine-year-old virgin?" she asked.

This was a whole new century. No one, absolutely no one, thought like that anymore.

"No. But I didn't expect a thirty-nine-year-old whore either."

The slap came from nowhere. Risa wasn't even sure she was the one who slapped him if it wasn't for the stinging in her right hand. He had pissed her off so much, slapping some sense into him was the only thing she could think of doing. The sound of the blow echoed throughout the hallway. He stood looking down at her. Even in anger she was beautiful beyond words. Her eyes sparkled. He wanted to pull her to him and apologize for hurting her. But his pride wouldn't let him. She had played him and he didn't like it. He had introduced her to his mother, for God's sake.

"Get out of my house," Risa said, fighting back tears. She had never had to put anyone out of her home.

"With pleasure," he said as he approached the front

door. He reached for the knob when she asked the question she needed answered.

"Was all this just to sleep with me?" she asked.

There were some men who went to any lengths to get what they wanted. Surely JD didn't have to create such an elaborate force just to bed her.

"If all I had wanted to do was sleep with you, I could have done that on the first day. You were that easy."

With that he was gone and a dumbfounded Risa could not bring herself to watch his retreating back as he got into his Jaguar and drove away. All she could do was close the door and lean against it for support before she slid to the floor in a crying heap.

# Chapter 12

Risa had the constitution of a horse. In her long professional career she had never taken advantage of the benefits offered to her like sick days and leaves of absence. She was a workaholic and overachiever. So when she called in sick on the next morning, warning bells and whistles went off. Totally unaware of this, she lay beneath the covers licking the wounds that JD had inflicted on her psyche. She had never misjudged someone so badly. He had pulled the wool over her eyes and concocted such an elaborate hoax just to sleep with her that she was doubting her ability to be a good judge of character. His behavior was totally unacceptable.

She was an adult and would have appreciated his honesty. If he had just told her that he wanted to sleep with her, she could have addressed it as she had before when faced with a man's apparent desire and rebuffed him kindly. But no. He came at her with deceptiveness so vile that she was physically ill. She had met his mother, for God's sake! She had shared food with his family. She played last night's events over and over in her head trying to pinpoint the moment that things went horribly wrong.

*The dinner went fine,* she thought. *Then we came back to my house.* If it were possible for her to blush, she would have at the memory of the things they had done. Oh, how he had made her feel with the physical release that was waves and waves of stored passion. He had released in her a siren she didn't know she possessed. She wanted to be everything he could desire in bed. She had given herself to him freely and without inhibition because he had touched her inner wanton. Afterwards he looked at her as if she had done something wrong.

She couldn't believe that he thought she was a whore because she appeared more skilled than she really was. The things she did with him were things she did for the first time because she wanted to please him. He brought out the inner hoochie that she didn't even know she had. And now to be punished for it? She couldn't stand it. It actually brought her to tears. She cried like a baby because she felt so deceived. This was a new millennium and she had fallen in love with a man with archaic morals and values concerning sex. Therefore, she was a victim to his outdated morals and values.

She was actually sickened by the thought that he was a man who allowed the double standard to effect their budding relationship. Why could a man have lovers before he fell in love, and yet if a woman walked down the same path, she was a whore? The unfairness of it was more than Risa could stand. For the first time in years she had opened her heart as well as her body to a man and had been rejected. Moaning, she crawled beneath the covers and decided here she would remain until the floor opened up beneath her and swallowed her whole. If that didn't work, she would remain in bed until she decided how to move forward.

As she lay beneath the covers she was startled when her doorbell rang. She was too drained to address it and decided to pull the covers over her head, hoping the person would go away. When the ringing turned to a persistent knocking on her front door, she decided she better answer it before her neighbors became alarmed. She managed to drag herself out of the bed and walk to the front door. As she looked through the peephole she was surprised to see both Helen and Cayce. Concern was etched on both their faces. Sighing, she opened the door. Something important must have happened at the station. She hadn't had the television on all day. She had just been playing the soundtrack to *The Bodyguard* over and over. She played it so much that her neighbor's cat left its comfortable perch on her windowsill in search of more quiet lounging quarters.

"What's wrong?" Risa asked her two friends.

"We're here to ask you that," Helen demanded with hands on hip, her very pregnant belly protruding as she waddled past Risa and took a seat on the down-filled couch and immediately put her feet up.

"Risa, look at yourself," Cayce cooed, steering Risa towards Helen who didn't move but immediately took her friend into her arms.

It was easier for Risa to bend down than have Helen get up from the overstuffed furniture. Risa's hair was in disarray. Her eyes were puffy and the old shirt she had pulled on was stretched out of shape. She didn't look like the Risa they were accustomed to. Eventually the two women managed to get Risa to take a seat on the couch and put her feet up. Once they had Risa settled, Cayce headed for the kitchen. She learned a long time ago that a girl pow-wow was best held over food. Risa didn't cook. But she kept a well-stocked kitchen. Soon Cayce was able to put together an entire smorgasbord of delectable delights. She was comfortable in the kitchen and knew how to take the most mundane and make satisfying fare. Unlike her boss, she had learned to cook at an early age. And unlike her boss's boss, she abhorred take-out. By the time she finished, they'd be having a man-bashing moment on full stomachs.

# Chapter 13

"Rack me up, bro," Larry said, indicating the cue balls on the pool table.

JD was so preoccupied in thought that he couldn't even remember the game. The balls had been sitting untouched for a couple of minutes. JD had lost two straight sets. This wasn't like him. Usually their pool games were heated trash-talking, competition-filled events. But not today. JD was pensive as he milked a beer and played haphazardly. He was forgetful and not very communicative. Big L knew there was something wrong with his friend but he couldn't figure it out.

JD had shown up with a six-pack of Heineken and a picnic basket that he had gotten from Daphne's restaurant. They sold them by the hundreds. He hadn't even checked to see what was in it. He knew his sister's reputation. No basket left her restaurant unless it had been double-checked. That meant there would be a whole roasted herbed chicken, a salad, handmade biscuits, macaroni and cheese, utensils, plates, napkins, and a dessert. She was even toying with the idea of selling the baskets over the Internet. Daphne, like her brother, was an entrepreneur. He was very proud of her. When he picked up the basket she wasn't there. She was at the new restaurant, Honey Baby's, which was scheduled to open in a couple of months. He was glad he missed her because he knew the first thing she would have asked him would have been about Risa. When he arrived home the morning after spending the night with Risa, his voice mail was filled with messages from his sisters saying how much they liked her and how pretty they thought she was. He would have to break the news to them that he had made a mistake. Risa wasn't the one he thought she was. But if this was the case, how come he could not get her out of his mind?

His face still smarted from her slap. In all his relationships, none had resulted in violence of any kind. As he reviewed the events of their night together in his mind, he was sure he had provoked her. She was feisty and didn't take any guff. He liked that about her. And in all honesty, he didn't mean to hurt her. But he was hurt after their lovemaking session and wanted to lash out at someone. She was the only one there. He knew it was wrong to behave the way he did when faced with her past, but he was only human. His mind was filled with questions that he might not ever get the answers to now. He wondered what kind of life she had before him that would have taught her such sophisticated lovemaking techniques.

He was a man of status and position. He could not have a woman with a past that could rear its ugly head and haunt him. He was a man with political aspirations to achieve within the next ten years. The woman he chose must be an asset, not a liability. Even in saying that, he knew that the real problem was that he literally saw red playing out fantasies in his head in which he imagined Risa with other men. It had nothing to do with his half-baked political ideal to eventually be the first Black mayor of Dallas, Texas. It had to do with being possessive and realizing someone else had played with his toy before him.

Although he grew up in a house that encouraged sharing, they all had their favorite toys that they didn't want anyone else to play with. Somewhere deep in his soul he knew he was being childish and immature, but he couldn't help it. He was consumed with wanting to know who she had been with. In his worst-case scenario, the woman he had bedded had bedded one or more of his associates. It might not be probable, but it could be possible. He couldn't think straight for thinking that it was possible that he knew some of these men Risa had been with. She wasn't a low-class woman. The men she would have been with would have been men of class and style. That added to the probability that they could have been men in his circle. *Who*, he wondered, *could have been there before him? Who? Who? Who?*

There were men who came to mind simply because of their reputations as lady-killers and playboys. Hell, based on reputation, he could be on that list! He kept reminding himself that all things weren't as they seemed. If they were, he wouldn't be tying his stomach in knots trying to create a list of possible suspects the woman he had slept with, who until last night, he had considered his and his alone. It was driving him crazy. And that was crazy with a capital *C*. CRAZY!

Who could have sampled the delights of that body? Who could have tasted the sweetness of her mouth? Who could have watched that delicious striptease that aroused him to a level of desire that almost made him compromise himself before their lovemaking session started? Who? Who? Who? He was grasping his cue stick so tightly, if it were possible for his knuckles to turn white then they would have.

"Hey, brother man? You want to stop and take a lunch break?" Big L asked, taking the cue stick from JD.

He was starting to get worried. JD had just been standing there holding the stick without taking a shot. Angela had taken the kids and gone to Carlie's house. The two men were left alone with some leftover meat loaf, yams, and greens. The two large men had already devoured that. It was time to start on the basket from Daphne's restaurant. Later they might even order a couple of pizzas if Angela didn't get back in time and start dinner. Sometimes Big L cooked. His specialty was Tex-Mex cuisine. He grew up on it and could whip up a smorgasbord of tacos, tortillas, salsa, burritos, and flautas quicker than most. His wife would always smile brightly when he cooked and not even complain when she helped him clean the mess he inevitably left. Every time he cooked he managed to mess up every available pot. To this day Angela couldn't figure out how he managed to dirty the coffeepot when he cooked. He didn't even drink coffee!

"Yeah. Yeah. I could eat something," JD said.

"Man, that Daphne sure can cook," Big L said and started unpacking the basket. JD took a seat at the large island that set in the middle of the floor. He liked this kitchen. When Big L and Angela had bought the house it had needed remarkably little work. The kitchen was the only room they had remodeled in the seventeen years they lived in the house. They had replaced the cabinets so that there were glass fronts and replaced the appliances with those of the modern stainless steel variety. They had stripped the floor of its original Formica and replaced with a patchwork of Spanish tile. Angela's kitchen had been featured in an edition of Dallas's *Beautiful Home* magazine.

Big L noticed that JD was preoccupied and kept up a commentary that he was sure would ease his friend into a discussion of what was bothering him.

"Man, that food last night was out of this world. I almost envy the man who lands her. Angela can cook too," Big L started. "But Daphne always manages to add a little something, something to her food. Did you taste those sweet little tomatoes?"

He loved good food and good times. Each and every day he counted his lucky stars for having married a woman who was as good a cook as she was a companion. He had learned to appreciate the delicacies that were soul food and took delight in introducing Angela to the foods of both his father's and mother's land. Coming from parents of two distinct cultures had cultivated his palette in an interesting and fantastic way. He was most happy when he got to wrap his mouth around some food from Daphne's restaurant, and couldn't wait until she opened the new restaurant.

"Want me to fix you a plate?" Big L asked. JD agreed absently. Still not getting the type of response that he wanted, Big L stopped and turned to his friend. "Okay, man, you're killing me. Killing me. What's up?"

He had a half a chicken in his hand and was just about to reach for the potato salad. Angela put celery seeds in her potato salad. A little sugar and garlic also played over his taste buds. If all things had been different and he hadn't spent a large portion of his life as an athlete, he would have been a very, very fat man instead of a very, very large man. His appetite did not allow for a sedentary lifestyle. Thank God for a home gym and four active children.

"I messed up," JD said as he put his pool cue down and faced the ex-teammate.

"I really messed up," JD repeated.

"Oh, woman troubles I see." Big L let out a sigh of relief. This was something he could handle.

Woman problems were an everyday occurrence for Big L. He had three as permanent residents in his house and a whole slew that were in and out. When he married a woman with four sisters, it was inevitable that he would have to deal with some type of woman problem. He began making the plates how Angela had taught him. He put a little of everything on the plate and arranged it prettily. Anything could be addressed over a plate of food. He and Angela rarely had disagreements, but when they did, they were so minor and insignificant that they made up before the morning sun cast its first light. Actually, he was hard-pressed to remember what their last argument was over. He was a very fortunate man. He hoped that his friend would be that fortunate. Right now, JD was hurting and he hoped that their conversation would ease his mind. He was sure all his friend needed was a good woman. It had worked for him.

"I feel awful," JD said, but it was unnecessary.

Big L knew that much. He could see it and feel it. On one hand he felt up to facing the challenge of making his friend feel better. On the other, he wished that Angela would arrive soon because she was so much better at tending broken hearts. She did it so much easier than he could ever do. As the eldest daughter, she was often the sounding board for her sister's man woes and frustrations. He watched amazed at the times she had given an encouraging word and offered a suggestion that turned everything around. As he watched his friend suffer, he wished that he had paid more attention when Angela was offering her pearls of wisdom. All he could think to do was feed him, give him a beer, and listen. Listening was always good. That he learned from his teenage daughter, Hailey.

"Daddy, sometimes I just need you to listen," she said to him during one of their frequent father-daughter outings. He tried to be a good father. He made it a point to spend some alone time with each child. When he and Hailey were together they would go for a walk in the park. She would talk and he would listen. She was a chatterbox. He learned so much from listening to her. The problem was,

JD wasn't saying anything. He couldn't listen if his friend remained stoic. JD was barely eating and he looked terrible. Big L was growing worried. He couldn't wait for Angela to return. She would know what to do. She had a knack for it.

# Chapter 14

"He said what?" Helen shouted. She literally saw red after listening to Risa give her and Cayce an account of the night before and her morning with JD.

She was pissed off. She was angry and darn near livid with animosity towards JD. How dare he treat Risa like this? She was a woman of quality and didn't deserve his scorn. Actually, from what she had heard, no woman deserved to be the victim of the age-old double standard. It was a new millennium, those archaic beliefs that a woman who was skilled in lovemaking had to be a whore were barbaric.

*How could JD be a victim of such inane and stupid thoughts?* Helen thought. She had known him nearly all his life. His sister Angela was one of her sorority sisters, Alpha Kappa Alpha Sorority, Inc. They saw each other at graduate chapter meetings. Angela was a liberated, freethinking modern woman. His sister Daphne was her favorite chef. Helen and Isaiah were regulars at Cornbread and Brie and were waiting with bated breath for the opening of Honey Baby's. She sang in the church choir with his sister Carlie. The girl had a pleasant voice and an even more pleasant personality. All his sisters were great girls. Even the really pretty one, Elisha. If Helen remembered correctly, she was a judge in the last pageant in which JD's youngest sister participated. She knew there was sometimes a double standard in the raising of girls and boys, but she couldn't fathom how JD could be such a caveman with his five female siblings.

Secretly, Helen was pleased when she saw the sparks between JD and Risa evident even on the tape of the interview she had watched. But happiness was a good thing and did not come with a price tag that was accompanied by pain and discontent.

*Just wait until I see Mr. Jones,* Helen told herself. *I'm going to give him a piece of my mind. By the way he was acting, obviously no one had ever done that before. Oh, well, Mr. Jones, there's a first time for everything.*

After her two friends left Risa's house, Risa began the task of cleaning up the evidence of their girl powwow. There was an empty Bluebell chocolate chip ice cream container, empty vanilla Coke bottles, half-eaten Mrs. Fields cookies, and an empty box left over from the pizza they ordered. The pizza came after the fried chicken wings and potato wedges that Cayce had fixed up. Risa ate so many carbs and consumed so much sugar that she knew she would have to spend more than her usual hour on the StairMaster. But that wouldn't be until tomorrow. She didn't feel like tackling the exercise machine. She didn't feel like doing much of anything except clear away the trash.

Declining Helen and Cayce's offer to clean the mess, she reasoned that it would be therapeutic to busy herself with as much JD nonrelated activity as she could find. But after dumping the empty boxes, straightening the pillows on her couch, and unnecessarily vacuuming the large antique Persian rug that covered part of her hardwood floors, she found herself still replaying the previous night's events. Her friend's reassurance that he was a cad, a caveman, and a bore did nothing to ease the guilt she felt over having been so easily led by her hormones.

Every time she closed her eyes she saw his well-defined handsome face and felt his skilled, gentle hands caressing her body. Although she was candid with Helen and Cayce and shared some of the most intimate details of her evening with JD, she was still too much of a Southern belle to give them the total unabridged version. They were, however, able to deduct for themselves what had taken place. It wasn't even necessary to read between the lines. All they had to do was look at Risa, who even through her pain, looked like a woman who had been well loved.

There was a satisfied, sated look to her eyes, a slept-on look to her hair and a having been loved look to her person. She was a woman who had been pleased beyond words. It was that obvious. There was no reason to read between the lines. It was written all over her face. So it was no wonder she felt like crap. How could he in one breath utter words of love and appreciation and in the next treat her so poorly? It boggled the mind and she continued with her busywork. Once satisfied that her house was back in order, she once again took to her bed. She needed to regroup and only the comfort of her bed or her mother's arms would appease her. Unfortunately her mother, Shelia Marcia Hooker James, was unreachable and had been for five days while she was out to sea on a senior singles cruise.

At the time of her departure, Shelia was hesitant to leave Risa with no way of contacting her, but Risa insisted that her mother take the much-anticipated trip. She was, after all, a grown woman and didn't need her mommy. But now five days later with her life in turmoil, all she could think was, *Mama, do I need and want you now!* So, with

Shelia absent she did the next best thing. She crawled into her bed with a box of Kleenex and the half-eaten pint of Häagen-Dazs chocolate chip ice cream. When Mama wasn't available, Häagen-Dazs was the next best thing. She had never found solace in food before, but on this day, Häagen-Dazs seemed to be the only thing to ease the pain in her heart and the burden on her soul.

# Chapter 15

As JD replayed his voice mail messages, he wondered how he was going to break the news to his family that he and Risa were no longer an item. When he told Larry, his friend looked at him with disbelief. Larry's initial response to the girl was genuine. He liked her. The ease with which she had fit into the Jones clan made her seem like a perfect match for JD. Plus she looked good. To get good looks and poise in one package was pretty damn good. He listened with rapt attention as his friend relayed his version of the events that led to their breakup.

"Well what do you think?" JD asked once the telling was over, bristling with self-righteous indignation, convinced that Larry would see things his way. He was shocked when the big man sided with the other wronged party.

"I think you're acting crazy," Big L said.

"What?" JD asked him again, damn near choking on his drink.

They had demolished the contents of the picnic basket and were working on the beers. Larry had also placed an order for three large pizzas. He had the local pizza parlor on speed dial. With four children, a working wife, and occasional gathering of ex-teammates of which JD was always included, he could get pizza, Chinese food, or Cornbread and Brie with the click of his finger. His son tried to show him how to order online, but he insisted that just as long as he had a finger and a phone, he didn't need to order takeout from the computer. He had just learned how to send e-mails, for Pete's sake. He was going to fight the technological age all the way!

"I said, you're being an egghead," he managed even though he was heavily involved in the fantasy football game on the big screen TV.

They had left the family room and was now in "Larry's space," which was a large room over the garage. At one time it was the maid's quarters, equipped with a bathroom and small kitchen. But the Wheatons had never had the need for outside help. Angela was supermom. She did it all. This room was designated as Larry's. With a house full of kids, Angela felt that he needed some place to call his own. She even decorated it to suit him. It was a man's room equipped with a big screen TV, Nintendo, satellite, and exercise equipment. The room was so perfect that Angela had friends who said that if their husband had such a sanctuary, they would never see him. Angela laughed, telling them her secret was to make sure that his small kitchen held the barest of necessities: beer, water, and juice. And she made sure the pool table was set up in the family room in the main house. In actuality she only said that for her friends' sake.

Larry was a dedicated and loyal father and husband. He used the room mainly to entertain his friends. It was the one place in the six-bedroom house that he could relax with his football buddies and not trip over toys. Today he was using it so that he and JD could talk man-to-man without Angela and the kids interrupting his friend's commentary. He wasn't sure when they would be back. So when he finally got JD to talk, he steered him towards the male sanctuary so that they could have some privacy. As he talked to JD, he worked his massive thumbs over the game keypad. Ironically, he played the game but steered away from the computer and Internet.

"All I got to say is, you don't throw away a Rolls-Royce because someone else sat in the seat," Big L reasoned.

"You do if you thought you were getting it with a thousand miles and you find out someone had played with the odometer," was JD's comeback.

"Damn, was it like that, bro?"

"Yeah." JD sighed, feeling both angry and frustrated. He knew that on one hand he was being ridiculous, but on the other, he felt justified in his anger and assessment of the situation. "I knew she wasn't a virgin. I'm not even saying I wanted that. There's something about a mature, sexy woman that I find appealing." JD paused for a moment as if searching for the right words. "I just didn't know . . . man, you don't understand . . . she was skilled. She was polished. You don't just develop skills like that from reading romance novels and watching Lifetime Television. Whoever was there before me . . . I will not try to fight a ghost again."

"Ahhh. I see." Big L nodded, with an "I get it now" smile creeping across his face.

"Do you, man?"

"Yeah, I do. Lucy's dead husband, Marcus, has you outgunned and outnumbered. It's like no matter what you do and say, he will always have done it better and said it better. It's like it's a cult that you don't belong to. He beats you in every fight."

"True that. Because he is dead, I can't take him on. And this thing with Risa . . . you can't understand. You married my sister."

"That doesn't make me stupid. I get it. It's like you are still fighting a ghost you can't see."

JD was shocked at his friend's insight.

"Yeah, it's like that. I wanted to be the teacher, not the student."

"I know. It's a special kind of pain. You don't want your lady doing tricks that have you whimpering like a little girl."

In all the years that they had known each other, no subject had ever been off-limits. However, in matters of the bedroom he always tempered his conversation. His wife was, after all, his best friend's sister. He had never been happy enough or drunk enough to tell JD that when he had finally bedded Angela, he had nearly gone screaming into the hills when he had discovered that he was lacking in the bedroom. His sweetheart had been more than eager to teach him. At first he hadn't been all too eager to learn. No man wanted to know that his woman was "the man" in the bedroom. It had been a blow to his overinflated ego. It had made him doubt his previous conquest and wonder who had taught her? Where was this elusive man? And if they were no longer together, why the hell not?

JD put his hands over his ears. "I can't hear this."

"Stop being a baby." Larry chuckled. " Man, you can't spend your days and nights turning that question over and over in your head. It will drive you nuts. Just know whoever she was with, she ain't no more. She is with you. So be the man that got her to the bed in the first place. Trust, it's fun learning a thing or two."

"Aaaarrrgh." JD moaned. "You're talking about my sister."

"And my wife."

"All I want to do is put a face to the guy, then I won't see him in every man."

"I get it."

"Do you, man, do you get what I'm saying?"

"I get it. But I just don't care. Man, all I can say is, if it's good, it's good. Does it matter which one whimpers first as long as they both whimper?"

Big L's words gave JD cause to think. For a moment the two men sat in companionable silence, both lost in thought.

# Chapter 16

It took Risa two whole days to shake the blue funk that surrounded her after she and JD parted with such terrible words. Every time she closed her eyes she could still see the angry look on his face and hear the hateful words he hurled at her with such venom. He called her a whore and said it like he meant it. It hurt terribly. It would take more than a day for her to recover. She needed the comfort of her bed to lull her into blissful contentment. She had laid in it for two whole days before she got the phone call from an old friend that made her stir from her hiding place. It was a welcomed surprise and made her get up and shake the sadness that covered her body like a shroud. And when she shook it, she shook it with a vengeance. She turned on her CD player and sang along with Patti Labelle's *New Attitude.* Then, adhering to more of Cayce's advice, she went and had a "Risa day."

She started with a manicure, pedicure, facial, and body wrap. It had been a long time since she pampered herself and she enjoyed it. Next, she made an appointment with her favorite hairstylist, Jerome. Jerome, like her, had once been stationed in Los Angeles. He decided that he liked being a big fish in a little pond better than being one of many little fish in an even larger pond. So Dallas became his place of choice. Jerome was one of the most sought-after hairstylists in the southwest. Women drove from as far away as New Orleans to sit in his chair. Risa got the last-minute appointment simply by relying on her celebrity status. Prior to this occasion, she always played by the rules and made her appointments ahead of time. This was the first time she traded on her clout and got him to take her without a prior appointment. He took one look at her and ushered her into his chair.

"My goodness, Ms. Risa James. Your hair looks listless and lifeless. Girl, you better get yourself over here in my chair pronto."

Risa complied easily, willing to let him work his magic without giving him instruction. She trusted him to make the best style decisions for her.

"Work your magic, boyfriend," she ordered him divaishly.

"I like that. Can I do whatever I want?" he confirmed in question. There was hint of mischief in his eyes as he stood watching her with his scissors in one hand and the blow-dryer in the other.

"Go ahead. I trust you."

With a loud cackle, he started on her. The result was that Risa's thick mane was cut, permed, flat-ironed, and streaked with a honey blond that came out light brown against her raven tresses. With shorter hair that framed her beautiful face, she looked younger, vibrant, and more alive. She hadn't had her hair cut in years. The occasional trim had been routine. But this drastic cut of several inches made an instant change in her appearance. If someone were to happenstance a guess at her age, it would be nowhere near almost forty. The last stop on Risa's list on "her day" was a shopping spree at a trendy local Dallas boutique.

Prior to her day, Risa had stuck with the classics and chose fabrics and hues for their quality and staying power. This was the first time she gave in to a whim and picked some mod fad clothes. Although she could well afford it, she never just splurged on a series of faddish apparel. She bought several outfits because they were fun. With help from a salesgirl who insisted that with her figure Risa could wear anything, she ended up in brown suede pants, a denim shirt, and three-inch-high stiletto black boots. She was a modern day cowgirl, trendy and sexy. There was nothing about her that looked like she was going to a hoe-down or anything else stereotypically Texan. But her out-fit hinted at the rugged heritage the state was popular for. Staring at herself in the mirror she was amazed at what properly placed accessories could do to an outfit. The sparkle from the golden hoop chain at her waist high-lighted the sparkle from the assortment of bracelets on her wrist. The earrings, which were large golden hoops, added just the right amount of sparkle and pizzazz. If she didn't know any better, Risa might not have been able to recognize her own reflection. She had never looked her age. As the expression went, "Good Black don't crack." But now in clothes that she would never have selected if left to her own devices she looked like she was a young, hip woman accustomed to the stares of admiration she was getting as she walked into her office at KKRL and took her seat at her desk.

"Risa! Risa! " Cayce said as she rushed into the office. "I thought that was you! You look marvelous!" the younger woman exclaimed. "I have those shoes!" Because Cayce was only five feet tall most of her shoes sported three-inch heels.

"Good. You can wear them tonight when we go out on the town," Risa said.

Risa made the impromptu decision as soon as she saw Cayce. It had been a long time since they had a girl's night out. The pressures and grind of the job had been too demanding to allow such an adventure.

"Aye, aye," Cayce said as she did a mock sailor salute then scampered away to her desk, happy that Risa wasn't going to let what happened between her and JD keep her from living.

It was about time her boss and friend realized she was an attractive woman with a lot to offer. Forget him if he couldn't figure that out. Hoping that Risa was stronger from her ordeal, Cayce couldn't wait to go out with her. Sometimes all it took for a woman to forget one man was to find another man. If Risa walked into a club looking like that, she would find another man. They would find her. They would swarm to her like bees to honey. Of this, Cayce was sure. She was ecstatic. Now, finally, Risa could start living the life she deserved.

Cayce sat down at her desk and started making calls. They would start by having dinner at Cornbread and Brie.

# Chapter 17

JD showed up at Angela's house two days ago looking big-eyed, puppy-dog sad and licking his wounds like a wounded bear. He alternated between moping about and growling. Only his youngest niece and nephew could get a smile out of him as they climbed all over him and demanded that he read to them or play horsey. Knowing he was in a foul mood, Angela made some of his favorite foods and watched with horror as he seemed to have no appetite and left his plate half full with untouched food. Looking to her husband for answers, she got nothing but a shrug and a helpless, "I don't know."

It was the safest answer Big L could give. Under normal circumstances he and Angela talked about everything. But he didn't want to talk about the JD-Risa situation until JD broached the subject with his sister.

"JD, honey, how's your food?" Angela asked.

Smothered potatoes and meat loaf were her two best dishes. She made meat loaf at least once a week. She made it still with hamburger and ignored Daphne's upturned nose. Everybody wasn't a chef at their own restaurant. But her family seemed content with her culinary skills. Neither her children nor her husband missed many meals.

"Fine," JD said between a half-eaten forkful. "I'm just not that hungry."

This alarmed Angela so much that she rushed to him and placed her hand on his forehead, pretending to check his temperature.

"I'm fine," he insisted, pushing her away from him.

Sometimes Angela was worse than his mother. Was it possible to have an overabundance of the nurturing hormone? If Angela didn't have too much of the mothering instinct, then she was close to it.

"JD, honey, you know you can stay the night. You don't look well enough to drive," she said, her mother-hen instincts kicking into overdrive. She was treating him as she would her own child instead of her adult brother who should be able to take care of himself.

"Get away. Get away," he ordered Angela, batting at her hands that were all over him feeling his forehead. When that didn't work she tried to look into his eyes. The eyes were the mirrors to the soul. She was sure she could tell what was wrong with him if he would just let her look into her eyes.

"I'm fine," he insisted, still playing with his food.

Angela immediately went to the phone and called in reinforcements. Totally oblivious to what Angela had done, JD retired to the couch in the family room. Hailey was on the phone and Jacob was playing a game on the Nintendo with his father. As he looked at them, it seemed to hit him for the first time just how much his oldest niece and nephew looked like their parents. In some families the children all looked like one parent or the other. In the Wheaton household, the children were a perfect combination of both parents. Sixteen-year-old Hailey had her mother's eyes, dark brown and inquisitive. Her hair was more like her father's, long, straight, and black. Her skin was like gingerbread. She would be a heartbreaker in a couple of years. Jacob was shaped like his father, thick and solid. When he gained some muscle mass, he would be formidable on the football field.

For a couple of days, JD wondered if he ever had children, would they look more like him or his new bride? Now that he wasn't going down that road with Risa, he might not ever know. There wasn't any other woman he wanted to have children with. Sighing, he turned his thoughts away from Risa. He didn't want to think about her right now. All he wanted to do was sit back and let his mind wonder. That said, he was haphazardly entertaining the twins when in walked Elisha and Betsy.

The girls took one look at their big brother's woebegone face and quickly gathered the youngest children. It was time for an intervention and that needed to be done without little ones present. While they entertained them, the doorbell rang again and Carlie rushed in past Big L who suddenly had a houseful of women, a despondent friend, four children, and a wife. Not knowing what he needed to do, he did the only thing a man in this position could do: he gave his teenagers the keys to his car and money for a movie and gathered the youngest children to his arms and abandoned his friend to the Jones women.

"Hey, what's going on?" JD asked watching his friend quickly exiting with a twin under each arm.

"Nothing, bro. Time for a bath," Big L said over his shoulder.

When you had little ones it was always either bath time or bedtime. Besides, he hardly ever got to draw baths and select sleepy-time stories. Angela always did it.

As he was leaving the room he saw JD being surrounded by concerned sisters. Big L made it upstairs just as his friend called to him to rescue him. Big L pretended not to hear it. He had done all that he could do. He wasn't really a coward, he reasoned while he picked out two sets of pajamas. He chose light blue with sailboats for his son and pretty pink ones with feet for his daughter. Angela never dressed the twins alike. He noticed that. He hadn't noticed there was a lot of blue in Edison's drawer and a lot of pink in Eden's until now. The two older children each had their own bedrooms. For now, the twins shared a room. It had twin cribs that could convert into twin beds, twin dressers, and a ton of stuffed animals. The furniture was white. A Winnie the Pooh theme was prevalent. It was a bright, happy room for bright, happy children. When they were older, they would be separated. Until then, they would share this room. To make the bath time more easy, he put them both into the same tub at the same time. He and Angela bought the six-bedroom house in anticipation of a large family. Back-to-back bathrooms separated the two bedrooms at the end of the hall. With the twins in the tub, Larry wondered how Angela made it look so easy. Sure Hailey and Jacob were helpful, but they were teenagers and Angela gave them responsibility without burdening them with their younger siblings. They both felt it was an injustice to saddle teenagers with the responsibility of raising children. They should be allowed to be children themselves. However, it wasn't frowned upon when they helped. An occasional helping hand was appreciated and encouraged.

As he watched his children play in the water, Big L wished he had brought the digital camera with him to capture them up to their chins in bubbles. There was as much water on the floor as there was in the tub.

"Daddy. I do. I do," Eden insisted, attempting to wash her own hair and pushing his hand away.

Her head was covered in thick black curls. Only Hailey seemed to have his straight black hair. The rest of the children had thick, curly, raven masses. Little Eden was so much her mother's daughter. She was very independent and insisted on doing so many things by herself. Edison cooed and played in the water like an average eighteen-month-old. He wasn't as bossy or as verbal as his sister. Like his father, he was easygoing. They were so young and yet they had two distinct personalities.

Eden was a Jones girl all the way. It takes a very special man to tame a Jones woman. Thank God he wouldn't have to worry about that for years with little Eden. Hailey, on the other hand, was another matter. He had many a restless night ever since she had started to mature. Then when she had started to drive, his nights of good night sleep were all but forgotten. His oldest daughter too was exhibiting Jones woman tendencies. His son, Jacob, had discovered girls and the wonders of being a teenager. *It was hard being the father of teenagers,* he thought. *It was harder still being the brother of a handful of sisters.* He knew that it took a special man to handle a Jones woman. *What kind of woman did it take to tame a Jones man?* He thought Risa would be that woman for his friend, JD. He hoped that the two of them would be able to work it out. He loved his friend and wanted him to be as happy as he was.

Despite JD's reservations, he felt that Risa could be the woman who could guide JD down the right path and that they could work it out. For a minute he wondered what was happening downstairs with JD and his sisters. He could easily go check once he put the kiddies in bed. Then again, he knew that the Jones women were downstairs giving JD their two cents' worth and took comfort in knowing that he escaped before he was called on to offer his opinion. He had already said his piece. In the end, he was just a man. Right now, his friend needed his sisters.

"For the hundredth time, I am not going to talk about this with you," JD said to his sisters.

His was on the couch and had his face covered in one of Angela's couch pillows. Illogically he reasoned if he couldn't see his sisters, they would just go away. Of course that made no sense. They were like four dogs with a bone. They kept asking him questions with the intention of having him finally give in. One of them was actually poking him in the shoulder trying to make him lower the pillow. He didn't know which one it was, but he thought it might be Carlie. She was the poker.

"Stop poking me!" JD yelled.

The poking continued. Four of his sisters were driving him crazy. There would have been five of them, but Daphne was meeting with electricians and had given her opinion via phone.

"Enough. Enough," he said as he sat up and faced them. Many a time their heated discussions were divided, with he and Daphne on one side and Carlie and Elisha on the other. Angela usually managed to hang out and be the swing vote. It was rare that all the girls banded together against him.

"She isn't the lady I thought she was," JD expressed.

"Well, why not? I thought she was very attractive," Elisha said.

"Looks aren't everything, Elisha."

"I know that," she said with a toss of her hair. "I'm not superficial," she was quick to assert before she tossed her hair again. She had just gotten her hair braided and was getting used to the new long tresses.

"I didn't say you were superficial. I said she wasn't the girl for me."

"She was smart," Carlie said. She refused to get into it with Elisha and JD. She was digging into her third helping of mashed potatoes. A perfect size eight no matter what she ate, she often joked that Daphne went into the restaurant business just to feed her.

"How's the sex?" Betsy asked. She had removed her shoes and was digging her feet into Angela's lush carpet. She had hardwood floors in her place and occasionally loved to slide her feet against the comforting, extra-thick carpet in her sister's home.

"Betsy!" Angela exclaimed.

"Shut up, Angela. You wanted to know too," Betsy said.

"You all can keep guessing," JD growled. He wasn't going to have this discussion with his sisters.

"So it was a sex thing," Elisha said, nodding her head.

"What do you know about sex?" JD demanded a response from his youngest sister. She in turn, wasn't put off by his growling and posturing.

"I'm in college." She said it as if that said it all.

"I don't send you to school to learn about sex!"

"Where else do you want me to learn it?"

Elisha had a great knack for getting JD's goat.

"Focus, JD. This is about you, not Elisha," Angela directed.

"Are you having sex?" JD demanded of Elisha.

"He went through this with all of us. He's worse than Daddy," Carlie assured Elisha.

"Who you telling?" Angela said as the girls shared a secret sister smile.

"My business is my business," JD roared. If they wouldn't listen to his reason, he'd scream at them and be intimidating.

"You made it our business when you brought her around," Betsy said.

"You made it my business when Carlie drug me over here," Elisha added.

"You made it my business when you showed up at my house looking like a lost puppy." Angela said.

"Okay. I'll go home," JD said as he began to gather his

things and storm off, leaving his sisters to discuss his fate without him.

Two days passed and JD managed to avoid his sisters by not answering his cell phone and ignoring them when they called his home phone, sent e-mails, and stopped by. For so long they had basically had an open-door policy. There was no need to call first. They were family. So each girl stopped by when she wanted to. Usually JD welcomed them with open arms. But for now, he wanted the solitude of his thoughts.

Wisely, neither one of them used their key to let themselves in. The boundaries between family members were lax but they still existed. Finally on the second day, tired of his own self-induced exile and trying to do something, anything to take his mind off Risa, he started returning phone calls. First on his list was young Hailey. Without much provocation, he agreed to dinner. Hailey loved Daphne, so Cornbread and Brie would be the perfect place to take the precocious teenager. That way he could have dinner and face his sisters at the same time. He knew how the grapevine worked. As soon as he walked in, Daphne would make the call. His sisters were so predictable. He just wished his feelings were. Even though he made up his mind about Risa, she was all he could think of as he drove to his sister's popular eatery.

# Chapter 18

At the last minute, Cayce was unable to have dinner with Risa. She and her new beau were getting hot and heavy and Risa insisted that Cayce spend time with the young man. It had been a long time since Cayce took the time to enjoy a relationship. Risa didn't want the two young people to get off to a bad start because the younger girl had to spend a night out with her boss. With her plans changed, she just decided to spend the night alone and curl up with a good book when her phone rang. The number was unlisted and Risa started not to answer it, thinking it might be a telemarketer. They always called at the wrong time. Sighing, prepared to give them the polite brush-off, she picked up the phone and was pleasantly surprised when a familiar deep baritone greeted her.

"Hello," Risa answered the phone.

"Hello?" the baritone voice said. "Risa James, a beautiful name for a beautiful woman." The deep cultured voice of Connor Ingram wafted over the phone line. Connor Ingram was a tall drink of water, as her mother would say.

Born in Jamaica, raised between England and New York, he owned an import-export business made successful through catalogue sales. Risa hadn't seen him in nearly three years. But she was glad to hear from him. He was a sexy, vibrant man used to getting what he wanted and single-minded in his pursuit of it. At the time he and Risa had met he was going through a rather nasty divorce and Risa provided a sympathetic ear and a shoulder to lean on. It never went farther than that because Risa was convinced that the timing wasn't right between them.

When he was zigging, she was zagging. When he was zagging, she was zigging. The attraction was one-sided and they just weren't a good match. Anyone seeing him would have been convinced that she was crazy. He was a Rick Fox look-alike with an edge that was as appealing as it was sharp. She was glad he called. He was a good conversationalist and despite the fact that they never connected intimately, he was a good friend.

"Hello, Connor. What brings you to my fair city?" Risa asked.

"I have some business to attend to and I decided to make part of my trip pleasure as well. Would you be interested in having dinner with me tonight?"

It was a Friday night in Dallas. The city was full of interesting and exciting things and he chose to call her. Patti Labelle wrote a book that Risa had read titled *Don't Block the Blessings*. Maybe his call was a blessing in disguise. She had a new hairdo and a new attitude. And the new man calling her wasn't JD. So Risa said the only thing a woman in her position could say.

"I'd love to have dinner with you." Her mouth worked without direction from her. She was on automatic pilot and decided to go with it. "Yes, I'll have dinner with you." She said it again just to see how the words tasted in her mouth.

"I heard you the first time," he said. "I'll be there in an hour."

Risa hung up the phone with a sense of anticipation. Hearing from Connor was the best thing that could happen to her right about now. She jumped from the bed and padded to her closet. Without giving it much thought, she selected one of her new "fun" outfits. He was a new man. He deserved to see the new Risa.

For a minute Risa felt just a little bit guilty. She knew that somewhere in the back of her head that she was using Connor Ingram to try to take her mind off of JD. But it was impossible. No matter how charming, how amusing or how incredibly attractive Connor was, he wasn't JD. He wasn't the man she recently shared her heart and her bed with. And although they could never seem to be on the right foot or the same page, there had never been an unpleasant or boring moment with Connor. He didn't deserve half her attention.

Risa tried to make a conscious effort to see him for what she was sure other women saw. She would have to be blind not to notice the furtive glances they got. He was a good-looking man and commanded attention. She really tried to be moved by the rugged good looks and cultured exotic accent that was a little Jamaican, a little British, and a whole lot of New York. He was a man of contrast. He was polished, but a little rough around the edges. He was good-looking but almost pretty with finely perfected features. He was a good dresser but flashy and chose clothes that screamed of money. Think of a rugged Rick Fox dressed like P. Diddy and you had Connor Ingram. He was interesting enough to make someone a good catch. That someone would not be Risa. He just wasn't the man for her. They had both realized it instantly and never started playing a game that could only end with one of them getting hurt. She hadn't wanted to hurt him. He hadn't wanted to hurt her. He just wasn't the right man at the right time for her. She wasn't the right woman at the right time for him. Realizing that, a comfortable friendship developed.

"Were it not for the fact that I see you sitting there, one could say I was dining alone," Connor said to Risa as they sat at the restaurant table.

"I'm sorry, Connor. My mind is a million miles away," she replied.

"Want to talk about it?"

"No."

"Come on. You listened to me when I was going through all that stuff with Justina. The least I can do is return the favor."

Justina Lucius and Connor Ingram had been childhood sweethearts who grew apart as they grew up. The beautiful Jamaican girl had been model pretty with perfect skin and a body that clothes were made for. Her face had graced magazine covers, billboards, and most recently television as the new spokesperson for a popular makeup brand. Even though she and Connor were no longer a couple she had managed to go on with her life so easily, it had devastated him. She and Connor hadn't been a good match for a long time and Risa was instrumental in helping Connor see that.

She had been a good friend to Connor in his time of need. Maybe if she allowed herself to open up to him, he could be a good friend to her while she was going through her ordeal with JD. It would be hard talking to him about it. Risa had never been that forthcoming with the personal details of her life. Only a select few people, mainly Helen and Cayce, were privy to her innermost thoughts. She knew that it would help to get a man's perspective on things. So taking that into consideration she began her tale.

Connor was her friend. She knew that she could trust

him. So swallowing her need and desire to be incredibly private, she poured out her heart. Afterwards she found herself in Connor's arms. Despite the fact that restaurant patrons turned to look at the stunning couple, Connor lavished her with attention. His ministrations were heartfelt and moved her. He gave her a hug, kissed her forehead tenderly and held her hand as he continued to listen to her. He didn't care that people were looking. He gave her his full attention and smiled at her with kind eyes that she seemed to notice for the first time. They were hazel and changed colors as he became more involved with their conversation. As she looked into his eyes she thought maybe she had made a mistake. Maybe she should give him a second chance. A man who could listen was a valuable commodity. JD had listened to her at first. Then he had slept with her. *Had it all been a ruse just to get her in bed?*

As if thinking about him made him materialize, Risa looked up to see the object of her affection, JD, stride into the room with a pretty girl young enough to be his daughter.

Risa hadn't seen him in days and yet he looked just as good as he did when she had first seen him. Brown was a good color for him. Dressed in a chocolate wool sweater and matching slacks he looked magnificent and commanding. His caramel camel coat created a good contrast to the color of his skin and the rich dark hue of his clothing. Compared to Connor it was like night and day. Connor sat across from her in a winter white wool suit. His shoulder-length curly hair was pulled back into a ponytail and the diamond pinky ring sparkled. Connor was a rough pretty boy, a smooth operator, a polished ex-thug. JD was debonair, elegant, manly. Both men made women's hearts go pitter-patter. She couldn't help but think how funny it was that just a few days ago she was about to turn forty with not a man in sight. Now she had one paying painful attention to her and one painfully trying to ignore her and doing a poor job of it. She was finding it hard to concentrate. She could feel JD's eyes on her. She knew when she had decided to keep the reservations that Cayce had made for their girl's night out at Cornbread and Brie that there was a possibility she would see if not him, his sister Daphne. But she refused to hide as if she had done something wrong. She had not. She was going to live her life. That meant that she was going to go to restaurants and to movies and to plays. She wasn't going to stay in her apartment, in bed, beneath the covers. *So JD be damned! Okay! To hell with him!* This was a popular restaurant. She was a popular person. She was going to enjoy her dinner if it killed her. Although she was no longer hungry she took a forkful of the tasty almond-crusted salmon and chased it with a sip of white wine. She could have a good time despite JD's sudden appearance.

The tension in the air was so thick it could be cut with a knife. But Risa pretended not to notice and forced herself to eat. She would die before she let him see that his presence upset her.

# Chapter 19

Lane Belle was Lucy Belle's sixteen-year-old daughter. She was a bright girl, serious about her choices and hopelessly devoted to JD. He had come into her life and filled a void that the death of her father had left. Not as oddly pretty as his niece, Hailey, she was cute in a girl-next-door kind of way. Short, bordering on petite, she was a fair skinned little honey with locks and horn-rimmed glasses. JD suspected she chose her incredibly studious look to distract from her natural cuteness. Unfortunately, as soon as she started talking, her natural animation drew attention to her cuteness.

When Lane had learned of her mother's breakup with the man she considered her surrogate father, she was devastated. Nothing her mother could say would convince her that the breakup was amicable and that she and JD weren't on the outs. Lane needed to see for herself. She had been calling JD for the past few days. When he didn't immediately return her call, as was his custom, she was convinced that he was no longer part of her life. When the call finally came, along with an apology and a dinner invitation, she was beside herself with joy. Just because her mother and JD were no longer a couple, she didn't want to lose him as her friend.

JD pulled Lane's chair for her before taking his seat. *She* was the first person he saw when he took his seat across from Lane. He did a double take that was almost comical when he realized it was *her*. It was Risa. She had done something to her hair and she was dressed in a provocative number that four days ago he would have thought her unable to pull off. Prior to the night he spent in her arms he would have thought her a tall slender sister unable to pull off the clinging red sheath. But having seen her body firsthand, he knew there were curves and substance to her hips and breasts. Her chosen wardrobe of the night showed off her slender curves to the maximum. Dressed in a red sheath that molded itself to her body, she looked radiant. In her ears and around her neck were the dainty fresh water pearls she seemed partial to. On her feet were three-inch red pumps that had a silken ribbon that wrapped around her slender ankles. H-O-T was the only way to describe her. She didn't look like the Risa he had first met and asked to marry him. Indeed she looked like the Risa who lured him to her bed with her siren's song and had him whimpering like a woman. She looked like the temptress who seduced him with her body and made him want her with his soul. He didn't know the man who sat opposite her. But he could tell from their body language that there was a familiarity between them that he found oddly uncomfortable.

This man was successful, or rather he looked the part. He had an arrogance and swagger about him that JD didn't like. He could feel the hairs on the back of his neck rise and feel the heat creeping up his neck. He wanted to take the man and give him what for. Just as soon as the thought occurred, JD realized he didn't have that right. He had forfeited that privilege when he stormed out of Risa's house half dressed and holding onto his pride.

Risa was by far the most beautiful woman in the room, JD thought as he tried to concentrate on Lane. He finally assured her that just because he and her mother were no longer dating, they, he and Lane, could maintain their friendship. Neither he nor Lucy Belle wanted to remove JD from her children's lives. Over the past four years both Lane and Richard, her twenty-year-old brother who was in his last year of college at the University of Houston, had become as important to JD as Lucy Belle had.

"JD!" Lane stated, her patience growing thin. She had repeated herself three times. He wasn't listening to her.

"Yes, Lane?" JD answered calmly in a tone insinuating that he had been listening all along.

"You're not paying me any attention," she said, pouting.

"Yes, I am. You're going out for cheerleader and there is a young man named Jamal that you find particularly appealing." He had heard everything she said. He grew up in a houseful of women. He knew how to listen even with his attention divided.

"No." She took a small bite of her honey-glazed chicken. It was her favorite dish. She ordered it every time she ate at the restaurant.

"I said I wouldn't be caught dead going out for cheerleader and Jamal gets on my nerves."

Well, that only went to prove that Risa drove him to distraction. While he was thinking of something to say, Daphne entered from the kitchen with a large tray of food in her arms. Although she owned the restaurant she wasn't above serving her guests if the waiters were busy. She would rather serve it herself than have it served cold. Seeing JD at one table and Risa at another she was momentarily taken aback. She recovered quickly. Deciding this was her

brother's issue she deposited the food at table ten where
the mayor and his wife were seated then ducked back into
her kitchen. She would serve her guests but she was way
too busy to have small talk with them. She saved that for
late nights when the restaurant wasn't as crowded. It was
nearly 9:00 P.M. They would be busy until almost midnight.
She was, however, going to take a minute to call her sisters. Let them handle JD and his crazy emotions.

Unlike the other girls, Daphne only got involved when
she had to. *What a shame,* she thought as she decorated the
lemon meringue pie for table three. She really liked Risa.
Unfortunately she didn't have time to dwell on it. Table
three was an important table. It was the local food critic.
Although Daphne wasn't fazed because of the critic's appearance she always wanted to make a good impression.
Sprinkling lemon zest and sugar on the meringue she re-
lived the moment when she won over the picky critic. It
was months ago with a soul food extravaganza that included five cheese-macaroni and cheese, honey walnut
yams, greens with red onions, and barbequed oxtails. Having given traditional soul food the Daphne twist she wanted
to make sure this meal was just as delightful. Risa and JD
were instantly forgotten as she scalloped the edge of her
pie.

Although Daphne quickly dismissed her brother and his
situation, Risa couldn't stop thinking about him or their
situation. Despite the fact that her stomach was doing flip-
flops she did manage to make it through dinner. She
made a good show of eating most of her food. If she had
not, it would have been too hard to explain. Daphne's
food was excellent. Only the sick would be able to pass it
up. Although her heart hurt she wasn't physically sick. So
she ate, listened to Connor, laughed at his jokes and
stared into his multicolored eyes. To the world she looked

like a woman enjoying her evening. Until that moment she didn't even know that she had theatrical talent. The night might have even ended without incident had Connor not taken their exit as an opportunity to stop by JD's table.

"Excuse me, Mr. Jones," Connor began, totally unaware that the man who had treated Risa so shabbily was sitting right in front of him. "I hate to disturb your dinner, but I couldn't leave this place without letting you know what a fan of yours I am." He reached out for JD's hand and didn't seem to notice the slight hesitation before JD took it.

"I am Connor Ingram, this is—"

"JD and I have met," Risa interrupted before Connor could introduce her as his date. "Really? I didn't know you were a football fan."

"I'm not." Her words hung heavy between them.

"Risa and I live in a small city pretending to be a large one. Our paths have crossed on many occasions," JD said, easing her out of what could be a sticky situation. Even though he had no obligation to her, chivalry made him come to her defense. He didn't like her looking uncomfortable and was mad at himself for even caring.

"As a matter of fact, JD was highlighted on an episode of *City Scenes*," Risa added.

This time when Daphne came out of the kitchen with her tasty treat she had reason to pause again. JD and Risa were having what looked like a civil conversation. Taking that as a good sign, she walked over to the table.

"I'm glad to see everyone getting along. When I saw you two I called in reinforcements. It isn't every day that a woman stops dating my brother. I am happy y'all can be civil towards each other."

As soon as the words were out of her mouth the mood around the table changed. Suddenly everyone realized they were characters in a play and didn't know the lines.

"Is this the lady that broke up you and my mother?" Lane asked in sixteen-year-old-innocence.

"She did not break up your mother and me," JD started.

"This is the jerk?" Connor inquired.

"Who are you calling a jerk?" JD said as he rose from his seat.

"I didn't know anything about your mother," Risa said to Lane, trying to ease the young lady's obvious pain.

Everyone was talking at once. The situation was getting out of hand. The two men were sizing each other up and Lane was shooting Risa looks filled with daggers and someone at the next table had taken out a camera. Realizing her innocent slip of the tongue could turn the situation ugly, Daphne stepped in with a loud announcement.

"In honor of the opening of my new restaurant, Honey Baby's, which will be opening in four weeks, desserts are on the house for everyone!"

People started clapping. Daphne bowed and Risa took this as an opportunity to steer Connor towards the valet. She did it quickly and refused to look over her shoulder at JD, although she could feel his eyes staring into her back.

They rode to Risa's house in silence in Connor's rented Mercedes. It was the largest one, spacious, black on black with leather interior that was as soft as gossamer thread. During the drive all Risa wanted to do was cry, but she didn't. Her mother had told her a long time ago, "Only cry for someone who will cry for you." She believed that. Just as she believed that it shouldn't have ended as it did.

In the beginning it was so good between her and JD. How could it go so wrong so fast? For the past couple of days all she had been doing was replaying their meeting, brief courtship, and out-of-nowhere breakup. What went wrong? What made it fall apart? It was hot and heavy until they made love. Being together was both their ideas. Just because he was so insistent wasn't a reason to blame him for their downfall. Nevertheless, she couldn't help but keep wondering if his adoration was just a way to get her into bed. This was a new era. Men didn't have to get sex with a promise of marriage and an introduction to the family. It wasn't necessary. Not that she would have slept with him with anything short of the rush of emotions and feeling she had for him. But the result was so unexpected that she wondered if her life was such a sheltered one that she didn't see it coming?

Did men drop women like hot potatoes just because they slept with them? Of course not. If that were the case, there would be a string of broken-hearted women everywhere you looked. Their circumstance wasn't normal. Their meeting wasn't happenstance. Her defenses weren't lowered because he smiled at her and promised her a golden ring. She let him into her heart and into her bed because he made her believe that she loved him. And it had to be love because only love hurt this badly.

"You should have told me who it was, Risa," Connor said, interrupting her thoughts. She didn't even notice that they had arrived at her home.

"I most certainly should not have," she responded. "You don't kiss and tell. Why should I be forced to?"

They were sitting in the car parked in her driveway. Connor left the motor running so that the heat would fill the car. It was thirty-three degrees outside in the cold Dallas night. It had been raining slightly for a few days. The thin mist was made dangerous by the chilly temperature. If it got just a little bit colder it would turn to an icy glaze that would make driving difficult. The streets would be filled with dirty sleet and the blades of grass on yards would be encased in ice.

"Is he the reason you don't want to be with me?" Connor asked.

"Connor, I don't want to hurt you," Risa said as gently as she could.

"Well, I guess that says it all."

Risa could feel the pain in his words. How long had he wanted for her, she wondered.

"No. It doesn't," she said as she took his hand in hers and looked into his eyes. "You are such a good man, Connor. I sometimes think I don't deserve you as a friend."

"Will we ever be more than friends, Risa? Can you learn to feel about me the way I feel about you?"

"No." She kissed his hand. "You deserve passion and love and good sex."

"Right now I'd settle for good sex." Risa laughed because she knew he was teasing her. It felt good to laugh. She hadn't laughed in days. "I'm serious," Connor added.

He leaned over and kissed her, stifling the laugh in her throat. His lips were soft yet demanding as they parted hers so that he could insert his tongue. She hadn't kissed a man since JD. And before JD she hadn't kissed a man in a long time. Connor's kiss was pleasant but it didn't solicit the same tidal wave of motion that JD's had. Part of her was curious as to whether or not she was missing the perfect man by not giving Connor a chance. But the kiss answered that question. No. Gently she pulled away from him. "Connor, Connor, Connor. What am I going to do with you?"

"You're going to let me walk you to your door," he sighed, turning off the motor and walking around to open her door. Even though he had been rebuffed, Connor Ingram was still a gentleman. And just like that he and Risa James became more than friends. Having both been losers in the game of love, they became comrades in arms and shared the heartache that cements special friendships. They would talk. They would laugh. Occasionally they would go out. But they would not date. Friends they were and friends they would remain. It was good to have another friend. Good friends were like ink pens. They were always needed. You could never have too many of them.

# Chapter 20

JD got Lane home without further incident. Then he found himself doing something he never thought he would do. Instead of getting on the freeway to drive to his Desoto residence, he drove instead towards Risa's Swiss Avenue house. Acting more like a stalker than he wanted to admit, even to himself, he parked his car two houses down and turned off his lights so that he could watch her and not be seen as she sat in the car with the other man. Just a few days ago she had been in the same driveway in another car with another man. He knew because he had been that man. If anyone had told him just two days later he would be watching her in almost this same situation and the man would not be him, he would not have believed it. But now, watching her, he didn't know what to say or how to feel.

Just seeing Risa with that dandy brought out feelings in him that he didn't want to address. The thought of her in another man's arms gave him a wake-up call he wasn't prepared to face. Was this man the one who taught her how to bring a man to passion's peak? Or was this man too another unfortunate victim who had been left trembling in her wake? Could he allow himself to forget her past? What was it about her that made him want her despite it? He didn't know. But seeing her with the other man made him feel like she was his favorite toy and someone else was playing with her. He didn't like it. He didn't like it one bit.

To make matters worse, almost out of nowhere it seemed, JD saw him kiss her. He saw Connor kiss Risa. He wanted to get out of his car and approach them. But what could he say? What right did he have? He threw this woman away without a backwards glance. Seeing her in someone else's arms brought up feelings he didn't want to admit to, jealousy and rage. She was his. He had her, but he didn't have her. His heart and his loins ached for her. He told himself it was physical and that she wasn't "the one" he was looking for. But his body betrayed him. He told himself that if the man went into the house with her he was going to drive off. He knew what happened in Risa's house. He knew what happened in her bed. He knew firsthand. But when his competition reached the door, he parted with a chaste kiss and a hug. Then the pretty boy drove off. Risa went into her house alone. JD felt triumphant. The thought of sharing her made him almost violent. This reaction was so unlike him. But so was sitting in his car parked outside of a woman's house in near freezing weather. What to do? What to do?

As JD sat parked outside Risa's house he was totally unaware of the sister gal network that was going on right across town. Daphne had called Elisha who called Carlie who called Betsy. No one called Angela because it was after midnight and she was a mother with four children. She could find out all the juicy details the next time she talked to any one of them. It didn't matter which one she talked to. They would share the incident in the retelling of it.

"You said what?" Carlie said to Daphne. She found the entire incident amusing.

"You know what I said. I'm not going to repeat it."

Daphne was up to her ears in a very warm bubble bath. She spoke to her sisters from her speakerphone. In her small, two-bedroom house, Carlie was putting embroidery on a pillow and Elisha, in her condo, was painting her nails. The nightly phone conversations were started so long ago that no one remembered when it even became a tradition. Thanks to technology they could all be on the phone at the same time. It didn't matter that they were in four different houses or that they were doing different things.

"So how did he look?" Betsy asked.

"Girl, JD looked mad enough to spit fire. She was looking good and that man with her . . . so not my type." Daphne made a derisive snort.

"Well, what did he look like?" Carlie jumped in.

"A pretty boy. Kind of like Rick Fox," Daphne analyzed.

"Now that's my type," Elisa chimed in, checking out her nails and holding the phone against her shoulder. She was a pretty girl and always dated the most popular, attractive boys. It was just how it was done.

"Too old for you. More Carlie's speed," Daphne said.

"Child, please. I am too busy to be bothered with a man right now," Carlie stated, admiring her handiwork with the pillow. It was very elaborate and would fetch a pretty penny if she ever decided to sell it. Carlie never sold any of her things. Her sisters called her a pack rat. One of her favorite things to do was item rescue. She loved to go to thrift stores and salvage lots, find an item, fix it, and create a work of art. The term *shabby chic* should have been invented for Carlie. She was very creative. Her siblings were sure she had everything she'd ever bought, made, or been given throughout her twenty-eight years. Her small house was filled with wonderful things that she had gussied up. If she ever opened a consignment store, she would already have all the merchandise.

"Well, I wish I had been there to see it," Betsy said. She spoke through her headset because she was doing sit-ups while they talked. She had lost twenty-five pounds and was determined to keep it off. She looked good as a size fourteen, but felt and looked better as a size nine. A tall girl, she was dark and sassy with a thick-layered sable mane, reminiscent of her mother's in her youth. Her dark skin and brown hair created a nice package. She never considered herself the beauty queen. That was her youngest sister's, Elisha's, role, but she was known to turn a head or two. Size was never an issue for her or the men who courted her, but she so liked trading clothes with her sisters and she couldn't do that unless she was a size nine. And try as she might, she could never squeeze into Elisha's dainty size sevens. As a perfect size seven, Elisha could wear her sister's size nines, but they couldn't wear her size sevens. Only Daphne, as a size twelve, stayed out of the clothing exchange. But even as a size twelve, Daphne was nearly six feet tall and carried her statuesque frame with dignity and grace.

"Me too." The others gave their consensus before they started talking about something else. JD's woman problems were interesting but not worth their entire phone time together. Soon they were talking about clothes, men, shoes, and men. JD and Risa were forgotten.

Even though his sisters forgot JD and Risa, JD wasn't forgotten by Risa and Risa wasn't forgotten by JD. As if watching the entire incident unfold before him, JD got out of his car and walked to Risa's front door. He knew that he did the action of his own accord, but he was being moved by a force so much stronger than he himself was.

For a moment he just stood on the porch undecided as to the best course of action. Then he raised his hand and knocked. Thinking it was Connor, Risa answered the door without asking who it was. They hadn't seen each other in years. To send him away to spend the night in a hotel room might not have been the friendliest thing to do. She could always put him up in her guest room. She had originally looked at the house because of its wonderful curb appeal. After taking a walk through it, she knew she wanted it because it had character. The room she chose for the guest room was large and spacious. It was decorated in soft blues and gentle greens. It wouldn't be too feminine for Connor. Despite the way they just ended their reunion, it had not been disastrous. He would be welcome to spend the night in her home. He was her friend. She flung the door open with a quick retort.

"Yes. You can spend the night," Risa said, beaming.

This wasn't what JD had expected to hear. He wasn't who she had expected to see. For a moment the two of them stood looking at each other.

"Sorry to disappoint you," JD said through gritted teeth.

She had just told the other man that he could spend the night. That said it all. He turned on his heels, convinced he had been right in his assessment of her, and started back to his car. With every step he cursed himself for being a fool. She wasn't thinking about him at all. Just a few days ago they were on their way to marital bliss and now she was seeing another man as if meeting JD had meant nothing. He had been an idiot to not go with his instincts and write her off.

For the second time in less than three days, Risa watched JD's retreating back as he got into his car and drove off. It was obvious that what they had wasn't over. It was obvious that he was fighting his demons as far as she was concerned. She, in turn, was fighting her demons as far as he was concerned. She didn't like this side of him, jealous, possessive, and volatile. But on the other hand, she could not get him out of her mind. Everywhere she looked she saw him. At every turn he was there. Their destiny was together. The question was what steps would be taken down that road. She didn't like what just happened and she wasn't going to let it end that way. So with the determination she was known for, she started upstairs with the intent of changing her clothes. Then she was going to go see Mr. Jones. She wasn't going to call and forewarn him. She was going to just show up on his doorstep and do as he did. He would not keep treating her this way and get away with it. He was going to get a piece of her mind.

# Chapter 21

JD started shedding his clothes as soon as he walked into his house. He had bought the four-bedroom ranch-style house in Desoto, a popular Dallas suburb, over five years ago. His mother helped him pick it out and had dropped several hints about what a great place it would be to raise grandchildren. Set on two acres of land, there was a pool, a pool house as well as a tennis court. Sometimes, with his whole family in attendance, the spacious house didn't seem large enough. Sometimes, like now, it seemed too large for him. It would have been nice to come home to a warm house, the smell of food cooking and a sexy siren like Risa. He had grown up in a house filled with warmth, good feelings, and wonderful smells. His parents still lived in the four-bedroom house of his childhood. Despite every attempt on his part to move them to bigger and better, they were content with the neighborhood they had grown old in. To compromise, they allowed for him to make some minor renovations. Having housed six children and two parents, growing up in his childhood home was a lesson in compromise. But no matter how crowded it got or how noisy it was, it always smelled like home. It was no wonder Daphne grew into the gourmet chef she was, having grown up at his mother's apron strings. His mother was a fine cook. To this day he couldn't smell the sweet aroma of cookies baking without smiling involuntarily.

Cookies always made him think of his mother. His mother baked cookies every Friday night. She had been doing it all of his life, just like she had been making her own sausage and biscuits. No processed meats or canned biscuits ever found their way into his mother's kitchen. His mother was a wonderful woman. Not just because she could cook. She was wise. She was smart. She was shrewd. Raising five girls in a one-bathroom house had taken all those skills. By the time she finally gave in and allowed JD to start working on the house, the first thing being to add a new bathroom, all the children had moved out.

She told JD that one bathroom was enough for her and Sam. But JD noticed his father sure did relish the addition of the new bathroom. For the first time in his life he could stay in the bathroom for as long as he wanted. That was the first time he had ever seen his father in near tears. When he added the new bathroom, Samuel Jones was moved to speechlessness. But truth be told, Samuel wasn't a real talker. His mother was the chatty one. Samuel spoke when he had something to say. That said, JD thought about calling his father and asking his opinion. He valued his father's opinion as much as his mother's. Both of them liked Risa, and although they approached a subject differently, they always managed to create a united front.

JD truly valued his parents' opinion. There were only a few times when they had been wrong. He still hadn't told them that he and Risa were no longer an item. But he knew they knew. One of his sisters told his mother and she, of course, told his father. His close-knit clan could be as meddlesome as they were loving. His sisters were a force to be reckoned with. No doubt his voice mail was once again filled with messages from them. He picked up the phone and checked just to verify his suspicion. He was a little surprised at the first voice. It didn't belong to Angela, Betsy, Carlie, Daphne or Elisha. The voice on his machine belonged to Helen Jeffries, station manager at KKRL.

"JD, this is Helen Jeffries," Helen said in her message. "I have a good mind to give you a good tongue-lashing. I would leave my number but I don't expect you to call me back. Risa James is a good woman and certainly deserves better than she got from you. Expect my call on tomorrow. You and I need to have this conversation. I don't intend to leave what I have to say to you on your machine." With that she had hung up.

JD winced. Although he wasn't related to Helen, she was giving him the same tone he got when he displeased his mother and that was rare. No doubt Risa shared their escapade with her friend just as he had with his friend, Big L. When he thought about it, he seemed to remember Helen being a friend of Angela's as well. Damn. The last thing he needed was Angela having the intimate details of his and Risa's relationship. Actually, based on tonight there was no relationship.

He was sure as soon as he had left she had called the other man and was right now entertaining him with her bodily delights. The thought of it had JD nearly beside himself with regret. If he hadn't have gone to her house, he would have never known. Then he could have surmised based on blissful ignorance. He didn't know what was better, pure speculation or actual knowledge. Either way, he felt betrayed by his emotions. He felt he was just another notch in her bedpost. And he didn't like it. He didn't like it one bit.

Dressed in nothing but his chocolate slacks, he walked

to the refrigerator and got himself a Heineken. He was
feeling lonely and despondent. There was a time when he
could pick up the phone and end the lonely feeling that
overtook him with just a phone call. But there would be
no phone calls tonight. He had gotten rid of his little
black book years ago when he started dating Lucy Belle.
Maybe he would call Lucy. If it was one thing, they still
were friends. When he had dropped Lane off, Lucy had
acted seriously happy to see him. There had been no animosity or mixed signals. Lucy would give him a woman's
opinion that didn't come from the same place as his sisters. Even as he contemplated the thought he brushed it
aside. He knew what kind of relationship he and Lucy
had. But he wasn't ready to parade another woman in
front of her. Not yet.

Sighing with a heaviness of heart he started towards his
bedroom. He was halfway there when his doorbell rang.
Frowning, he went to the door. He opened it without looking out the keyhole. This was Desoto, Texas after all. Bad
guys and bogeymen didn't ring your doorbell at 1:00 A.M.
He didn't know what he expected, but he didn't expect
Risa. He wasn't prepared for her. She had only taken time
to change her clothes before she rushed out after him.
Dressed in jeans and a sweater, she stood on his porch.
The weather hadn't changed. It was still cold. A light drizzle fell from the sky. Her new hairstyle hung limply and
framed her face. She was damp and shaking in the cold.
Her teeth chattered. She thought she looked like a drowned
rat and yet she was the most appealing thing JD had ever
seen. His anger dissipated in an instant. He stepped aside
and she entered. She had been to his house before, but
she never looked at it. It was decidedly masculine with bits
and pieces of original African art and thick, heavy, leather
furniture.

"What brings you out in the cold, wet, night, alone?" JD

asked. He hoped she was alone. It would be really bad
form to show up on his porch with his competition.

"We need to talk," Risa said steadfast. She faced him
with a determined tilt of her chin.

"Where is your friend?"

"He's in his hotel room," Risa said and she could tell by
the expression on JD's face that he didn't expect to hear
that. "I don't know what you expect or want from me, JD.
But I will not be treated like this." Even angry she was
beautiful. "I will not have you glaring at me and I will not
have you showing up at my house unannounced." He
couldn't keep his eyes off the rise and fall of her chest. He
could make out her breast beneath her sweater. "I will not
have you proposing marriage to me and I will not have
you renege just because your ego got crushed." He wanted
to kiss her. "I am a woman fully grown. You weren't my
first. But if you keep acting like this, you won't be my last.
I wanted you to be my last, JD." She glared at him. He put
the beer down and pulled her to him.

"I'm glad the dandy is in his hotel room," JD said right
before his lips found hers.

It was as if an electric shock went through her body. Although she didn't know it, she had been waiting for this
kiss. She had been waiting for this reaction from him. As if
starved for the taste of her, his lips devoured her. He
traced the outline of her lips with his tongue, sucking and
tugging on the pouty pieces of perfection. She had to
breath through her nose because his lips were so demanding on her mouth. Her arms went around his neck. He
hoisted her onto his hips and held her effortlessly as they
kissed. She managed to free her mouth from his so that
she could taste other sections of his skin. He tasted like
chocolate and salt and moon drops and rain. It was myth-
ical and magical and carnal the way he made her feel.
There was a throbbing in her heart and in the center of

her woman's place as he tongued her. He walked over to the oversized leather couch and deposited her without preamble. The leather was soft and pliable beneath her body. Good leather. Quality. He was a man who appreciated good things. The leather felt good beneath her. At first she didn't know what he intended until he unzipped her jeans and drew them from her long legs. Looking at her in her sweater and small strip of pink satin he was aroused to the ultimate. The pink satin looked delicious against the chocolate of her skin.

He spread her thighs and placed his face in the center of her. She was already moist. He licked and sucked allowing his tongue to do what his fingers had earlier. Involuntarily, her thighs framed his head as she pulled him in closer to the center of her. All she could do was moan as he brought her to a magnificent, shuddering climax. And still her body was quivering with desire for more of him. Looking into her passion-filled eyes he was, for the first time, distracted. There was so much he wanted to do. There were so many ways he wanted to take this. He pulled her sweater from her exhausted body and had to steady himself when he saw that she was braless. She had rushed into her clothes too fast to stop and put on a bra. Two perfect mounds of flesh with hard pinpoints of licorice ecstasy met his eyes. He devoured her flesh with his eyes. She was perfection personified. He had to suckle.

He took little tasteful licks of her flesh. He tasted her skin. He rubbed his face into the scent of her. She smelled like honeysuckle and rain and moon drops. It was mystical and magical and so damn good. All this he did while he was still dressed. Blindly she reached for him. He pulled away from her and kept himself out of her reach as he played her with his hands. Again she moaned, almost driving him to madness. Knowing that he could get another magnificent reaction from her he slid his fingers further into her moistness. The thin pink satin thing she wore was in his way. Impatiently he tore it away. He heard the little mew of protest from her but shrugged it off. Little pieces of satin and lace could be replaced. His large hand covered the all of her.

Her woman's place fit nicely into his large hands. He could feel her warmth and smell her desire calling to him like a pheromone that was chemically perfected for his senses. Placing her legs over his wide, muscular shoulders made it easier for him to reach his target. He placed his finger in his mouth. Once it was wet he slid it into the juncture at her thighs. She couldn't control the movement of her hips. She couldn't control the sounds coming from her mouth. It was a good thing he lived alone because the words she uttered were meant only for his ears.

Like a master composer he played a melody on her body. He created a symphony of sensation as he brought her closer and closer and closer until she thought she could not stand it any longer. When he thought her pleasure was unbearable, he finally let her finish. Exhausted, she stared up at him. The only sound in the room was that of their heavy breathing. He was still dressed. When she reached for him this time he did not pull back. He took her hand and kissed it gently but stopped her short of removing his slacks. Then taking her by surprise he lifted her into his arms and carried her to his bedroom. No words were necessary. He laid her on the oversized bed and stared at her beautiful body before he removed his clothes and joined her on the bed. His desire was evident and yet he made no attempt to join with her. At her confused look he merely kissed her long and deep. He tasted so good, she thought. She tasted so good, he thought.

"This night, my love is for you," he said. Then he crawled into the bed and pulled her to his overheated body. And that was how they fell asleep. She sated. He naked and triumphant because finally he had done it. He had tamed the wild beast that clawed at him saying she was too experienced for him. He claimed it by claiming her. This would be his wife and the mother of his children.

Risa left him asleep in his bed. His passion was still aroused and anxious. It wouldn't have taken much for her to stay and address it but she chose not to. This all didn't play out the way she had wanted it to. Dressing hurriedly, embarrassed by her lack of control, she snuck out like a thief in the night, fulfilled and a little bit ashamed of her wanton behavior. She didn't plan on giving in to his ardor. She planned on being strong and letting him know just how she felt about him and this whole situation. But when she was faced with that perfect, chiseled chest and those fantastic eyes, she wanted nothing more than to lay with him again. When he took her in his arms and started kissing her she knew that she had lost the battle to stand strong against him.

This time their lovemaking was more intense than the last. Without even entering her he had brought her to the pinnacle of ecstasy. Her skin burned at the memory of his touch. His tongue and fingers were as skilled as other parts of him that made her blush with the memory of what they had done. No matter how good the sex she wanted more than the perfection found in a physical release. She wanted a meeting of the minds as well as the bodies. That prompted her to pull on her jeans and sweater and get out before she was lured once again into the comfort of his arms and found herself a victim to her own desire.

She was unable to locate the wispy piece of satin that she wore over to his house and left it somewhere beneath the tangle of covers on JD's bed or maybe his couch. She was too intent on getting out of his house to find it. The decision to leave him was a difficult one. Laying in his arms with his naked body cocooning hers so effectively she only wanted to wallow in the contentment she had felt. His body was a perfect fit to hers. His smells and taste were the perfect complement to hers. But she could not allow herself to fall victim to his charm.

Her tryst with JD suddenly opened her eyes to the fact that she was desirous of a relationship. But based on his reactions, it could not be with him. Although she loved him, she could admit that to herself now, she had to think of herself first. The laws of self-preservation did not allow her to be in a relationship that would have her walking on eggshells so as not to shatter his fragile male ego. She wanted to be uninhibited and free in the bedroom. But her reaction brought out a side of him that she didn't like. During the act he was as caught up in the rapture as she. It was afterwards that she could not stand. So before he awakened to once again berate her and judge her morals and past, she ran. Again she reminded herself that first and foremost she had to think of herself. Her heart could not tolerate displeasure from him. So trying to put as much distance between them as she could, she got into her car and drove home. She had to get away from JD.

JD awakened with a smile on his face, a song in his heart, and an apology on his lips. But when he opened his eyes, his ladylove was nowhere to be found. The only evidence of her presence was his rampant, excited member and a wisp of pink satin that clung to his left foot and had the power to arouse him because it immediately had him thinking of Risa and how she looked in it. He realized then that he truly did love her. It didn't matter what she had done or whom she had been with. What happened before he and she were a "we," well, that was history. As she lay beneath him moaning his name and giving into abandon, he felt her reaction legitimate and genuine. So it didn't matter that she was more skilled than he expected or desired. Her reaction to him made him feel triumphant and powerful and loved. Knowing this he could only be ashamed of his earlier behavior. He wasn't raised to be a chauvinist or to devalue women based on outdated morals and someone else's values. He didn't know what made him behave like such a caveman but he was truly sorry. His behavior almost cost him his ladylove. He had to let her know just how truly apologetic he was for his momentary lapse and could not wait to share this news with Risa.

He threw back the covers and padded naked to the bathroom expecting to give her a delightful surprise in the shower. His shower was large. Designed to his specifications it held two comfortably. When he had bought the house he had made only a few changes. A wall had been knocked out; mirrors, tile and double showerheads had been added. The bathtub was oversized and had Jacuzzi jets. It was a magnificent modern design and one of his favorite rooms in the house. The bidet, obviously added on a spur-of-the-moment whimsical fantasy by the architect, was removed. There was a funky hip vibe to the bathroom. Unlike Risa's ultrafeminine bathroom, his was more practical than pretty. But he loved his bathroom. They were going to have to learn to compromise if she found it too sterile for her taste. There were none of the little soaps, lotions, and pretty towels. His bathroom was his one sinful indulgence in decadence. Only the bathroom at the downtown gym, of which he was a member, rivaled the water pressure in his favorite room.

He tiptoed to the bathroom expecting to surprise Risa. To his disappointment, she wasn't naked awaiting him in the shower. Thinking there weren't many places she could be he headed towards the kitchen. He was hungry and hoped she had found breakfast fixings. Noticing her absence in the kitchen he figured that's why he had not smelled any delightful aromas wafting through the house.

He didn't know if she could cook. Well, if she couldn't, he could. If she needed or wanted more instruction, there were his sisters and his mother. If she didn't want to learn, they could eat out. It didn't matter as long as they were together. Surprised that he was alone, he immediately went to the phone and dialed her. He got the answering machine.

"This is Risa. Leave me a message and I will get back with you," JD heard her recorded voice message and smiled at the sound of her voice.

As a reporter she had a brilliant command of the English language. He liked everything about her voice especially the timbre, pitch, and Southern twang that was appealing.

"Let's set the date," he said into the phone, knowing if she were there that she would pick up. Convinced that she hadn't made it home yet he went back to the bathroom. As soon as he finished his morning toiletries he was going to buy a ring.

Risa didn't hear the phone message because she wasn't at home. When JD called her and left that message she had just walked out the door. After having arrived at her house with a new sense of purpose to get on with her life and forget JD, she had taken a shower, changed her clothes, and headed to her mother's house. Her mother had just arrived from her cruise earlier that morning. The two of them were going to play catch-up.

# Chapter 22

"Risa. Risa. Hello, darling!" Shelia Marcia Hooker James called from her front porch. Her mother was very Southern so it stood to reason that she would have a mouthful of names. Southerners loved to have a mouthful of names. Everybody seemed to use them all the time. Risa herself was Risa Elizabeth. Named after both her grandmothers, she was happy that she didn't have even more syllables attached to her surname.

Shelia was a well-preserved sixty-year-old given to extravagance and the ornate. Dressed in a fur-lined leather coat and matching hat, she had on high-heeled boots and didn't look a day over fifty. Weighing not one pound more than she did the day she got married, she was an unlined, wrinkle-free Southern beauty who would die before she let her gray hair show or left the house without full makeup. She waved anxiously at her daughter and literally skipped off her porch to greet her only child.

Risa was so happy to see her mother that she almost burst into tears just so she could be taken into her arms and fed Campbell's tomato soup. Her mother always gave her Campbell's tomato soup when she was down in the dumps. Marcia was convinced it cured everything from the common cold to a broken heart. Despite their obvious differences the two women shared a mother-daughter bond that was very strong. Risa actually liked her mother. She found Shelia a delightful kook, charming in her eccentricities.

"Don't get out of the car. Don't get out of the car," Shelia said as she opened the passenger door and got in next to Risa. After planting a big kiss on her daughter's check she immediately started giving directions. "I have a surprise for you. We're going to breakfast."

Risa was about to tell her mother that she wasn't up to going out when she decided to indulge her instead. Part of her new resolve was to get out of her rut. If that meant having an impromptu breakfast with her mother instead of their weekly Sunday brunch, then so be it. So listening to her mother's instruction she turned the car around and headed in the direction she was told.

It wasn't until they were pulling into the parking lot of Cornbread and Brie did Risa realize that she was once again at the popular eatery. Listening to her mother and coming from Shelia's house instead of her own, Risa had no idea this was their destination.

She was about to inform her mother of all the drama that had occurred at the restaurant then decided against it when she saw how excited her mother was.

"Your father had to pull some strings to get us in here today, but he did," she said proudly.

It never ceased to amaze Risa that her parents could be such good friends *after* their divorce. Her mother always called Frederick Walter James, DDS, "her father." And Dr. James always called Shelia "her mother" when talking to Risa about his ex-wife. As far as Risa was concerned, the two never should have gotten divorced. They spent more time together as exes than they ever did when married.

They had just come back from a cruise together, for Pete's sake! True enough, they had had two separate cabins, but she was sure they spent time together. She wouldn't even be surprised if some of that time was spent noodling under the sheets. She was an adult and knew what happened between men and women. Her mother and father had been married forty years. Their divorce had gone into effect three years ago. And yet neither the sixty-year-old Shelia nor the sixty-five-year-old Frederick seemed to spend time with anyone else. She wouldn't even be surprised if Frederick Walter joined them for breakfast. She wasn't disappointed.

As soon as they were ushered inside, her father was the first man she saw. Dressed impeccably in his traditional three-piece suit, he cut a dashing figure. Standing six feet tall he wore a pair of two-toned wing tips and even had on cuff links. Her mother called him stodgy but to Risa he looked like an English gentleman or a chocolate-colored Mr. French. Her father was always fully dressed and owned only one pair of jeans. Those, she bought him. Once, to get a smile from her, he wore them. But he also had had on a denim jacket and vest. To this day, Risa has no idea where he found the two pieces to complete his denim ensemble.

"Daddy," Risa said excitedly, rushing to his table.

He immediately engulfed her in an awkward embrace. He wasn't a very demonstrative man but always made an attempt for his daughter.

"Hello, Risa Elizabeth," he said. He always called her by her full name. "Shelia." He nodded to his ex-wife, acknowledging her presence.

"Freddy," she said as she smiled at him.

* * *

Dr. James or Frederick Walter. He didn't seem to mind as he pulled out a chair for his ex. Risa could have taken her seat but knew that her father felt it his responsibility to uphold the rules of chivalry. She allowed him to pull out her chair and sit between the two of them. It didn't matter that she was an adult. She felt a momentary rush of excitement at having her parents together. All children of divorce harbored a secret desire to have their parents re-unite.

"Well," Shelia began. "Let's play catch-up. You can start with that ridiculous haircut." Risa opened her napkin and busied herself with the menu. *Ouch*, Risa thought. Her mother was definitely back. God, had she missed her.

# Chapter 23

When JD showed up at Elisha's condo with a stupid grin on his face and his credit card in his hand, his youngest sister knew exactly what was needed: shopping spree! She was a marathon shopper. Unlike Carlie, who was a notorious pack rat, and Daphne, who was so cheap that Elisha often told her that she had the first dime she ever made, Elisha shopped for the sheer fun of it. She didn't bargain hunt like Angela or stick to the clearance aisles like Betsy, whose motto was, "If it's not on sale, I don't see it." Elisha bought what she wanted when she wanted it. Although she had her own money from pageants, contests, and scholarships, her older siblings indulged her, and her money, for the most part, remained untouched.

She often counted her lucky stars for their generosity. As long as she was in school and made good grades, then the following happened: Angela paid her credit card bills, Daphne's restaurant kitchen was opened to her, her parents kept up the maintenance on her cost-effective Jetta, her prize as second runner-up in the Miss Strawberry Patch pageant of last year and JD footed the bill for her condo. She was living a charmed life and she knew it. Her free ride was going to come to an end upon graduation when her family was going to expect her to pull her own weight and be the adult she always said she was. But until that time, she was having a ball!

"What's my limit?" she asked her brother excitedly while they perused the jewelry case at Vine and Blake, an upscale jewelry store located in the Galleria Mall in exclusive far north Dallas.

"It doesn't matter," JD answered.

"Just how much money do you have?" Elisha asked rhetorically as she had the clerk show her yet another ring. Initially, when they entered the store they were ignored until one of the patrons rushed up to JD and asked for an autograph. Overhearing the exchange, and seeming to realize for the first time that the good-looking African American couple might actually be able to afford the costly baubles, two clerks nearly bumped into each other trying to help them. The honors went to a very effeminate young Asian man who complimented Elisha on her panache, flair, and style. Dressed in purple suede jeans and a lavender oversized Irish wool sweater imported from Dublin, she was indeed giving off much flavor. She had on a pair of deep-purple boots and had removed the leather gloves from her slim hands so that she could try on the rings. She wore her sable hair in shoulder-length braids and had small diamond earrings in her ears. Her coffee-colored eyes were excited as she compared one ring to the other. She was a striking girl, pretty, and used to having attention paid to her.

"So, girlfriend," the clerk, whose name tag read Adan, started, reaching for a three-karat diamond as he deftly replaced the smaller one she had just removed from her hand. "When is the lucky day?"

As the two of them chatted and Elisha let him know that

JD was her brother and not her beau, JD busied himself with daydreams about how he was going to present the ring to Risa. He hadn't decided if he was going to go the truly romantic route and get down on bended knee or if he were going to put the ring in a tasty treat over dinner and have her bite into it. He quickly nixed the last idea after suddenly having an image of Risa chipping one of her beautiful teeth on the diamond. He was snapped from his reverie by the excited chirping from Elisha and the sales clerk, Adan. The two of them had found it. And by found it, he took it to mean they had selected the perfect ring. He started over to them but was sidetracked by a sparkle that caught his eye. He stopped to see what it was and saw in the display a simple platinum band with three small diamonds in the center. This was the ring. Simple. Elegant. Perfection. Risa.

"I want this one," JD said.

"That one? It's so plain," Elisha said, holding out her hand with the three-karat rock.

JD shook his head in the negative. He had made up his mind. "I think this is it."

"An excellent choice," Adan said, dropping the flamboyant air he had used with Elisha.

He was all business as he unlocked the display case for JD. Although not as large or as ostentatious as the ring Elisha had chosen, it was twice the price.

"Okay, seeing it out of the case and on my hand, I guess I can see the appeal."

"It's beautiful."

"Too plain for me." Elisha continued to scrutinize the ring.

"It's not for you."

Elisha ignored JD as she held out both hands to look at the two rings she wore. In the end she agreed with JD.

"Simple, dainty, but making a statement. Yes, it is the perfect ring for that woman I saw you with."

"That woman? You know her name."

"Yes, I know her name. Why all the secrecy, JD?"

"Are you kidding me? I don't have any secrets from you guys. The Jones women network works faster than the Internet. As soon as I kissed her y'all knew everything including her ring size before you had met her."

Elisha knew he was right but didn't give him the satisfaction of an answer. She just reluctantly held out her hand so that the clerk could remove the ring and place it in its case.

Elisha hated parting company with the three-karat ring she still had on her other hand but managed to do it without tears. For a brief moment she wished she too were getting engaged just so that she could get the ring. But that wasn't the case. Sadly she removed it and handed it back to Adan.

"This ring is a one of a kind, sir. It is a magnificent choice. Your lady will be pleased because it is a testament to perfection." Adan chatted happily as he went to have the ring sized and gift wrapped.

To show his appreciation, JD let Elisha pick out something for herself, making it clear that the three-karat ring wasn't on the list. Pouting just a little, she decided to let her new friend, Adan, help her select a bauble that would turn her frown into a smile. In the end they settled on a diamond and ruby broach. It was shaped like an apple and caught Elisha's eye. All in all, JD was happy. Elisha was happy. Adan got a huge commission and Risa was going to be dumbstruck. It was a good day for JD.

# Chapter 24

"I'm sorry. Run that by me again," Dr. Frederick Walter James said as he swallowed a piece of the delicious carrot cake he was eating and faced his daughter.

"She said he asked her to marry him but she said no," Shelia repeated. She had stopped eating somewhere in the middle of Risa's story. The peach walnut pancakes with homemade syrup lay cold on her plate. She was too upset to eat and didn't realize that Risa had, of course, edited the past week's events for them. "I just don't understand. Risa, why on earth would you say no?"

Risa thought long and hard on what she was going to say to her mother. On one hand she wanted to confess everything to get her mother's opinion and her empathy. On the other hand, Shelia was still her mother and therefore not privy to all the delicious sexual details.

"Maybe this boy isn't the right one for our little girl," her father said. He only called her his little girl when he sensed her distress or was coming to her rescue as her knight in a three-pieced suit of shining armor.

"Boy? Girl? Your daughter is almost . . ." she whispered, "forty."

As soon as the offensive number was out her mouth, Shelia turned to make sure that no one heard her. From her reaction, you'd swear that Risa had uttered a profanity in church or been caught doing something unspeakable that brought shame and disgrace onto the family. All she had done was remain single.

"And? I heard on the radio that forty is the new thirty," her father proclaimed.

With that declaration, Frederick Walter James picked up his fork and started back on his carrot cake. Risa was shocked. When did her father become hip? When did he stop being so stoic? When did he start listening to something other than big band swing on the radio?

"That is just a bunch of hogwash that unmarried forty-year-olds say to justify their spinsterhood," her mother spat. In this, her mother was very old-fashioned.

"Really, Mother, do you hear yourself?" Risa asked.

"Of course I hear myself. Do you hear me?"

"Mother, why is it so important to you that I get married?'

"Every woman needs to get married at least once in her life."

"But you aren't married."

"I don't have to be married. I've been married. I'm getting married again."

"What?" Risa wanted to make sure that she heard her mother correctly.

"We're getting married," her father clarified, speaking louder as if that would make everything clear to Risa.

"I don't understand," she said with a confused look on her face.

"Your mother thinks it's time to make an honest man out of me. We're doing everything married people do."

Risa almost gagged on her iced tea. She could not be having this conversation with her parents. She knew her father was a little spunky lately and her mother was positively glowing, but the thought of it being from a rekindled sex life was more than she wanted to know. She knew her parents had been together for forty years, but to actually think of them together was enough to make even to most liberal squirm. They were, after all, still her parents.

"Congratulations," she stammered, still trying to wrap her mind around their declaration.

"We're not talking about us. We're talking about you. Risa, I just want you to be happy," her mother stated.

"I can be happy without a man, Mother."

"It's not *a* man I'm talking about. It's *the* man." She covered Risa's hands with her own. "Can you be happy without *the* man? I couldn't."

Shelia smiled at her husband of forty years. When he smiled back, she patted his hand affectionately. They really were meant to be together. Risa's father was the man for her mother. Her mother was the woman for her father. Risa realized her mother had a point. No matter how much she wanted to ignore it, JD was her man. And she couldn't be happy without him.

Just then, unbeknownst to Risa, Lane Belle entered Cornbread and Brie in a huff. She and her mother had just spent their once-a-month mandatory mother-daughter day getting facials, manicures, pedicures, and body wraps. They had even gotten their hair "did" as the locals said in the colloquial slang. Under normal circumstances she endured these indulgences with disdain and contempt because she felt that all it did was perpetuate the stereotypes that women were vain creatures. But today, despite herself, she enjoyed every mud pack and cucumber facial. She liked the way she looked and felt wonderful. Her sixteen-year-old mind saw this as a betrayal of all the feminist values that she held dear. In admitting that she enjoyed herself, it was admitting that her mother had been right all along and that no matter how hard she tried, it was her birthright to be a pampered Southern belle.

Lane was predisposed because of her genetic makeup. She hated it when her mother was right. Aaaarrrrgggghhh. That said, she was a little huffy when she started towards her and her mother's regular table. It didn't matter that JD and her mother were no longer together. He said that nothing would change. Therefore, their regular seat should be waiting for them. So when she entered the dining room, a few steps before her mother, who was showing Daphne her new belly ring, she almost started screaming when she saw Risa in her seat at their table. Did she live in the back room of the restaurant? She couldn't get away from her!

There were other restaurants in the city. Risa knew this because not only had she seen them, she had actually eaten at them. But it seemed like on this day everyone in the city was at Cornbread and Brie. She looked up and noticed the pretty teenager enter just as she was about to excuse herself from her parents and go see JD. Leaving him as she had done was a cowardly way to behave and she needed to make things right. But her confrontation with JD would have to wait. It seemed there was a very angry teenager glaring at her. She was as prepared for Lane as she was for the girl's mother who appeared in the room surrounded by a cloud of admiration.

Dressed in nothing more than faded jeans, an oversized sweater, high-heeled stiletto boots, and gloves, she managed to look marvelous in her apparent effortlessness. She was a well-preserved and stunning beauty who made heads turn as she strode towards her daughter. For a brief second, Risa felt an uncharacteristic moment of self-consciousness. This was the woman who had shared JD's heart, life, and bed before her. The older woman was intimidating in her confidence. Her mother always said men were creatures of habit and followed the same MO. So in other words, if his last girlfriend was a big-busted beauty there was a pretty good chance that his present one would be as equally if not better endowed. Looking at this woman who radiated a sexual confidence to herself, Risa could see nothing they had in common. Ever since she met JD, she had been a bundle of nerves and had lived on the edge, giving into impulses and desires that had lain dormant for years. This woman was a lusty strumpet who embraced life and lived it to the fullest. It was in her bearing and character. Surely JD had chosen each one of them for their differences and not their similarities, because he unfairly judged Risa for being just as vivacious in bed as Lucy was in life.

"I'm so sorry," Lucy said apologetically. "Please forgive my daughter for standing over your table glaring at you as if she has had not an ounce of home training. We are regular customers here and usually sit at this table."

Her voice was cultured and strong and possessed a definite Southern drawl. She couldn't lose the accent if she tried. And it was possible she would never try. The accent was alluring and appealing. It was no wonder the age difference meant nothing to JD. There was no doubt in Risa's mind that the older woman had her share of admirers, young and old.

"It's not a problem. Would you like to join us?" Frederick Walter volunteered, always the gentleman.

It is amazing what forty years would do to a relationship. Shelia Marcia Hooker James didn't even flinch when her husband offered Lucy Belle a seat. She was secure in her relationship and didn't feel in the least bit threatened. Lane, on the other hand, wasn't having it. She was annoyed and wanted everyone to know it.

"Mother," Lane started, everything in her voice indicating her utter dislike of this decision. She was immediately shushed by her mother.

"We don't want to interrupt your mealtime. We'll wait at the bar until a table opens. I am sure the food will be just as good no matter where we sit."

She flashed a smile, showing a perfect set of teeth. Risa knew it took everything her father had not to ask her who her dentist was. He had been a dentist for over forty years and took pride in his work. A good set of teeth usually indicated to him a colleague who had a work ethic much like his own. Although his practice had expanded to include two other dentists, he still kept regular office hours. He'd had some of his patients since they had been children. Loyalty ran deep in southerners.

"We'll let you get back to your meal. Again, I am sorry we interrupted you," Lucy said with a firm hand on her daughter's shoulder as she ushered her away.

They were halfway across the room when Risa saw Lane say something to her mother, which made the woman turn and look at Risa. Across the room their eyes met; JD's former lover and his current love shared the kind of moment that is seen in movies. In an instant Lucy Belle sized Risa up. She did it skillfully and surprisingly without malice. But she was thorough. Risa felt as if she had been dissected under a microscope, examined, and put back together without a scratch. It almost left her drained.

"Excuse me," Risa said to her parents as she rose from the table and headed towards Lucy Belle.

She was halfway across the room when she realized she didn't know what she was going to say to the beautiful older woman. But she had to talk to her. As if sensing Risa's presence behind her, Lucy turned and the two women stood facing each other. Risa was almost a head taller than the petite beauty. But the height difference meant nothing as the two women looked into each other's eyes. Lucy's look to Risa was filled with curiosity and nothing more.

"Yes?" Lucy said.

"I'm Risa," Risa said with confidence.

"I'm Lucy. Lucy Belle. I should have recognized you from your show. I can see JD's attraction. You are a beautiful young woman." There was no malice in her tone or anger in her demeanor.

"So are you."

"Beautiful. But no longer young." She said it without regret and even laughed, creating a musical and magical sound.

All around them people were eating and going about their business and yet Risa felt as if the two of them were the only two people in the room. Lane scurried away as soon as the two women started talking.

"Teenagers," Lucy said as if that summed up everything. "Let's get a drink at the bar."

The two women made their way to the bar. Although it too was packed, they managed to snag a couple of glasses of wine and a small space in order to talk. Whenever the place was packed and there was a wait Daphne had her staff supply free wine to her patrons who were old enough to partake. It was another reason Cornbread and Brie was so very popular. The wine was free-flowing and of good quality.

"So, girlfriend, what's on your mind?" Lucy bluntly asked, which started a free-flowing conversation between the two women.

While Risa and Lucy were talking, JD was on his way to the restaurant. He had made an impromptu stop by Risa's house and noted her absence. He checked his messages and called her again. His ladylove was missing in action but he still had to eat.

"Of course you love him. JD is totally lovable," Lucy said, taking a sip of her wine.

Risa's parents had long since said their good-byes and the two women were now occupying the table vacated by Frederick Walter and Shelia. Lane had retreated to the kitchen with Daphne. She had always been fond of JD and his sisters. Daphne was her personal favorite. And if she stayed in the kitchen she wouldn't have to be part of a conversation that she found obscene in its civility. Outside in the restaurant the wine and comfortable atmosphere had Risa and Lucy dishing the dirt like old friends.

"I love him. I'm just not in love with him. And he isn't in love with me. I wish you two the best," Lucy Belle said as she toasted her newfound friend.

Risa took another sip of wine. It was her second glass and she was getting a little light-headed. She had never developed a tolerance for alcohol and usually drank wine. One full glass was her limit. But today she felt like celebrating. She was giddy and happy and elated at her newfound discovery of her feelings for JD. She had searched for love and suddenly it had been offered to her on a silver platter. A thoroughbred had passed her the bit. A runner had passed her the torch. She would accept her banner with pride because JD was a good man.

"We had a long, mutually satisfactory union," Lucy added.

Risa didn't know what to say to that and it seemed totally inappropriate to agree. JD's prowess had never been in question. Both women knew that firsthand and had the decency not to elaborate on it. This was the first time in her life that Risa had knowingly been in such close proximity to a woman with whom she had shared more than conversation. While in college she was the unknowing third in a love triangle between her boyfriend and a sorority sister wannabe. Once she found out, she pledged to never man share again. Now years later she found herself in a situation that wasn't exactly the same, but could have a decadent and obscene air about it if she hadn't known of JD and Lucy's relationship. She liked Lucy Belle. She found her confident and very entertaining. They would be able to talk about something other than JD. She was sure of it. The wine and comfortable surroundings would make conversation easy. She wanted to be hip and cool and talk about the man they shared and compare notes on the bedroom etiquette, but she was way too square to do that other than in her head. It would take more than wine to make her that cool.

# Chapter 25

JD ate at Cornbread and Brie so much that he asked Daphne to set up a delivery service so that he wouldn't have to drive into the city everyday just because he had a taste for apple walnut fritters. She, on the other hand, told him he had better darn well make the drive. He lived outside the city limits and having food delivered wouldn't be feasible. It wouldn't arrive hot and therefore the taste would be compromised. She was such a perfectionist, his middle sister.

He pulled into the parking lot and walked through the front door with the intention of getting a takeout basket. He thought it would be a good idea to show up on Risa's front porch later and surprise her with the basket, a bottle of wine, and the ring. It couldn't get any more romantic than that. He chose to do something that would be a perfect Hallmark moment and make her heartstrings sing. As soon as he entered the restaurant he made a beeline for the kitchen. He saw Lane and Daphne at the same time. Daphne was standing over the stove stirring a pot. Lane was sitting at a table eating a slice of lemon pie. All around them was the hustle and bustle of a busy restaurant.

There were waiters, cooks, busboys, and dishwashers. It was a hive of activity. JD's presence could have gone virtually unnoticed had Lane not looked up from the pie she was enjoying with such relish.

"JD," she exclaimed and jumped from her perch. Before he knew it, she was in his arms. "My mom's outside with that woman."

JD looked to his sister who merely shrugged as if to say, "You got yourself into this, get yourself out," and continued with what she was doing.

"Lane. Lane. Lane Marie. Your mother and I are still friends. It's okay. It's okay," JD said as he stroked her back. In his head, all he could think was it was inevitable to have this confrontation with the teenager. Although they had dinner the night before, it seemed that they had merely glossed over a problem. He had been a constant in her life and she was reluctant to see it end. No matter what he said, she could not believe that he was going to still be there for her even when he continued his life with Risa. This was a problem he, as a single man with no children, wasn't prepared to handle. He needed the help of Lucy Belle.

"She's in the dining room," Daphne volunteered, "with Risa."

JD's heart did a flip-flop. No wonder he wasn't able to find his ladylove. She was right beneath his nose. The fact that she was with the other love of his life was somewhat daunting, but the only way to handle the Lane situation was to call in reinforcements, so he would have to put his own discomfort on hold.

Placing a comforting arm around the teenager's shoulder, he went into the dining room. Although he knew what to expect, the sight of Risa and Lucy sitting at a table drinking and chitchatting like old friends was a little unsettling. There were men he knew who would have been excited by the prospect of seeing two very sexy, beautiful women together knowing that they shared a special kinship. He wasn't one of them. The thought of them comparing notes was intimidating. In an instant his mind raced over the possible key points of their conversation. *Did they compare his lovemaking skills and dating technique?* he thought. *Did they describe how his face looked when he kissed or how his body reacted when he was aroused? Did they say how many times he brought them to bliss or did they discuss his shortcomings?* Although he had just conquered his fear of being not as skilled or as polished as Risa in the bedroom he could not face the thought of approaching the two of them with a grin and a "give it to me, I can take it" attitude. So with much trepidation he marched Lane Marie over to the table.

Risa saw JD approach and had a momentary intake of breath at his appearance. As always he was impeccable in his dress. Charcoal-gray slacks, a charcoal cashmere sweater, and black boots that were spit-shined to a reflective tint highlighted a man who was used to commanding attention. She could see the women look at him with admiration and took delight in knowing he was hers and hers alone. She almost suffered a momentary bout of remorse when she thought of her newfound friend, Lucy Belle's, loss. That thought was immediately replaced with pride as she beamed at him. Lucy's loss was her gain.

JD was looking at Risa with a mixture of desire, possessiveness, and expectation. The past was forgotten. She was looking at him with new eyes, seeing him for the sexy, desirable man that he was. She was beside herself with wanting him. She was beside herself with needing him. Everything in her being said to forget the past. They could start fresh with a dual effort.

Risa and JD's eyes met over Lucy Belle's head. As always there was an instant connection. It took everything she had not to get up from the table and rush into his arms. She liked the way she felt in his arms. She liked they way her skin felt pressed against his. She liked the song they sang with their bodies. The physical connection was so perfect between the two of them it made everything all right.

"Look what I found," JD said, indicating Lane.

He didn't really know what to say and he knew his introduction was weak. But he had to say something and this awkward moment could be made so much worse with the wrong choice of words. Lane looked from one woman to the other. She was confused. Even through her teenage eyes it was obvious that there was no animosity between the two women.

"Hello darlings," Lucy Belle said, taking her daughter by the hand and raising her cheek to JD's lips for a kiss. He didn't hesitate as he obliged. "I have just spent the past hour speaking with your delightful new companion. You did good for yourself, JD. I like."

For the second time, Risa realized there was no hostility or hidden message in Lucy Belle's actions or words. Lucy Belle recognized that as long as Risa and JD were together, there was no chance that she could continue her relationship with JD. So as a lady and a true Southern belle, she conceded with skill and grace.

"Are we okay? It's important to me that we are okay," JD asked his ex-lover.

"We'll always be okay," Lucy assured him as she gathered her reluctant teenager to her bosom in an impromptu bear hug.

"Honey, JD and I are friends. JD and I will always be friends. Now Risa and I are friends. Everyone is friendly. It's important for you to know that everything is okay," Lucy assured her daughter.

"Nothing changes between us, pumpkin," JD confirmed.

Lane wasn't JD's daughter. But his concern for her well-being was obvious in his demeanor. If he didn't love her, his feelings for her were so close to love that the difference was indiscernible. Risa knew then that he would be a good father. If the child was born of their union, or if they adopted, which had been her intent before meeting him, the child would come into a house that had two loving parents, not just one. She heard so many stories of where the burden of raising children fell solely on the mother's shoulders. Even with today's modern standards, there were so many men who reverted to the old-fashioned notion that a child gets love and attention from its mother and discipline from its father. JD wouldn't be like that. He would be sensitive and caring. He would be the perfect father for a little girl. He knew how to relate to a girl's delicate psyche. But being a man, he would be clumsy and awkward while doing it. His discomfort was endearing. Looking at him her eyes filled to the brim with tears brought on by love. This man was so perfect for her.

"I want to go home," Risa heard herself say.

Lucy Belle arose from the table in a movement that was as seductive as it was simple. And although her movement was as natural to her as breathing, it had an effect on so many men that Risa thought their table was going to be rushed. Only JD seemed impervious to her unconscious seduction. He had eyes only for Risa.

"Let's go, sweetness," Lucy cooed to her daughter as she put a protective arm around her shoulder.

For all her sophistication, Lane was still a teenager. It would take a little time and a lot of patience to make sure that she came out of this unscathed.

JD watched the two of them leave the restaurant. He was still uncertain as to how to handle the situation with

Lane. Unlike her older brother, Richard Marconi, she was fragile and raw. He would handle her with kid gloves. His concern for her welfare was still foremost in his mind.

"Well," Risa said when they were alone.

"Well." He echoed her sentiment.

For a moment they just looked at each other.

"Let's get out of here," JD said as a courtesy.

No words were necessary between them. He just said the words so that he wouldn't appear rude by taking her by the elbow and escorting her out. He needed to be alone with her. What he had to say did not require an audience.

"I have to take care of the check first," Risa said.

"No you don't." JD snatched the tab up off the table and placed it in his pocket. He'd take care of it later. He was walking so fast that Risa found it hard to keep up with his long-legged stride.

"You're going to have to slow down if you don't want me on my face," Risa protested as her three-inch heels made a clickety-clack against the pavement as she followed him.

"I want you any way I can have you."

JD stopped abruptly and turned to her. There was so much he wanted to say. But he wanted to do it just right. He knew she could see the desire that was evident on his face and body. He didn't want her to think this was all about sex either. It was more than sex. If he got his way this would be the woman he would spend the rest of his life with. She would be the mother of his children, his partner, and soul mate. Telling her he wanted her was unnecessary. She could see that. She had that effect on him. Telling her he loved her had to be done under the most ideal circumstance. The parking lot of his sister's restaurant wasn't the right place. Coming immediately after his confrontation of sorts with young Lane wasn't the right time. Whatever the ideal moment they would have to move from this spot in time and do it soon. Their two cars were taking up prime space in the rapidly filling parking lot. The valets were busy.

"My place is closer," Risa offered without the trepidation she felt just hours earlier.

No matter what the outcome she would be with JD for the duration. It took them only a moment to decide how they would meet up. In the end, they decided to take both cars.

Risa usually followed the rules of the road. But faced with the prospect of having another tête-à-tête with JD she actually ran a stop sign. In the event she ever made it to court she could have contested it on the grounds that she was blinded by love. It wasn't really a blatant disregard for the rules of the road. It was instead more of a rolling stop. JD was fast behind her.

His Jaguar kept pace with the BMW easily. But unlike Risa, he made it a point to stop, fully. He was a Black man driving a Jaguar. He would not miss his special time with Risa on a technicality. Why give the police an out? He respected and admired the police. He understood the necessity of a police force. If there were no police there would be chaos in the streets. He was a strong believer in the creed that we needed the police like we needed government. There was a reason for rules and regulations. He also knew that all policemen weren't bad. He knew that all policemen weren't good either. As a Black man in these days of racial profiling, he always made it a point to follow the rules.

He wanted to be with Risa more than he wanted a ticket. He would scold her later on her reckless behavior. They made it to her place in record time. No sooner were they inside was she was in his arms. Past awkwardness was pushed aside as they found a familiar and common ground.

Clothes were discarded in a tangled heap as they sought to press skin against skin. Chocolate mocha almond fudge satin blended with carmel frosty crème brûlée and created a fantasy dessert of sweetness and decadence. His lips were on her. Her breast pressed against his chest. Perfectly formed orbs excited him to frenzy. He lifted her slight frame easily and carried her to the bedroom. He had only been there once before but he hadn't forgotten the way. Once in her room, there wasn't either the time or the desire to pull back the embroidered linen comforter.

Her taste was exquisite as indicated by her choice of surroundings. Each time he entered her home he felt a sense of contentment and euphoria. He would love to have her woman's touch in his home. He deposited her onto the bed and stood just for a moment to look down at her tempting treats. God, how he wanted her siren's touch against his skin. Standing at the foot of her bed he could only look in awe at what was sheer perfection. His eyes drank in the sight of her. There was at first chocolate-brown skin with traces of sienna beneath the satin of it. Then there was long hair splayed against the pillow in a haphazard passion-inspired array. Her eyes were misty with desire. Lips pouty with wanting. She was a lady named seduction and she lay, waiting for the union of their flesh. She was a sexy, seductive, siren poised and eager to oblige.

"Oh, my God, Risa, you take my breath away," JD stated.

Looking up at him she too was struck almost speechless by what was male perfection. His body was honed and cut with defined muscles and ripples. The dark skin and Michael Jordan good looks were fantasy inspiring. Rising to her knees, she reached out to him and drew him into her warm embrace. She wanted to taste him as much as she wanted to feel him. The time they spent apart had been too long. She wanted to join without preliminary, but he wouldn't let her.

"You are a delicacy to be savored," he said, drawing one of her long fingers with the well-manicured nail into his waiting mouth.

As he sucked it Risa felt a tug in her most sensitive spot. This reaction was surprising because what he sucked was just a finger. It seems in the few hours they were separated JD had let his imagination run free. He was doing new and innovative things that inspired awe in her. As he drove her to distraction with gentle flicks of his tongue and long slow kisses against her hand he placed his other hand between the juncture of her thighs. She opened herself to him. He smiled, delighted that he brought her to this level of ecstasy.

"I have you where I want you," he said as he began to tease her with delicate kisses from her breast to her navel, avoiding her most private parts, yet making what he touched desirous of his mouth as if it were used to the touch and taste of his tongue.

Risa squirmed beneath him anxious for him to end the torture of her flesh and join with her. He only smiled, excited by his mastery of her response. It seemed that he was a quick study. When the game had first started she had been the master. As they played, he was quickly becoming her equal. This he attributed to the earlier phone conversation he had with Big L when he was on his way to Cornbread and Brie.

*"I think you were just scared."*

*"I was not scared,"* JD had answered quickly, knowing deep down in his heart that he had been.

His meeting and courtship, if you could call it that, of Risa had happened so fast that it took him by surprise. His reaction to her both physically and mentally was just not something he had expected to happen from a brief encounter. Truth be told, they had only met days ago. Yet the raw emotion and roller-coaster ride of feelings were those of a relationship that had lasted for a longer period of time. Although he hadn't put in the time he had put in the commitment. He had moved to levels with this woman in a matter of days that other couples only experienced after serving time. With Risa it had not felt like a "sentence" or "time spent."

The days had run into each other, as had his feelings, which let him know that this was no chance encounter. This woman, this tall, slender beauty forced him to examine emotions and notions that he was now ashamed to admit that he hadn't known about himself. Until he was ready to commit to her, he had been a dyed-in-the-wool, card-carrying chauvinist. He just hadn't known it. If anyone had asked him his feeling on women and their place or if he were a chauvinist, he would have responded with something to the effect of, "Chauvinist? Me? I have five sisters!" That was before he had met a woman, asked her to marry him, and then bedded her in less than a week! Before that he had been an athlete for most of his life and spent many a day in the locker room, and therefore knew that there was a double standard where men and women were concerned. He was supposed to be the all-knowing bedroom guru. She was supposed to be the willing eager apprentice, not the other way around and this made him treat Risa with antiquated ideas and notions that he could no longer subscribe to.

If JD had been a younger man he could have blamed his earlier behavior to ignorance learned from listening to locker-room stories and gossip that surrounded the girls that put out too fast. No one ever condemned the boys or discouraged their actions. The girls were the ones who had to pay with their reputations. And although he and Risa were adults who did not have to answer to anyone he was concerned with her past. He had wanted and needed to know who had indoctrinated her into the world of sensual delights. He was obsessed with her sexual past. This obsession almost cost him his prize possession. Had it not been for his friend pointing it out to him he might have not recognized how ashamed he was of his earlier behavior. Thank God for friends. He would not continue to chide himself over his earlier behavior. He had righted the action and corrected the wrong.

A long time ago his father said to him, "Anybody can make a mistake. The bigger mistake is in not fixing it." He was fixing it. Oh yes, he was fixing it. He wished he could tell his friend how he was fixing it. But he could not. Now that he and Risa were back together, the intimacies of their relationship were no longer to be shared between friends. He wouldn't continue to kiss and tell. He couldn't kiss and tell. This wanton had him under her spell and he didn't want anyone to prejudge her based on his earlier actions. This was his woman, his prize, and he wanted her treated like the lady and Nubian queen that she was. In saying that he and his friend had come to the line that they would not cross. They both knew what it was. Big L was married to JD's sister. Big L couldn't go there with JD and JD wouldn't go there with him about Risa. Risa, Risa, Risa, she lay beneath him moaning with desire. He was surprised they hadn't set off the water sprinklers they were both so hot. It excited and terrified JD. He was afraid to mess it up again. But it was a fear he would happily face if she kept making that sound beneath him.

"Awe," she let out a breath of utter contentment as he moved within her. It was a sweet sound. It was a delicate sound. It was a sexy sound. It was a sound that made him want to please her. His largeness was the perfect size for her sheath. Without having to be told, she wrapped her legs around his moving back. With her heels she pulled him into her as far as was humanly possible. She starred into his dark chocolate eyes as he appeared shocked and then delighted by her reckless move.

For a fleeting second she chastised herself because she didn't want him to revert to his old way of thinking that her skill had come from many lovers and not from her desire to please him. She didn't know about the conversation he had in his head about his earlier deplorable behavior. All she knew was that he only smiled at her. It was a pure masculine smile of utter enjoyment as he rode her like a beautiful horse. Risa's body performed as if trained to respond to his touch. She felt herself soaring to heights that were soon to be legendary once she entered them into her journal. She could only call his name as she lay beneath him glorying in his touch. Each time they made love it was better than the last. Each time skin touched skin they moved to another level.

"JD. Oh, JD. I missed you," she breathed against his neck. They fit so good together, the time spent apart seemed an eternity instead of a few hours.

She arched beneath him and let out a squeak of delight as he skillfully and effortlessly flipped her over onto her stomach. All this he did without missing a beat as he, once again, slid into her warmth from behind. He placed his hand beneath her flat stomach and the bed and raised her to her knees. Her back was subject to the warm kisses that he had been treating the rest of her exposed skin to. Her long hair fell over her face in a cascade of supple curls as he ran his fingers through it. Even massaging her scalp, he managed a moan from her. It was so good between them. So raw and so perfect. Every position solicited the ultimate in feeling. It was like reaching the top of Mt. Everest, lassoing a unicorn, and landing on the moon all it once. In other words their union was indescribable.

Once it was over they lay panting like greyhounds after

a strenuous race. Neither one of them could say anything. Naked, strained, and exhausted, they drew strength from each other as their bodies touched. Words weren't necessary. Exhausted, JD reached for his pants. Risa watched, confused, because it was too late to reach for the small package that was so necessary in a modern relationship. Actually they'd been so heated that she had grabbed one from her nightstand drawer thinking she could get to it faster. His getting his own now was just an afterthought unless he was ready to go again. As she ran her hand lovingly and passively over his magnificent maleness, she knew that it wouldn't take much to make her dream a reality. Instead of a tiny package of protection, he withdrew a small velvet-covered box.

Risa saw it but wasn't prepared for it. For a moment she stared at the treasure in his hand. She had dreamed of this moment but she never dreamed of it unfolding like this. In her mind's eye she had a moment much like that seen in spoofs of romantic rendezvous. She had been running in slow motion through a field of flowers to her awaiting lover who had gathered her into his arms so that they could ride off into the sunset on a white charger named Prince. It happened like that . . . not like this, naked and wanton pressed against sweaty skin while her lover looked at her smugly as he held out the velvet-covered box. And yet this was just as sweet. Her heart almost stopped and she felt her breath catch as she sat up in bed to get a good look. For whatever reason she felt that this moment deserved that she be seated upright instead of pressed against her lover's side. Delicately she took the box from him. It was light in her hands and seemed magical like a lucky talisman.

"Open it," he coaxed.

"What's inside?" she asked.

"Our future."

All she could do was open the box. She wasn't blinded by glare or struck dumb by gaudiness. Instead she was lulled into a sense of contentment by the mere beauty of it. The simple structure of it. It was simple and perfect and just right for her. She slipped it onto her finger and was not surprised that it fit. There would be no reason to have it sized. It fit perfectly. That was surely the sign that she needed. She answered him with a kiss. It was tender and long and sweet and perfect and just right for the two of them. Again, words were not necessary. With the simple gesture of the presenting of the ring their pasts had been eradicated and their future secured. This was her man. She was his woman. Let no man put their union asunder. They were as well as married. No ceremony was necessary. Like words it would be unnecessary and repetitive. All they needed was each other. That night they slept in each other's arms as the couple they were meant to be.

# Chapter 26

Shelia Marcia Hooker James was beside herself with excitement. Finally someone had listened to her. She knew that her daughter would be happier with a mate than without one. There was someone for everyone. It was just a matter of time that Risa found that someone and she finally found him.

Shelia had taken a much-needed vacation and her daughter found the love of her life. He just fell out of the sky into her arms. How lucky was that? Just days ago Shelia and her husband, who became her ex-husband and who would soon be her husband again, had laid in bed bickering over the merits of their only daughter getting married. She was for it. He was surprisingly against it. He just wanted his daughter to be happy. If that meant being married, or single, he could live with the outcome. Just be happy. Shelia was mortified that on this subject they didn't see eye to eye. She felt strongly that to be happy her daughter needed a significant other in her life. True enough, Risa had been quite successful on her own. Risa was a woman who should be proud of her own accomplishments; sharing that with someone only made it better. Her parents' two opinions on the opposite ends of the poll was just one of the things they had bickered about.

Throughout Risa's life they had made it a point to present a united front. Now that Risa was an adult he felt that it was okay to show dissention in the ranks. She still didn't. She would get Frederick Walter to see her point or else. Together they were going to get that girl married and that was that. It didn't matter that she had known him less than a week. It just didn't matter. As a matter of fact, she had been thinking about just how to tackle this particular point when Risa beat her to the punch. Risa called her with a song in her heart and a giggle in her voice. She, Risa James was getting married, and not to just anybody, but to JD Jones. Not only that, but the date had already been set.

Shelia didn't know how to react. Should she jump for joy or scold Risa on the inappropriateness of springing this on her with such short notice? How was she going to get a decent wedding together? The wedding she dreamed of for her little girl would take a year minimum to plan. She was too busy trying to get her ex-husband to set their wedding day. Now that they were a couple again everything was such a negotiation. Dividing her time between Risa's upcoming nuptials and Frederick Walter's growing stubbornness was enough to break an ordinary woman. Shelia Marcia Hooker James was no ordinary woman. She was a woman getting ready to organize the wedding of her thirty-nine-year-old daughter to one of the city's most eligible bachelors. She was a woman possessed.

There were invitations and phone calls and decorations and choosing a location and, and, and. There was finding the dress and getting the food. Actually getting the food was the easiest thing. It helped when the groom's sister owned one of the hottest eateries in the city. That said, her husband of thirty-seven years and ex of three had better give in on some of his new demands or she wasn't going to be able to give Risa her full-undivided attention.

Just last night they started yet another negotiation to determine which house they would live in. Shelia felt that logic dictated that they reside in the house that they had raised their child in. In her mind the house where they spent the first thirty-seven years of their married lives together should be the house where they spent the rest of their days. Frederick Walter, on the other hand, had gotten a taste of independence in the short time that they were divorced. For the first time in his life he gloried in the excitement of purchasing sheets and dishes and furniture. He found that there was a difference in the quality of thread count and discovered quite by accident that he really didn't particularly care for dainty paisley prints, flowers, and doilies. He liked deep, rich colors and was partial to heavy leather furniture and overstuffed couches.

His spacious two-bedroom condominium sported very masculine leather, modern pieces, and sparse decorations. There wasn't a knickknack anywhere to be found and he liked it. So at sixty-five in the twilight years of his life he had his first bachelor pad and he didn't want to give it up without a fight. If he had his way, they would sell the large four-bedroom house filled with country classics and French things he could care less about and move into his new space.

He had his hands full with Shelia and her excitement over Risa's upcoming wedding. Deciding where the two of them would cohabitate could take a backseat until after the glorious day. It had been a long time since he had seen Shelia so happy. She was focused and on a mission. It made him happy to see her so thrilled. Focusing on their daughter's upcoming nuptials actually managed to take ten years off her already youthful appearance and give her an extra spring to her step. Already a good-looking woman, she was even more attractive when she was on a mission. He was indeed a lucky man. He hoped his new son-in-law would realize what a prize he had in acquiring a James woman. He did.

"I don't care," Risa said for the hundredth time. She and her mother were in her bedroom. She lay on her bed with a pillow over her head and her mother was sitting on the floor.

Shelia was surrounded by bridal books and had samples and swatches of material before her. They had ordered a pizza and Shelia had been going on for what seemed like hours about this and that. She was as giddy as a teenager. Watching her mother sitting on her floor eating pizza and chatting had Risa reminiscing of her own college days. That, she was sure, was the last time she talked about her wedding with anyone. Back then they all talked about having it all and how they were going to accomplish it. Back then she pictured a dream wedding with Mr. Perfect in which she wore her grandmother's wedding dress.

Risa had seen a picture of the gown when she was younger and thought that it was the most beautiful thing she had ever seen. She remembered the dress and how she wanted to look in it, but she couldn't remember who she had pictured as Mr. Perfect. Thinking about it, she was sure back then it had been Denzel Washington or some other movie star leading man. Now, she could only picture JD. He was her leading man. He was her Prince Charming.

Maybe she could get her mother to go into those trunks she kept in the garage. She knew her grandmother's dress had never been destroyed. The problem was in finding it in the things that Shelia had kept once her mother passed away over seven years ago. So consumed was she with the dress that Risa had stopped listening to Shelia over an hour ago. She didn't care about the food or the reception. She didn't care about the invitations or even her shoes even though everyone stressed how important shoes were because she was going to have to be standing in them for hours. The only things she really cared about were that all JD's sisters, plus Helen and Cayce be bridesmaids and that she find her grandmother's wedding dress. Those were her only concerns. She knew that marrying into this family would instantly give her the sisters she never had. She could not and did not want to alienate them. The wedding dress was the only thing she wanted just for herself. She would find it.

Risa was snapped out of her daydreaming by Shelia tugging on her toes to get her attention. "Well, Risa Elizabeth . . ." her mother said, using her full name whenever she wanted to get her attention. "You had better care about something. If you don't say anything, those girls are going to take over. That little one even wants to make your dress. I will not have my daughter in a handmade wedding dress."

By that little one, she meant Carlie. In a family full of leggy beauties, she was the shortest. Risa had seen some of Carlie's handiwork firsthand and was pleased with it. She and JD had stopped by to pick up a sweater she mended for him and Risa saw a house filled with handmade embroidery and stitchery. Carlie's quaint home was just like something out of *Better Homes and Gardens*. She was a public relations professional who seemed to have a temperament more suited to that of design or decorating.

"Carlie is pretty talented. I've seen her work," Risa said. Suddenly she had a thought and set up in the bed. "Mother, you are a genius. I think Carlie can alter Nanna's dress for me."

"Mama's dress? What would you want with that old thing?"

"I'm going to get married in it."

For the first time since she and Shelia had been talking about the wedding and all the particulars, she was excited. By including Carlie in the alteration of the dress, she would get everything she wanted.

"Come on, Mother," Risa said, jumping up.

"Where are we going?"

"We're going through the things in your garage."

"The garage? Risa, it is filled with junk!"

"No, Mama. It's filled with dreams."

Risa took Shelia by the hand and helped her from the floor. The two of them had a lot of trunks to go through. They wouldn't be able to do that if they sat there eating pizza and making wedding plans.

# Chapter 27

"There's got to be a tactful way to handle this," Angela stated.

She was leading the discussion from behind her buffet. The table was laid with cookies, cakes, and all types of pastries. They even had frappe, a punch made with ginger ale, lime sherbet, and frozen strawberries. This was a menu left over from their days as children when they had tea parties with their mother's good china once a month. When they were children they used to look forward to the monthly gatherings. They got to dress up and sometimes even wore hats and gloves. Their mother had a picture that Angela had gotten enlarged and framed last year that depicted all the girls in their frilly, pastel outfits, hat and gloves included at one of their high teas. Taken over thirty years ago, it was a family keepsake. It was a very funny picture because they had even gotten JD to join in. He had on a tie and an old fisherman's cap. No matter what they had said or did, they weren't able to persuade their brother to dawn one of the frilly, Easter bonnets. Even at a young age he knew that if he did, they would have been able to black-mail him forever with that picture.

Times were so much simpler then. Back when they played dress up and sipped tea and ate finger sandwiches they could not have foreseen this day and how the mood would be so different around their childhood tradition. True, as they grew into adulthood some of the menu changed, as did their palates, but never their desire to spend time together over good china and conversation. That said, they had chosen this avenue to discuss their latest family problem, Shelia Marcia Hooker James.

"Well, you try. She is impossible. She actually told me she wanted me to use her mother's recipe on the cake. Does she know who I am?" Daphne asked in a huff.

Her next venture, Honey Baby's, was an eatery that handled nothing but dessert. She had just won a $15,000 honorarium from *Southern Chef Cooking* with her coconut pineapple cake recipe, for Pete's sake. She didn't need anyone telling her how to bake a cake.

"Girl, I think she knows and doesn't care." That came from Betsy. Betsy always told it like it was. She didn't pull any punches. She summed up Shelia's bossy personality in a few seconds flat.

"I told her I would be able to hook up the wedding dress. She asked me if I had ever been married." Carlie too was a little pissed off.

Of all the girls she was the only one who had been planning her wedding since she was twelve. It was going to be a fairy-tale affair. The only problem was that she didn't have a prince, yet. Once she got the news that JD and Risa were going to tie the knot, she immediately pictured a design that would complement Risa's lithe frame and gentle curves. Of course she would confer with Risa, and she was willing to work night and day to make sure that it was done. Who else could say that they had their own personal tailor on call twenty-four hours?

"I think that if this is how it's starting, we better be prepared for a whole lot worse," was Elisha's comment.

She was still excited over the brooch she got when JD selected Risa's ring. If she had her way she was going to turn herself into her brother's personal shopper. That way she could always get a little something for herself. As long as JD didn't mind she was game.

It was the Saturday before the wedding. The five Jones sisters were having an emergency powwow at Angela's. Each one had run into Shelia and had come away holding her tongue and being as polite as they were taught to be. It was very difficult because Shelia was a force to be reckoned with. Like Carlie, Shelia Marcia Hooker James had lived for this moment. She had been planning her only daughter's wedding ever since she knew the life growing inside of her was female. Now that this moment was here she was going to play it out just like she wanted it. The problem was that the five Jones sisters were pretty independent and didn't kowtow easily. They were going to have to reach a compromise without alienating their brother's future mother-in-law. They were all afraid that if Shelia had her way, it was going to be Shelia's wedding, not Risa and JD's. The girls knew they needed reinforcements and therefore did the only thing they could do. They broke out the big guns. They called their mother.

All JD heard was yakkity yak, yak. He wasn't really paying any attention. He didn't care about the food or the clothes or the location. He didn't care that his sisters were in an uproar. He didn't care about anything other than Risa's happiness. He had gotten her call from her cell while she and her mother were "treasure hunting," as she called it. So as far as he was concerned, if she wanted Carlie to make the dress, Carlie would make the dress. If she wanted Daphne to make the cake from her grandmother's recipe or from Daphne's award-winning coconut pineapple one, it was okay. He didn't care about the groomsmen or anything other than his father being his best man and Big L standing to his right.

For the past two days his sisters had been calling him, paging him, e-mailing him, and showing up on his porch with ideas for this and pictures of that. He told them to talk to Risa. They complained they couldn't talk to Risa without talking to Shelia. That said, JD got the fallout. Right now, he lay on his couch listening on the phone while Shelia bent his ear with a whole new slew of suggestions. Actually he had stopped listening well over ten minutes ago.

*My goodness, that woman loved to talk!* he thought to himself. He hoped his future bride didn't develop this annoying habit as they went into their sixties. No matter what she was saying, he discovered that a well-placed "uh-huh" or a "really?" or an occasional "I'll see what I can do" was finally enough to get her to calm down. She was certainly excited about something. He didn't care as long as Risa was happy. Maybe his mother would be able to get everything straightened out. He didn't know why she had been called in, but listening to Shelia go on and on, he was glad that Lillian Jones would be the one to handle Shelia. Of all the women in his life, she was the most equipped to do the job.

By the next day, everybody seemed to be up in arms and Lillian couldn't figure out why. It seemed very simple to her. It was all figured out. Daphne would prepare the food. Her fourth daughter would make her coconut pineapple seven-tiered wedding cake. She would use Shelia's mother's recipe for the groom's cake. Carlie would make the dress by altering Risa's grandmother's linen wedding dress. Found well-preserved in a cedar chest in the back of the garage, it was in remarkably good shape.

The gown was actually very beautiful. It was a cream-colored dress with layers and layers of lace. Risa was several inches taller than her grandmother and at least thirty pounds lighter. Once she put the dress on, it came to her calves and not to the floor as it had done on her grandmother. Also, because of the difference in body type the bosom was awfully low and showed more of Risa's breast than delicacy would allow. The difference in measurements would require all Carlie's skill to alter it without damaging the fabric or the authentic pearl buttons. Now an antique, it was beautiful in its delicacy and superb in its original design. Risa had made a good choice. The dress and the ring transformed her into the beautiful bride that she had once dreamed about and forgotten as she had climbed the ladder of success. Although the dress needed more than a tuck here and there, Carlie was up to the challenge. The first hurdle was to get it cleaned without damaging the fabric. Carlie accepted the challenge excitedly.

They would have the wedding at St. Luke Community United Methodist Church because both the bride and groom belonged there. There was such a large congregation that there were four Sunday services. Risa had attended 8:00 A.M. service, JD 10:00. Looking back there were times when they had spoken in passing with her leaving and he entering. The reception would be in Angela's beautiful backyard. These choices allowed everyone to participate and contribute. There was no reason to argue about it. It was the most logical set of choices and Miss Shelia would just have to agree. Lillian wasn't concerned at all. She was sure she'd be able to get the other woman to see her side of things.

The two mothers met for lunch at Honey Baby's.

Daphne's new venture was scheduled to open in a couple of weeks. She moved it back a couple of days to accommodate JD's wedding. Lillian had chosen the location for several reasons. One, it wasn't the overcrowded, extremely popular Cornbread and Brie. Two, it was a beautiful location filled with Carlie's personal touches, hand-embroidered pillows, strategically placed portraits of the family, and comfortable slip-covered furniture. It was like having a tea party in someone's home. It also gave Shelia the opportunity to taste Daphne's sample menu, which included both the bride and groom's cakes, Jamaican chicken breast, stuffed shrimp, lemon-glazed green beans, white asparagus, and red walnut cabbage. To her credit, Daphne had taken both the bride's and groom's favorites and created a wedding menu that would have made Martha Stewart speechless. As a mother of six, experiencing her second wedding, this one being her son's instead of her daughter's, Lillian wasn't as frazzled as Shelia. On the contrary, she was virtually the grand guru of advice and suggestion. By the time she finished, Shelia didn't even care what color the invitations were. All she wanted was for Risa and JD to be happy. That had been the ultimate goal from the beginning.

"She really isn't that bad," Lillian said to Sam as they prepared for bed. They had been married for well over forty years and had a nightly routine that rarely varied. He slept on the left closer to the door. She slept on the right closer to the window. He slept in blue cotton pajamas. She slept in blue satin pajamas. They both drank a cup of warm tea before bedtime and no, it didn't mean that they had to get up in the middle of the night. He started a sentence. She finished it. They were like a well-oiled machine.

"From the way the girls were talking, you'd think she had two heads," Sam said, amused by the whole ordeal.

He liked the young lady that his son had chosen. And as

an older, wiser man, he knew that when a man married a woman, he married her family. Look what Risa would be getting by marrying JD. Had JD thought what he was going to be getting by marrying Risa? A mother-in-law that was a shrew could ruin the best of marriages. From the contrasting stories he had heard, he deduced that Shelia was neither a shrew nor a busybody. She was just a meticulous woman who liked having things go her way. Sam recognized this quality instantly because he lived with this type of woman.

When his daughters were over, these types of women surrounded him. He had nurtured and raised them. So Shelia's little idiosyncrasies didn't faze him at all. It seemed the kettles were looking at the pot. At first they saw shades of red. Now they all saw black. His wife was a magical woman. She had gotten both sides to compromise without lifting a finger or breaking a sweat. She was very diplomatic and should have been a politician. Her forty years as a schoolteacher was time well spent, but he often wondered as to what the state of the union would have been if she had geared her energies towards Washington.

"What are you smiling at?" Lillian asked.

"Oh, I was just thinking about you. You always make me smile," Sam answered.

When he said that, Lillian stopped brushing her hair and turned to her husband. She loved this man so. He always managed to say the right things to make her insides turn to jelly.

"I love you too," she responded.

She crossed the room and got into the bed. She kissed her husband long and deep then lay down. If her son could have just a fraction of what she had with this man with the woman he had chosen, then surely he would be a happy man. What every parent wants for their child is happiness.

# Chapter 28

"She wasn't that bad," Shelia said to Frederick.

He was lying in the bed reading a copy of the *Wall Street Journal*. As of late, he had taken to wearing just the bottoms of his pajamas and sleeping with his chest bare. He was a sixty-five-year-old man and strangely she still found him appealing. His body was good. He had never gone to fat or lost his boyish build that had always tended to be lean.

"The way you were talking about her girls, I expected a woman with two heads," Frederick stated.

Shelia was polishing her toes. Ever since they had officially gotten back together and Risa had announced her upcoming nuptials, it was like she was reverting back to the Shelia she was as a young housewife. She had boundless energy and was feeling youthful and vibrant. No one would guess her sixty-three years even though she wouldn't admit her age. And truth be told, if pushed, she would hint at fifty and that was it, not a day over. If she could get away with it, then so be it.

"No. She is wonderful and those girls, my goodness, Risa is about to get five sisters."

Hearing the wistful nature in her voice, Frederick put down the newspaper.

"Did you ever want more than one child?" he asked.

Tonight they were in her house, formerly their house. Shelia had actually finally decided to give some thought into giving up the large four-bedroom house in order to move into Frederick Walter's condo. The house was large and they didn't need all that space. Their only child was grown and gone as the expression went. Even though the house was filled with memories, she was up to making some new ones in a new place.

"No, Walter." She called him Walter when she was really serious. "One child was all I ever wanted or needed." She closed the fingernail polish and took her husband by the hand. "And if you're trying to tell me you want another one, you're going to have to settle for a grandchild."

She could always make him laugh, this woman. He knew then that he had made the right decision in choosing to remarry her.

"Risa, they're beautiful!" Cayce exclaimed as she modeled her bridesmaid dress.

The room was filled with all the girls: Angela, Betsy, Carlie, Daphne, Elisha, Cayce, Helen, and Risa. Everyone was very happy with their dresses. No one made comments like she had heard in weddings that she had taken part in. No one thought the dresses looked like curtains or that they wouldn't be caught dead in the gowns. On the contrary, everybody was trying to figure out where they were going to go so that people could see them in their dresses. Risa too was pleased. She wanted to make sure that the dresses would be functional as well as beautiful. She wanted the girls to be able to wear them again and not have any bad feeling about being forced to wear a monstrosity.

The dresses were absolutely gorgeous. They had evolved
from a sketch in Risa's head, to the beautiful creations
that Carlie had manifested. Pale pink with gauze and lace,
they were wispy fairy-tale dresses that highlighted everyone's assets. Some girls had great legs, or fantastic breasts,
or a small waist. And one, specifically Elisha, had it all. But
she wasn't the one getting married. Risa was. So she was in
no way intimidated by the bevy of beauties that surrounded
her. The dresses were beautiful and the day was beautiful.
Risa was happy. Carlie was a godsend. She had even managed to make Helen's maternity matron of honor dress
just as appealing. Lined up in their pink finery, the girls
looked like a sorority of divas poised to meet the press.

"If our dresses are this nice, what is the wedding dress
going to look like?" Cayce added.

Risa had been waiting for this moment. No one other
than Carlie had seen the dress, not even Shelia or Lillian.
Risa and Carlie had been working well into the night and
were excited to present their masterpiece. Originally, she
had been doing this for Shelia. Risa could have gotten married in the courthouse. She was more concerned about
spending the rest of her life with JD then all the hoopla
that surrounded the wedding. But as the days went by, she
got more and more excited.

While everyone watched, Risa pulled her wedding dress
from its protective garment bag. There was an audible
gasp from the room. Even Angela, who thought no dress
could rival her own, had to bow down to her sister's mastery and skill. The dress was a masterpiece. It hung just
above Risa's ankles. Carlie added a sheer pink strip of
satin to the hem. Above that she stitched a strip of cream
fringe. She had taken the buttons off and sewed them
back on in more strategic locations. She had also taken it
in at the waist and created a bustle with the extra fabric.
What she ended up with was a modern version of an an-

tique turn-of-the-century gown. With Risa's height and slender figure, it hung like a dream.

"Carlie, I'll say this yet once again, you need to open a store," Helen said, looking at the dress. "There are so many people who would pay you big bucks for the things you do."

"She doesn't listen," Elisha said, looking at herself in the mirror. Carlie had made her last two pageant dresses. She never doubted her sister's skill. The girl had a knack.

"You guys," Carlie pooh-poohed the idea.

She made a good living as a mechanical engineer. The dress and pillows and slipcovers were things she did to relax. She never contemplated the thought of trying to make a living from her hobby. She had read of people who did these things. . . . Step out on faith. She had never taken the thought seriously for herself. She needed the comfort of a steady paycheck, benefits, and 401(k) plan. Even though she had a hefty nest egg, she wasn't ready to make that leap just yet. But judging from the reaction she was getting from the women, it might be something to contemplate.

"Risa, you are beautiful." That came from Betsy who was chewing on a piece of licorice.

"Thank you," was all that Risa could say. She was looking at herself in the mirror. The image she saw was like a dream come true.

Over the past few days she had actually thought of all the what-ifs. What if she hadn't selected JD as one of the bachelors for her episode on eligible men? What if there had been no chemistry? What if he hadn't of left Lucy Belle? She could drive herself crazy with the what-ifs. She decided to just accept the meant-to-bes'. She was marrying JD because it was meant to be.

# Chapter 29

"No, I haven't seen the dress," JD said.

He, Big L, Sam and Frederick were having a boy's night out. It was Lillian's idea that they do so and to his utter amazement, he was enjoying himself. The four men decided to make an evening of it with dinner and games of pool. They were at a local T.G.I. Friday's that had several pool tables. The bachelor party wasn't until the night before the wedding. Both Frederick and Sam would be absent on that night.

"They are making a big secret of it. But if you must know, I don't care about the dress," JD said.

"We know," the men chorused.

"It's all for the women, the invitations and the dress and the food. Who cares? We just want them happy," Big L said.

"Keep them happy," Sam added.

"Hear, hear," the men chorused again.

JD never felt left out that he wasn't part of the decision-making process. If he had his way, he and Risa would have been married at the courthouse. The marriage was a formality for their parents. He knew that in his and Risa's mind they were already married. What was marriage but a commitment? They had committed themselves to each other, physically and spiritually. The ceremony was to unite the parents and families.

Originally, at the beginning stages of the planning of the grand affair, the hoopla seemed to stress Risa out. But as they got closer to the big day and as their mothers got closer, the stress seemed to dissipate. Risa became a smiling ball of happiness. His sisters stopped bombarding him with messages and even Helen had been civil to him. By the way the women in his life were treating him he wondered if he should announce his engagement every day. It seemed like once he did this all the women in his life treated him extra special and bent over backwards to accommodate him. As the only boy in a houseful of women he got used to special attention. If he wanted, he could easily have women catering to him. That is, all except young Lane. She had finally agreed to speak with him and she was going to be at the wedding. But it had been a rough and rocky road to her forgiveness and understanding. In the end, JD had to enlist the help of his niece, Hailey. As a teenager herself, she understood the intricacies of Lane's emotions. One good thing that came from it, though, was that the two girls had gotten closer.

"Rack 'em up," Sam said.

JD was thirty-nine years old and didn't know that his father was a pool shark. When it hit him that the two older men had somehow formed a bond when no one was looking and decided to take the two younger men down a peg, it was too late to recover. They had been playing for over an hour and the score was remarkably in the favor of the two older dapper dudes. JD was sure that the two men had worked out hand signals and coordinated a take down that was going to be memorable. The funny thing was that he was enjoying himself. He had always been way too competitive to be a good looser. But the time spent with the important men in his life was more important than winning a pool game. It seemed that getting married was bringing in all the pieces of his life.

# Chapter 30

"Really, honey, I don't think I am being unreasonable," Shelia said.

Risa and Shelia were shopping in the lingerie department of Neiman Marcus. To Risa's amazement she was more conservative than her mother. For each tempting treat she selected, her mother chose one a little more risqué. As Risa fought back a prudish gasp, Shelia held up a lavender sheath made of the finest silk. It was so sheer that Risa could see her mother's well-manicured hands beneath the fabric. There were delicate little purple daisies placed in strategic spaces on the fabric. Nevertheless, it would leave little to the imagination.

"I can't wear that," Risa said, fighting back a stammer.

She quickly looked around to make sure that no one saw her with the delicate piece of fabric. If she didn't know any better she would think she were in Frederick's of Hollywood instead of the tasteful, upscale, Neiman Marcus. The $475 dollar gown could hardly be used for sleeping. It was an instrument of seduction and she was embarrassed that her mother could handle it so casually.

"Of course you can wear this. You have the height and you have the breasts. Take it," she encouraged, throwing it on the pile with the other pieces that she had selected.

For their honeymoon, a cruise to Alaska, it was Shelia's contention that the newlyweds would never leave the cabin. Therefore, they needed to have as much excitement as possible in the small stateroom. The purple gown would definitely facilitate it.

"Mother, are we standing in Neiman Marcus talking about my breasts?"

Over the past week, Shelia had been changing slowly but surely. Risa was seeing a new Shelia, one who was carefree and reckless and relenting. She wasn't sure if it was because her mother was getting remarried or if it was because she, as her only daughter, was finally fulfilling one of her mother's lifelong dreams, having a dream wedding to a dream man. Risa didn't know and she didn't care just as long as her mother remained the carefree, happy woman that she had become.

The new Shelia was a little much. She was flamboyant and bold and approving and just fun. Risa had even laughed at her suggestions that their roles had been reversed. She was more like her mother used to be and Shelia was more like her daughter used to be. Either way it went, she could not possibly buy that gown. It screamed that she wouldn't be wearing it long. She was still too much of a puritan to let people know what went on behind her closed doors.

"Oh, give it to me for goodness sake," Shelia said as she snatched the bundle from Risa's arm and marched up to the cash register. Before the salesgirl could ask them if everything had been to their satisfaction, Shelia had pulled out her credit card. "Everything was great. You were delightful."

The salesgirl smiled at the compliment. She was a

young girl, polished and sophisticated. Shelia was a regular Neiman's customer. The salespeople bent over backwards for her and others who flexed their buying power on a regular basis. Risa's head was spinning. Her mother was buying her lingerie. Sheer, sexy, expensive lingerie. She still couldn't believe it.

"As I was saying," Shelia went back to her original train of thought. She wasn't about to let herself get sidetracked by Risa's prudishness. "I think I have been more than flexible. There is no reason for us to have two houses. We need to pick one and stick to it."

Shelia and Frederick had been vacillating between the two houses. Just as they thought that a decision had been reached, one or the other didn't want to give up their space. Risa could understand. She and JD were faced with a similar decision. Whereas JD's house was larger and had both a pool and a tennis court, Risa's house was more centrally located. Whereas JD's house was the more expensive of the two, Risa's house was in a better school district. Whereas JD's house seemed like the logical choice, Risa loved her house. She had picked everything from the paint on the walls to the light fixtures. She didn't want to see it all go away just because JD's house was in a different league than hers. The two houses couldn't even be compared because of the price difference and neighborhoods. Because JD's was larger, more expensive, and had more amenities, it outclassed Risa's humble abode. In the end they decided to keep JD's house and Risa's things. With her furniture in his house it wouldn't seem like such homage to masculinity. Once they got back from their honeymoon they could look for yet another house.

The new house would be *their* house. It wouldn't be Risa's or JD's. It would be theirs. The other two houses would be sold. This was the only decision that put both houses on the same playing field and allowed each person to start from the same line. In a new house that was theirs they could start traditions and forge memories that were fresh and came with no baggage. Once the decision had been made, they decided it was something they could both live with. A new house was the best thing for their new life together. Interestingly enough, Elisha expressed some interest in purchasing Risa's house. She liked it from the moment that she had seen it. Each time she set foot in the house, she liked it more and more. She would have chosen different furniture and arranged it differently, but she liked the overall feel of the house and could easily see herself leaving her condominium for it. She would be graduating soon. Maybe if she played her cards right she could take the money she had saved and use it as a hefty down payment. It was something to contemplate.

Risa was touched by Elisha's interest. When she was a senior in college she hadn't thought of buying a house. All she wanted at twenty was to get her career started. Today's twenty-year-old was so much different from the twenty-year-old she had been. Elisha was like the young salesgirl, polished and sophisticated. She wanted to be taken seriously and was conscious of her finances. Unlike Elisha's family members, Risa had knowledge of just how much money Elisha managed to horde away from beauty pageants and competitions. She had a vague notion of how much the girl had saved by not paying rent or credit card bills also. At first glance Elisha might appear to be nothing but flash and fluff, but Risa saw a very determined young lady filled with the entrepreneurial spirit that seemed to have infected both JD and Daphne.

"So, I don't know what I am going to do," Shelia continued, taking the shopping bags from the salesgirl. "Your father is making me crazy."

She was dressed in a green wool suit and three-inch heels. She wore a green beret and looked as ageless as always. Risa was having a hard time keeping up with her mother's long-legged stride as they headed out of the store. They had a long day planned and her mother's boundless energy was enough to make even the strong weak. Nevertheless, Risa kept up. Shelia was a handful but she was indeed entertaining.

# Chapter 31

The funny thing was that Betsy and Cayce planned the bridal shower. These two had developed a bond of friendship that was interesting to say the least. Of all the Jones sisters, Betsy was the most subdued and conservative. But that wasn't saying much. The Jones women were dynamic and individualized. Betsy was just the more conservative of the group. She and Cayce had become fast friends discovering, to their amazement, that they had a lot in common. They were sorority sisters who had both majored in journalism and multimedia applications. Whereas Cayce had chosen to go into the television production end of the business, Betsy had decided on public relations.

As the media director of JD Jones Enterprises, Betsy was instrumental in having JD appear on Risa's *City Scenes* program. For indirectly introducing them, Risa owed Betsy her gratitude. When she supplied each girl with their bridesmaid's gifts, she made sure that each gift included a handwritten thank-you note and a very special trinket that showed her appreciation of each one's own personality. So each girl got a set of beautiful pearl earrings to wear with their ensemble. Betsy's trinket was an all-expense-paid weekend for two at a local bed-and-breakfast. Carlie's was an antique brooch that Risa picked up years ago when she had traveled to Egypt. She was delighted to see Carlie's eyes light up once she saw her gift. Each girl was special, but both Carlie and Betsy, in Risa's eyes, had gone above and beyond the call of sister-in-law girlfriends.

By the time Risa had shown up at Betsy's house for the "surprise" bachelorette party, she wasn't surprised at all. Betsy had a split-level duplex in old Oak Cliff. She had it converted into a single-family dwelling and inherited a lot of space after the renovations. It was decorated in earth tones and Afrocentric touches. It was very inviting. For the party, the girls laid out a feast fit for Nubian queens. To everyone's amazement, Daphne didn't supply the meal. Betsy and Cayce cooked themselves and had created a Haitian, Cuban, American buffet completed with fried plantain. The girls were seated on Betsy's overstuffed furniture, on pillows spread around the room and even on the floor. It was a big, sorority-mixer-slumber-party feast. The only thing missing were the men. At least that was until the stripper showed up.

Now Risa knew that bachelorette parties usually had strippers, but she wasn't prepared for the guy that showed up. He arrived dressed like an African warrior. He was at least six feet, four inches, and more sinewy than thin. He was lean, possessing not an ounce of excess body fat. His muscles were defined and heightened. The expression "cut" came to mind just looking at him. He was the color of deep, dark, ebony with no highlights to mare his authenticity. He had a skullcap of tight, black, twists. His eyes were so brown they were the dark chocolate of Hershey's kisses. His nose was long, wide, and defined. He was an ebony warrior, a Zulu king. He was a proud Black man who taunted them with his masculinity. He was Shaka

Zulu incarnate. He was young, at least twenty-three. For a moment Risa was embarrassed that they were treating him like an object. But when he winked at her, she realized it was all in fun. He was a college student paying his way through graduate school. This was an easy and enjoyable way to make some quick cash. The next thing she knew she was getting his information so that she could do a show on him and students like him and the creative ways in which they supplemented their incomes.

"Risa, for Pete's sake. Can you take a break from work if just for a minute?" Cayce exclaimed when she saw Risa questioning the young dancer.

"What?" Risa said. She had the decency to look sheepish although she was formatting the show in her head.

"This is a party!" Cayce exclaimed, pulling Risa into the middle of the floor where some of the girls were dancing. "Nobody is working. Especially you. We're having fun!"

Yes, Risa was having a good time, but she couldn't help but think of her upcoming episode. She was where she was because of her strong work ethic. Every time she executed a dance move she checked to see the whereabouts of the young dancer as he mingled with the girls. Everyone was very polite and treated him like a guest instead of a hired object of sexual stimulation. She was sure they were nowhere near as raunchy as men got during a bachelor party. She knew the women where getting a thrill out of stuffing dollar bills into his loincloth and making fake passes.

Everyone seemed to enjoy his performance except young Elisha. Risa's keen reporter's sense seemed to notice what no one else did. He wasn't paying Elisha any attention. Elisha was a very pretty girl and used to getting attention from men. The fact that the young dancer was making his way through the crowd without so much as a backwards glance at Elisha had her bristling. She did everything she could without being obvious in her attempt to get his attention. But the young ebony Apollo wasn't having it. He spoke to the women. He danced with them and basically kept them entertained.

*Hmmm,* Risa thought as another show idea surfaced. *What would it be like to be the girl who always got the guy and suddenly you find yourself without a date on Friday night? Now that would be interesting. People always interviewed the pretty girl but they never ask her how it feels to be treated like the ugly girl.*

"Really, Risa. Take a break," Helen scoffed, grabbing Risa by the arm and twisting her around so that they could dance to an old Temptations tune, "Ain't Too Proud to Beg." Even though Risa hadn't said anything, the two women had worked together so long that she could tell when Risa's mind was working in overdrive.

"She can't help herself. She is a workaholic," Cayce said, moving to the music. The women danced with each other easily. The Motown music was timeless and classic. It never went out of style. This was the music they had all grown up listening to. That went for each generation present. Cayce was enjoying the music just as much as Shelia and Lillian. Their age differences meant nothing as they danced the night away. All in all everyone had a great time. Except Elisha.

"Did you see him?" Shelia asked her new fast friend, Lillian. The two women were each in their own houses lying in bed next to their husbands and talking on the phone like teenagers.

"I would say that I was almost in shock," Lillian concluded. "He was indeed something to look at. I wasn't sure what to expect.'

The men didn't know what to make of the conversation. But they did like the turn of events that had their wives acting like women half their age. Neither of them had ever been lacking in the love department—on the contrary, they were all spry and agile. Their sex lives had only gotten better as they had gotten older. It wasn't something they discussed, but rather took for granted, as they remained as sexually active in their twilight years as they had been in their youth. Also, there was something about planning the upcoming nuptials that had rejuvenated the women. There was pep to their step and a song in their respective voices. The budding friendship between the two of them gave them both a renewed energy that was invigorating.

"I still can't believe that I saw a stripper," Shelia whispered the last word as if it were something naughty that she was indulging in.

"Well, you did and you liked it," Lillian stated before the two burst into identical sets of giggles.

In their respective houses the men rolled their eyes and continued with their activities. Neither one was going to let his wife's newfound friendship get on his nerves. On the contrary, both Sam and Frederick Walter were as pleased as punch. It would make things so much easier all around if the women became friends. They encouraged it.

Meanwhile, while the mothers were bonding by reliving the events of the bridal shower, Risa and JD were packing some of Risa's things. They decided the transition would be so much easier for Risa if she moved into JD's house until after the wedding. They were spending so much time together that it became a chore to carry her things around in an overnight bag. And the drawer she had grew into an entire closet, and the bathroom down the hall from his was suddenly very feminine with pink rugs and a frilly shower curtain. He didn't even remember her changing it out. What color had it been? Purple? No, it was green, maybe. He didn't remember. He only used the master bathroom.

"You're going to take this, aren't you?" JD asked expectantly as he held up the Neiman's bag that Risa had forgotten to unpack. From the look on his face, she knew that he had been in it.

"JD, you aren't supposed to see that until the wedding," Risa said with a pout.

"That's the wedding dress. Not this." He held up the lavender piece of fluff that her mother had insisted on buying.

"Put it on."

"If I put it on, we'll never get out of here."

Risa had packed two boxes. JD, on the other hand, had watched television, drank a beer, and looked through all her old picture albums. She wasn't really angry with him because he had carried her boxes to his car without complaint.

"Maybe we should spend the night here," JD said as he held up the negligee.

He was smiling at her in that drop-dead gorgeous kind of way that let her know just how much he wanted her. "Come on," he teased. "I dare you." He held the gown out to her. Accepting the challenge, she reached for it. Before she could turn and go into the other room, he stopped her. "No. Here. In front of me." For a minute she hesitated. "Don't be shy now. I've seen it all."

And he had, just as she had seen the all of him. Giving tit for tat she reached for the zipper on the top of her velour warm-up suit and pulled it down. It was powder blue and soft as down. The top was trimmed in white. The bottom had no such trim. As she pulled the zipper past her breasts she saw his eyes widen when he realized she was braless. He liked her breasts. He liked the feel and taste of them. She removed the top and discarded it with very little effort. Standing topless in front of him she hooked her thumbs into the waistband of her sweatpants and had them pulled down to her feet before he could scrutinize her technique. She stepped out of them and stood before him in a pair of sheer blue panties. There was a time in her life when all her underwear was beige, black, and white. She had just started to embrace the sensual side of her nature and replaced the sensible underwear with thongs, bikinis, and snippets of color and hue that fascinated her. She became a frequent shopper at Victoria's Secret and was glad her body supported the fashions. But that didn't mean she was completely comfortable parading in front of JD. That was something she was going to have to grow into. She might as well start now. Summoning her courage, she walked naked to him and donned the purple sensation. It was so sheer that he could see through it. Dressed in it she seemed to excite him more than she had standing naked before his eyes.

"Now you," she said amazed at her own boldness.

"You want me to wear that?"

He was sitting on the floor with his back against the couch. The fire was burning in the fireplace and illuminated his face and his desire. He was dressed in gray corduroys and sweater. On his feet were gray socks and he was as sexy as if he lay before her bare to the bone.

"No. I want you naked," she chuckled.

"Your wish is my command."

He pulled his sweater over his head without preamble. His pants and socks were the next to go. In nothing more than his gray Calvin Klein boxer briefs he was a magnificent creature. A sexy beast. As soon as he hooked his thumbs into the waistband of his boxer briefs she crossed to him and stopped him.

"No. Let me," she said.

In a move that was becoming second nature to her, she straddled him and placed her hand on his maleness. With little effort it was in her hand and free of the boxer briefs, which were open to reveal his manhood for her. He didn't need to take them off to be exposed to her probing hands or her desire. He kissed her nipple over the purple rosebud that covered her breast. He teased her to excitement without her having to remove the delicate piece of fabric. When she moaned, he knew he had achieved his goal and laughed against her stomach. Taking his hands, he inched the gown up above her waist. With her most sensitive part bare to his touch, they coupled while they were partially clothed. The more they did it, the better it got between the two of them. Risa couldn't imagine what she had been doing before uniting with JD. Whatever it was, it was mere practice for this glorious union.

Faster and faster he worked her against him. His hands worked themselves against the sheer fabric that felt like a sexy sensation beneath his hands. It was so sheer that his tongue was able to get to her flesh through the fabric. The combination of the tongue and the fabric brushing against her skin was driving her crazy. She was working her passion into a frenzy of sensation. Faster and faster she rode him until the inevitable result occurred. Biting her lip to keep from screaming in sheer delight, she collapsed against him.

"Do you have another one?" he asked.

"Don't tell me that reaction was because of the gown," she said.

"Okay, I won't tell you."

He kissed her and skillfully removed it. Naked, she remained on his lap.

"Now you," she whispered.

Her words were just the encouragement he needed before he too was as naked as she.

"Again?" he questioned.

"Do you have to ask?"

Laughing, they coupled one last time in front of the fire before they fell asleep in each other's arms with just the wool throw from the couch to cover them. It was the last night they would spend in Risa's house and they had spent it in a blaze of glory.

After a lot of reorganizing and a little elbow grease, Risa managed to get the last of her clothes into JD's closet. His house was large and most of her things had been placed in one of the guest rooms. But it made no sense for them to share the master bedroom and she have to go down the hall to dress. As she stood back to observe her handiwork she finally agreed to herself, if not to him, that the decision to sell her house had been the right one.

This house was larger. It had a pool and a tennis court. There were four bedrooms. It was the only logical move to make that she move in. But she was anxious to find another house, one that would be *theirs* and not *his*. Although he made her feel welcome, she just didn't have that feel of belonging that she felt in her house. This house was too cold, too masculine, too "not her." Even though she had moved in some of her furniture, it just wasn't right. She wouldn't feel completely at home until she found the perfect house for them to start their lives in. That said, she started out. She had an appointment with a Realtor in thirty minutes. She wanted to get the house thing situated before they went on their honeymoon. That way, when she returned they could transition into their life together without downtime.

# Chapter 32

"I think it's the only logical choice," Elisha said as she took a bite of her Cobb salad.

"That's because you want the house," Betsy said, looking down at her entrée, a steak, baked potato, and asparagus, deciding which to take a bite of first.

The two sisters were having lunch at Cornbread and Brie. Daphne was away at Honey Baby's. Angela was at a school function and Carlie was out purchasing a new car. She had their father with her and was determined to get the best deal possible.

"But that's what happens when you get married late in life," Elisha said between forkfuls. She had started a diet and was on a new workout regime. Although she didn't need it, she was still miffed that the young stripper from the night before hadn't paid her any attention. To add insult to injury, she discovered that they both attended the same school. Funny how when she saw him on campus she hadn't given him more than a sideways glance. But having seen him near naked at the bridal shower, she had seen him in a whole new light. He, on the other hand, didn't even glance her way when she passed him on campus. She wasn't liking that at all.

"Late in life?" Betsy scoffed quickly, running down the age range of her siblings in her head. Angela was holding steady at forty. JD was a prime thirty-nine. She was soon to be thirty. Daphne was twenty-six, and little Elisha was a baby at twenty. Nevertheless, she wouldn't call JD's decision to get married at thirty-nine a decision made late in life. Thirty-nine was prime. It wasn't old.

"Yes. They're both getting up there," Elisha said.

"Elisha, really . . ."

"No, listen to me," Elisha insisted because she had given this a lot of thought. "Getting married well into your thirties creates so many problems. Between them they have two houses and three cars. They have to buy another house, for Pete's sake."

Betsy had listened with everyone else when JD and Risa informed everyone that they were going to sell both houses and get another one. If placed in that predicament, she wasn't sure what she would do. She loved her place. She would hate to give it up. And Daphne said that she never would. Even for true love she'd keep it. But knowing Daphne, she'd rent it out.

"And what about kids? She's forty," Elisha added. "If she had a baby today, she'd be a fifty-year-old woman with a ten-year-old."

"Forty is the new thirty," Betsy said.

"Believe that if you want to. But I am going to be married by the time I am twenty-five. I am going to have my kids by the time I am thirty. Trust me, I'm going to do it so that by the time I'm forty I'll have kids I can communicate with. A ten-year-old at fifty would drive me crazy." She stabbed another forkful. She really wanted her sister's baked potato. But she had to work on her figure. She couldn't load up on carbs and not expect to be affected.

"I don't care what they do. I just want everyone to be happy," Betsy said as she pushed her potato towards her sister. She had seen her eyeing it. "You're too skinny anyway."

Elisha couldn't help herself. She dove into the potato. That would just be another lap in the pool. She had a pageant coming up and she wasn't coming in second this time. The title of Miss Dallas was one she had coveted for some time.

"All I'm saying is that selling both houses and buying another one is the only thing they could do so that they could start on equal footing. The man I marry will come to my table with the same or more. . . . I'm not mad at Miss Risa. She did good. And JD didn't do too bad for himself," Elisha said as she started on what was left of her sister's steak. The steak wasn't that bad. It was protein. It couldn't hurt her; nevertheless, she had resigned herself to doing two extra laps tonight. No pain no gain. There was something to that.

# Chapter 33

JD looked at himself in the mirror and just had to crack a smile. He looked good even if he had to admit it himself. The tux was a classic cut with black pants and a white coat. He had tried on one with tails and even the all black, but there was something about the white coat and black pants that added a grace to the timeless, ageless perfection of the tuxedo. Elisha insisted that for his upcoming nuptials he should look as good as his bride. Risa insisted that it wasn't just her day but his as well. All eyes should be on them, not just the bride. They would be a striking couple.

With Elisha's urgings he was doing everything he could to look good for Risa. His younger sibling insisted it would make his future bride's heart swell with pride that other women would think him attractive. The thought never occurred to him. He didn't think that women were as pompous as men and liked to show off their significant other. But if they did and Risa was one of those women, would she be proud? Considering that, he turned to catch a glimpse of himself from behind. He had a strong back, wide shoulders, a narrow waist, and a high, firm ass. For a man in his late thirties, he looked good. He knew that and if he didn't, women made him aware of it by their actions.

JD had been known to turn a head or two in his day. Jokingly, he shook his butt then laughed at his actions. He wanted to make Risa proud, not embarrassed. When he said it out loud, Elisha almost cheered. Finally he was ready to let her have her way with him. She promised him Risa would be proud of the result she created. So JD sat back and let Elisha run the show. The fact that she had appointed herself as his personal shopper hadn't missed him at all. As a matter of fact, he enjoyed her company on their little outings. She had a great fashion sense and enjoyed spending his money.

He had picked her up after her lunch with Betsy and the two headed to the tailor's. Originally Carlie was to join them, but it seemed like she was too busy enjoying her new car. She ended up getting a new BMW and was digging the ride. Everyone told her it was time she got a new car. Her old one, a 1984 BMW, had served her well. In her role as senior engineer with JD Jones Enterprises, a new car would look better in her parking spot. The one she bought was black with cream leather interior. It was sleek and sharp. She liked it and was happy she had remained loyal to BMW. Since her old one was still in good shape, she chose not to trade it in and had instead given it to her niece, Hailey. This earned her massive brownie points on the aunt scale. She was happy because, so far, Elisha—being the closest in age and temperament—had been wearing the crown. They all spoiled the children mercilessly and had been trying hard to stop trying to outdo each other.

"The white coat is perfect," Elisha said, bringing JD's thoughts back to the chore at hand. She was standing behind him and peering at his reflection in the mirror. "The rest of the men are going to look so dapper."

Every now and then, Miss Sophisticated, Elisha, would say something so out of character that JD would have to laugh at her. *Dapper* seemed a word more a part of his mother's vernacular. Of all his sisters she looked more like his mother. He could see the same eyes and the same tilt to the lips when she smiled. She had always been a pretty girl. She would be an even more beautiful woman. The man who she chose to marry would have his hands full with her.

To reward Elisha for using her fashion sense on this little shopping spree, JD agreed to look at her proposal for purchasing Risa's house. Once he discovered that she was indeed serious, he felt that he owed it to both his sister and his lover to see that a fair and equitable arrangement was reached. He wanted both parties to be happy. He was happy. He was so happy that he would buy Risa any house she wanted. Hell, he would build it for her. She could design it. Whatever she wanted, if it was within his power, she would get it.

"Stand still," Elisha said as she picked an imaginary piece of lint off his shoulder and adjusted his tie. "Yep, this is the one."

She had already made up her mind about the tuxedo. But there was something about the way his eyes sparkled when she looked at him in the mirror that said, "Yes, this is it."

"Yes," she repeated. "This is the one. Give it to me so I can go pay for it."

She held out her hand for his credit card. He handed it to her and quickly pulled off the tux so that she could hang it up. Once she was gone he got dressed. The wedding was just days away and suddenly he was getting butterflies. Risa, on the other hand, was like a fluttering butterfly herself as she was on the hunt for their new domain.

Risa had seen five houses before she found the perfect

one. She found it by accident. She was on her way back to JD's house to meet him for dinner. As fate would have it, a water main had burst in the cold. Traffic was rerouted. For the first time in her life she turned down a street she had never noticed before. She had grown up in Dallas. She had gone to college in this city, left this city and came back to this city and had never seen this street. And the funny thing was that the street was just a few blocks from her usual beaten path. Nestled between historic South Boulevard and the popular Martin Luther King Boulevard was a quaint little street whose name was covered by over-grown ivy. The houses were large and well structured. The yards were manicured and landscaped. There was a feeling of peace and serenity about the street. She was driving down it about the turn onto the detour when she noticed the "For Sale" sign.

The house was located mid-block. It was a large red brick structure with a porch built for a porch swing. There was a large willow tree out front and a cluster of yellow roses beneath the window. She pulled her SAAB over to the curb and got out. From where she stood she could see a chimney in the living room and another off to the side. So the house had at least two fireplaces. Curious, she walked up to it and looked through the large front bay window. There were hardwood floors and beautiful hand-carved moldings on the wall. She liked the house. She went to the front door to see if she could get a different perspective through the glass at the top of the door. For some reason she turned the doorknob when she approached the entrance. To her surprise it was unlocked.

"Hello?" she called as she entered cautiously. "Hello?"

When there was no answer she went inside. In the foyer was a table. On it was a flyer giving the details of the house. There was also a note that read: *Back in fifteen minutes. Feel free to look aroun*d.

Dallas was so unlike Los Angeles. Never would a Realtor have left the property so exposed in the jungle that was LA. Risa didn't know when the fifteen minutes had officially started, but she took this time to check out the house. Once inside it was actually larger than it appeared from the outside. There were four bedrooms, two baths, two fireplaces, a kitchen, a separate butler's kitchen, a formal dining room, and a sunroom. In the backyard was a pool and a barbeque. Although not as large in square footage as JD's house, it was bigger than hers. There was a combination of the modern and the classic. It was as if someone had taken the best of both their houses and molded it into this one house. She knew then that this is where they would start their lives together. It was just meant to be.

She immediately took out her cell phone to call JD. Before he could even get out a "hello" she was telling him all about the house.

"Wait a minute. Wait a minute. Slow down," JD said. He was driving and Risa was speaking loudly and excitedly through the headset connected to his cell phone.

"JD, it's perfect!" Risa exclaimed.

He loved her enthusiasm. He wished they were together. They couldn't be together 24-7 though.

"Okay," he said.

"No, JD. It's perfect. You don't understand. Puuuurrrrfect," she literally purred over the phone. In his mind's eye he could see her standing in front of the house speaking on her cell phone. He wondered what she was wearing. It was cool out so she was probably dressed in something befitting the weather although he would prefer her in next to nothing or better yet, naked and smiling in his arms.

"Okay. Then make an offer," he instructed her.

It would be unreasonable for him to conjure up pictures of her naked. Especially when he was driving. It made for a rather uncomfortable situation.

"Don't you want to see it?" she asked.

"You said it was perfect. That's all I need," he said, taking her word for it.

"Oh, God, JD. I love you," she said right before hanging up the phone.

Laughing, JD put the phone back into his breast pocket. It looked like he wouldn't have to build her a house after all.

# Chapter 34

*A glance, a touch, a kiss says it all.*
*We were meant to be together.*

*Risa Elizabeth James and James Derrick Jones*
*Invite you to a glorious celebration of our union*
*as we unit in Christ*
*Please join us at St. Luke Community United*
*Methodist Church*
*On the fourteenth day of February in the year of*
*our Lord 2007*

Risa looked at the invitation for what seemed like the hundredth time. She still couldn't believe that within a few short hours she would be Mrs. JD Jones. She would join a very prestigious group in becoming yet another Jones woman. It still seemed like a fantasy. It seemed as if just yesterday she was lamenting over the fact that she had been so busy living her life that she had missed a very important deadline. Now, all the pieces of the puzzle were falling into place. A new man. A new house. A new life. All in the matter of weeks, not years, weeks. It happened just like it was supposed to. It was meant to be. She was meant to be JD's wife. She was meant to have him in her life. She was meant to have him at this time.

If they had met at a different time when they were in different places in their lives she wasn't sure that the events would have unfolded into this end. It takes life experiences to determine how one would act in any given situation. Prior to this time in her life, the mini-dramas that she and JD had experienced might not have led down this road to marital bliss. And it would be blissful. She knew that. She looked at the way he treated his sisters and the relationship he had with his mother and she knew that she was getting a man who would love, cherish, and honor her all the days of her life.

She put the invitation back into the envelope and placed it in the wedding memory book that she received as a gift at her shower from her soon to be sisters-in-law. It hadn't taken long for the girls to give in and embrace her as one of them.

The church was beautiful. In addition to flowers there were balloons and doves. White, silver, gold, and black created a sophisticated allure of romance. The birds were placed in golden cages around the room and were part of the decor. Once the bride and groom departed for their honeymoon the doves would be released into the air. The aisles were lined with lilies and daisies. JD had spared no expense and the church looked it. One couldn't calculate love based on the money spent; however, if they could, then JD loved Risa tremendously.

He couldn't wait to see her face when he presented her with his gift later that night on the plane. He had gotten her a diamond and emerald necklace that he was sure she would love. It would look good against her skin and wasn't so ostentatious that she couldn't wear it with many outfits. The jewels were small but numerous. It was simple. Plain. Beautiful. Just like Risa. She would love it as he loved her. Unbeknownst to him, she had gotten him a gift as well. It was a set of onyx cuff links. They could be worn with many of his shirts. Each time he put them on she wanted him to think of her. As they both prepared for the big day they were excited, happy, and elated. Finally, they would be able to begin their lives together.

From her vantage point outside the sanctuary, Risa could see inside the church without being seen. The double doors were closed and she stood on tiptoe looking through the glass at the top of the doors. The church was packed, filled with friends, family, and business associates. Everyone was facing forward so no one saw her.

"Risa," Shelia whispered with urgency. "Will you please behave?"

Risa almost burst into laughter at her mother's scolding. From Shelia's tone, Risa would swear that she was a teenager and her mother was a disapproving parent.

"I just wanted to see," she clarified.

"You don't have to see them. Let them see you."

Shelia reached out and brushed an imaginary piece of lint from Risa's dress. Reluctantly, Risa moved away from the door. Her bridesmaids stood in ascending order by height and looked as beautiful and glamorous as she did. She didn't have to hope that JD looked as magnificent. She did, she knew that they would present a dashing picture. That would make her mother happy. Shelia had a storybook wedding planned and the picture-perfect bride and groom completed that image. Truth be told, Risa felt like JD. She didn't care if they were married in burlap bags as long as they were married. But being glamorous and beautiful did add a boost to her ego.

"Smile," Shelia said.

Before Risa could do anything, Shelia snapped a picture. For a moment the flash from the digital camera momentarily blinded Risa. When her vision cleared she saw Lillian tactfully leading Shelia through the double doors. Lillian was dressed in a pale champagne dress with matching shoes, hat, and purse. Shelia had on a champagne-colored shirt and aqua-blue beaded top. Stunning. Simply stunning described both women. One of the things Risa was grateful for was the bond that was forming between the two mothers. Like she and Lucy Belle, it was never too late to make friends. Speaking of Lucy Belle, Risa wasn't shocked in the least when her new friend had dropped by the house with a tasteful crystal bowl as a wedding gift. Lucy Belle had graciously accepted an invitation to both the shower and wedding knowing as she did that the only way to avoid possible uncomfortable feelings from mutual family and friends was to address the issue head-on. Risa could applaud her for that. She didn't know if in Lucy Belle's position if she could put on such a brave front. It endeared her to the woman.

Risa had caught a glimpse of Lucy Belle entering the church. She had arrived in grand style in an off-white silk dress. It was perfect for winter in color and texture and looked fantastic coupled with the off-white fur coat that she wore. Against her chocolate skin the white was amazing. Her daughter Lane and son, Richard appeared at her side. It was the first time that Risa had seen the young man. He was tall and possessed movie-star good looks. He was darker than his mother and sister and was very comfortable in his skin, exuding a confidence beyond his years. It was the special woman who could have children their age, look so good, date a man ten years her junior, and appear at his wedding looking fantaboulous. Risa had to give it to her.

From inside the sanctuary the wedding music began. Upon hearing it, Risa's heart literally skipped a beat. It was about to happen.

"Risa, are you ready?" Angela asked as soon as the music started. The melody drifted to their location easily.

"Yes," she replied. And she was.

The procedures started off without a hitch despite Risa taking a deep breath when the minister asked if there was anyone who objected to the union. Speak now or forever hold your peace. She had a moment of concern simply because young Lane Belle had looked quickly to her mother then to the uniting couple. To Risa's relief and delight, the young girl smiled and gave them the thumbs-up sign. She was happy the young woman had finally come to terms with their union. After waiting for what seemed like an eternity for the pastor, the good reverend Moses Holland began to continue with the service. Risa let out a relieved breath when he began to speak again. He had been Risa's pastor her entire life. She had been baptized in this church and had served on the youth usher board and teen choir. It was when he started to speak again that everything went haywire.

Risa heard the moan before anyone else. Then she heard the faint, nearly inaudible, "Damn it." Risa turned her head just as Helen's water broke. It seemed like everything from that point went into overdrive. Isaiah, who was the videographer for the event, put down his camera and ran to his wife. She tried to shoo him away.

"I've been in labor for the past half hour. I'm okay," she insisted.

"For the past half hour?" Isaiah exclaimed. "Helen, when are you going to learn that you can't control everything? You can't tell the baby when to come."

It was the first time that Risa had ever seen him buck up to Helen. He was usually a mild-mannered guy who deferred to his wife. But in this instance, he was a little hot under the collar.

"Come on," he continued. "We're going to the hospital. Risa will understand."

"I understand," Risa insisted.

For the first time in her life Helen was being overruled by the masses. No one listened to her and she didn't like it. Despite her insistence that they continue with the service, she was being ushered towards the parked cars. They were going to continue with the service when Helen let out a sound that didn't sound comfortable and was far from ladylike. It was then that the ugly reality of her friend's age hit Risa square in the face.

"JD," Risa said as she turned to her intended with a concerned look on her face.

Somebody needed to take control of the situation and she was too raw to be the one. As far as she was concerned, Helen needed to be on her way to the hospital and that was that. Helen could be a handful and she was very close to creating a scene with Isaiah. Risa didn't want to be on the receiving end of her wrath as well.

"I love you, dear, but I know my body more than any-one," Helen insisted.

"You're going to the hospital," JD said to Helen and grabbed Isaiah's camera on their way out of the church.

He took control of the situation to avoid a potentially ugly situation between husband and wife because hor-mones were flying. So despite Helen's insistence that JD and Risa say their I do's over her contracting uterus, she was rushed to the hospital in the limousine that was await-ing the bride and groom.

The emergency staff at St. Paul's Hospital wasn't pre-pared for the full wedding party that descended on them. Risa was the first one through the doors in her beautiful wedding gown followed by a very dapper JD. They rushed in and demanded a gurney, which arrived at the limou-sine just as Isaiah emerged holding his protesting wife who had somehow managed to make up with him in the back of the car. The bridesmaids and groomsmen were next followed by family and friends. The emergency room wasn't large enough to hold everyone and an announce-ment had to be made to have everyone who wasn't imme-diate family ushered out. This left Risa, JD, and Isaiah.

"I'm her husband," Isaiah declared.

They put Isaiah in a surgical gown and mask and ushered him into the delivery room.

"I'm her sister," Risa lied.

"And I'm her brother," JD lied.

They both lied in unison. They hadn't consulted with each other before they made their announcements. They were just on the same page.

"Where I come from, sisters and brothers don't get married," the nurse said with an understanding smile.

She was a large woman standing nearly six feet tall. She weighed at least three hundred pounds and was the color of gingerbread. Although large and formidable, she had a kindness to her face and softness to her voice.

"Look, why don't you two just wait out here? We'll keep you posted," the nurse said. She said it like it could possibly be their idea to stay in the waiting room. But everyone knew it was her decision.

"I'm really her sister," Risa tried again.

"Sure you are. Now have a seat."

JD took Risa by the hand and took a seat. This was an opponent he didn't want to face. In a battle of wills he was sure the competent nurse would win. This was her domain and she was boss.

"It'll be okay," JD insisted as he comforted Risa and led her to the uncomfortable waiting room chairs where they took up residence while Helen delivered her first child. It was as they were seated that Angela came to inform them that everyone, nearly the entire wedding party, had taken up residence in the parking lot. Basically they had commandeered it. If there were too many of them for the waiting room, they would be in the large parking lot. He could only admire their tenacity and determination. He realized a long time ago, sometime in high school, that he had trouble on his hands with five pretty sisters. As pretty girls it was an unwritten rule that they got away with murder.

JD had watched his sisters wrap many a man around their little fingers, starting with their father. So it did not surprise him when his eldest sister informed him that they had cleared it with a parking lot attendant. You could get more flies with sugar and more cooperation with a smile than with anything else. So he was sure that with five Jones women bearing down on him, the attendant could only fold. By the time they finished with him he would have thought it was his idea to have a makeshift tailgate party in a secluded section of the large parking structure. On most occasions JD's sisters were independent enough to handle their own situations and rarely needed him to be the overprotective big brother. This had been one of them. It seemed all his life he had been surrounded by strong, independent women. He liked it. Women who stood on their own two feet were more of a partner than a servant. That was what he liked and what he needed. He squeezed Risa's hand.

"What is that for?" she asked.

"I love you," he answered.

"Me too."

She made herself as comfortable as possible in the impossible chair. JD did the same as he reflected on the day's events. When he was in the church awaiting his bride and had looked up to see his beautiful sisters walking in, he realized what a lucky man he was. His siblings were good women and good sisters. They supported and loved him. He was a lucky man. As they walked towards him he thought that they looked like angels. All this had been going through his mind until Risa appeared. Then all thought except for his love for her was erased from his mind. If his sisters were beautiful, Risa was ten times more so. If his sisters were radiant, Risa was ten times more so. If his sisters were breathtaking then Risa was ten times more so. She was the most beautiful woman he had ever seen. Her radiance and her bearing made his heart smile and his spirit soar. All was well with the universe, then Helen had gone into labor. But be that as it may, he could neither blame her nor be upset with the outcome. He held his ladylove's hand and soothed her brow. They hadn't been able to complete their union but they were still together. And for that he was grateful. As he stroked her brow she looked up at him.

"I love you," Risa said.

He smiled at her and said, "I know. You told me."

"I wanted to tell you again."

She kissed him and placed her head on his shoulder. They were a picture-perfect duo dressed as bride and groom and ready to be placed atop a wedding cake. They were sitting like this when they fell asleep. They were awakened by the nurse.

"You can see your sister now," the nurse said. She smiled at them both, going along with the lie, and led them to Helen's room.

While they slept in the waiting room, Helen's hospital room had been transformed into a beautiful sanctuary. It was filled with flowers. Surely someone had bought all the flowers from the gift shop. There was no rhyme or reason to the arrangements chosen. There were roses and lilies and daisies and daffodils. Someone had even brought in some balloons from the church. Helen looked radiant as she sat up in bed with a little chocolate kiss surrounded in a pink blanket. Risa knew instantly it was a girl. Isaiah stood next to the bed. He was smiling from ear to ear and videotaping their entrance into the room.

"Look at your goddaughter," Isaiah said.

Helen held the baby up for Risa to see. She rushed to

the bed and looked down at the beautiful baby. She had a head full of black curls and expressive dark eyes. She was a beautiful, wrinkled, chocolate kiss.

"She's beautiful," Risa said, her eyes filling with tears.

"Yes, Little Breann is the most beautiful baby ever," Helen said, beaming. "Are you guys ready?"

"What are you talking about?" Risa asked.

"Are you kidding? We have a wedding to finish," Helen declared.

JD and Risa looked at Helen with confusion as she signaled to Isaiah. He in turn opened the window. Outside the window stood the bridesmaids and groomsmen. There were too many of them to fit into the room. The good reverend preacher pastor Moses Holland entered the hospital room from the hallway. Risa had a moment of total confusion. How and when had this all taken place? Surely Helen hadn't been in any condition to arrange anything. Just then she got her answer.

Lillian, Sam, Shelia, and Frederick entered with more flowers from the church.

"Hurry, hurry," Shelia exclaimed. "That rather large nurse said we had ten minutes before she had to shoo everyone out." Shelia quickly began placing the flowers in the room.

"What—" Risa sputtered.

"Isn't it obvious? We're having a wedding," Lillian explained.

"But—"

"No need to protest," Lillian said.

"Somebody has to get married today or somebody is going to miss their plane and their cruise and their honeymoon," Sheila stated. By *somebody* she of course meant Risa and JD.

"But—" Risa tried to start again.

"Shush," JD put his fingers to Risa's lips. "I don't care where we get married as long as we get married. I love you."

"And I you," Risa said.

And just like that Risa and JD were married in the private room of Helen Jeffries at St. Paul's Hospital, pronounced husband and wife, destined to live happily ever after because it was meant to be.

# Epilogue

R isa looked out at the breathtaking view of the tundra from her hotel suite at the beautiful Alaskan Hilton. After they were announced husband and wife, she and JD had just barely made their plane. Once they landed they quickly boarded the ship and their honeymoon started in earnest.

Everything that had happened before had been merely practice. For the first time, totally committed to each other, having said their vows before God and man, the newlyweds dedicated themselves to each other in a show of love that did not include one, or even the thought, of the small, convenient Trojan packets. They felt skin against skin within skin and sang a song of love that was meant to be sung with no barriers and no resistance. The five-day Alaskan cruise was so amazing that the newlyweds decided to take an additional week soaking up the Alaskan wonderland.

The beautiful hotel suit was a welcome change from the room aboard the luxury liner. As Risa looked out on the picture-perfect view, all she could do was once again was thank God for the life she had and the choices she had made. For a minute she couldn't believe that there had almost been a moment when she would have given all this up. She was truly the luckiest woman in the world, if not the happiest. Turning from the window she took in a sight just as breathtaking. Her new husband of six days lay asleep in the bed. He was dressed in a pair of flannel pajama bottoms and naked from the waist up. His finely chiseled torso lay comfortably against the navy-blue sheets and matching down comforter. Sleeping the sleep of the fully sated, he looked peaceful and sexy and virile even in sleep. She crossed to him and took her position next to him. Absently, he reached out and pulled her to him. Aligning herself with his body she laid in his arms and took her position as the next Mrs. Jones.